GRANT
&I

GRANT & I

INSIDE AND OUTSIDE THE GO-BETWEENS

ROBERT FORSTER

OMNIBUS PRESS

London / New York / Paris / Sydney / Copenhagen / Berlin / Madrid / Tokyo

TO LORETTA AND LOUIS

'In him morality is discovered far from its official haunts.'

FROM ALAN BENNETT'S
EULOGY TO PETER COOK

CONTENTS

REEL I

I Go Back To June 1957

We lived next door to the Smiths. Many years later with The Go-Betweens, I would share a record label and a stage with a bejewelled and beflowered band of that name. But in 1963 Mr and Mrs Smith were our first neighbours, having built a house and moved into Glenmore Street, The Gap a year after we had. I used to watch Mr Smith. He'd rake leaves in the morning, chip away at things under his house, and at his leisure go shopping. And he had time for me, as did relatives and friends of my parents who on each weekend visit would ask, 'What are you going to do when you grow up?' This had to be settled, it seemed, when I was six. I didn't know, and so piped up 'fireman' or 'ambulance driver', the glamour professions fancied by a boy wishing to please adults stooping down from the clouds to speak to him.

My heart wasn't in my replies. I couldn't imagine what activity would occupy my future, and then I did. Running up to my mother in excitement to declare, 'I know what I'm going to be when I grow up, I'm going to be like Mr Smith.' She laughed. Mr Smith was retired.

And there it is. I knew then, and you could say I've been retired ever since.

I knew other things as a boy in suburban Brisbane. I'd see my father's overalls, still dirty after being washed, spinning on our backyard Hills Hoist clothes line. One pair for every day of the week. And as much as I loved my father, I knew I'd never do what he did, work in a place that turned your clothes black. That realisation came at seven, as did seeing the days rotating in the drying wind, week in, week out, and knowing a life as regular as that was not one I was going to live.

My parents Mary and Garth, my younger brother Tony and I were in a frontier suburb. The success of a city in those years was measured by its sprawl, and with our neighbourhood encircled by low mountains, Brisbane was hitting a western edge. Young families were arriving, not rich or poor, and there was a zest in the air, an early-sixties crackle that came with those settling into the freshly carved streets. It was as if young Jack Kennedy, not jowled Menzies, were our leader.

The Forsters were part of a migration that in my younger years had me flipping between what songwriter Jonathan Richman later called 'old' and 'modern' worlds. My mother was a single child from Toowoomba who later moved to Sydney; my father was the youngest of three sons, and part of an extended family living in and around a large dilapidated Queenslander in Hendra called Cranbrook. Last painted in about 1900, it had once caped acres of inner-city land. If it sounds like there was money about, there wasn't. A fortune can be spilt as well as squandered in a generation, particularly when there are thirteen children. The sons, including my grandfather, were assigned trades – boilermaker, fitter and turner, the latter taken up by my father – to work their lives at Forster Engineering Works in Mary Street, in the city. My mother occasionally took my brother and me there after school. It was a dark, grindingly loud, cathedral-sized workshop caked in grease and full of ancient pulley-operated equipment. Our uncles and grandfather nodding to us from behind machinery, our eagle-eyed spinster aunt Sibbie in the front office dispensing Nice biscuits and tea. The business was a perfectly preserved piece of Edwardian industry still operating in the sunlit sixties. It was to fold and be sold, along with Cranbrook itself, in the mid-seventies.

Born in nearby Clayfield in 1957, I touched with baby fingers and explored in first steps old-world Brisbane, and smelt it too. A musty scent had escaped the great houses in the years before the First World War, settling over the tennis courts, red dirt and hedges of an elevated group of inner-northern suburbs. Exposure for me was at its most potent at Cranbrook, the home of Sibbie and her unmarried elder sister Marcia, where an aged, bedridden uncle was rumoured to reside in a back bedroom. The closets housed the nineteenth century – swords, bug-eaten military uniforms, flags and seafaring trunks brought by the family from England in 1833. I got a quick whiff before being whisked away to the gum-treed hills and construction of a new home. The call of my aunties – 'What are you doing moving *way* out there?' – in our ears. To them The Gap was Birdsville, not a few miles across town.

My parents were intent on a fresh start. But I was to carry something with me, a feeling instilled, never to dim, that even when I think of it now causes a smile to spring to my face: I was the golden boy. The firstborn amidst first cousins, the eldest male child of a sparser generation within the wider family, and I sensed it – a most loving welcome. I was coddled and indulged, the centre of attention wherever I went, a situation, judging from the photographs of myself beaming in the arms of relatives and friends, that I not only appreciated, but knew how to encourage. Confidence was never going to be a problem for me. The main offender, to the mild disgust of my father and grandfather, was my grandmother, a fragile, eccentric woman prone to hypochondria who would light up in my presence. From her and others I discerned that great things were expected of me; does every golden child feel that?

There was no less love at home, though it was of a more regular kind, and it was a self-assured, well-mannered boy, untouched by trauma or unfortunate incident, who was taken to the newly built local primary school to begin formal education. My mother's one constant story from my early school years: I was asked to stand before the class and talk about a pencil for a minute if I could – I was stopped after five. Imagination and, it must be admitted, an attendant ability to bullshit were at play here, but what pleases me each time I hear this story is the object of my oration. Not a holiday photograph or a treasured toy from home, but a pencil; it is the mundane and everyday that draws the inspiration from me.

Memories of my own, intact and strong, date from my last years at primary school, when I am ten or eleven. I am good at cricket, scoring a century in an inter-school game, and bounding over a hill ahead of a herd of breathless kids to gain a cherished certificate for third place in the cross-country. I am also doing well academically, my work neat, my attention on the teacher. This increasingly sets me apart from my peer group, who as pre-teens in the late sixties come under the influence of wilder forces out in society and the high school down the road. Hair is now longer, spitting an art, and swear words harsh to my ears curl around the first names of teachers. I resist. A contrariness of behaviour that will often have me swimming against the tide comes in – if rebellion is on, I will play it straight; when straight is needed, I'm the funniest guy in the school. This mule-kick attitude will define me.

Opposite us lived the Mitchells. Noel and Dell and their children Andy, Peter ('The Bean') and Julie. Noel was an architect and their home, long and open-plan, was how houses would look ten years into the future. They were the first bohemians I met and I was intrigued. Noel's Buddha-like sandstone sculptures dotted the bamboo garden, and exotic black and red fish swam in a concrete pond. Their cats were Burmese. Andy was my age, and Tony The Bean's, the younger brothers sidekicks to their older siblings. The four of us walked the mile to school down a stretch of Waterworks Road, hunting for matchbox tops and money as we went.

Andy was fanciful and mischievous; more artistic than I, he drew, winning prizes. Our final year at school was a momentous one for us both. I was the opening batsman in the cricket team and had been given the responsibility of ringing the school bell. The cross-country fell on the day of the Apollo moon landing, and to my frustration Dell insisted we watch it from her home – one small step for mankind, one cross-country not run, *and* I'd been training. The whoosh of the months intensified into a fire-storm when Tony and I learnt from our mother that Noel had died. We were too young to be told how – a daughter of visiting friends blurted out the truth, measuring our shock as she did. It was suicide. We grew older in a day. Noel's death leaked poison into other events, of importance and triviality. The death of my mother's father, Grandpa Charlie, weeks after he visited from his New South Wales farm; Australia's four–nil loss to a genius South African cricketing side, and glimpsed newspaper reportage of the Manson murders made 1969 a strange year to be twelve.

The turn of the decade, as it would in the future, seemed to have more significance than the click of one year into another. I was inoculated against much of the subsequent drama in our street, divorces mainly, by being sent to Brisbane Grammar School. 'Grammar', founded in 1865 – the Australian equivalent of Europe's 1410 – was an imposing set of church-like buildings perched on a hill at the city's edge. I was back in the old world to mix with boys from all over Brisbane, some of whom had grown up in the moneyed suburbs of my birth.

I was soon to discover that there are two kinds of parents who send their children to private schools: those who can afford it and those who make themselves afford it. After being a stay-at-home mum for most of my primary school years, my mother had taken a job as a nurse's aid in the geriatric ward at Prince Charles Hospital. In conjunction with that, my father was out of overalls and working as a salesman. I was grateful for their hard work and sacrifices, while blinking at the magnitude of the change. The school was a bigger stage, the height of it immediately apparent when a sifting of first-year students had me grouped not in either of the two smart classes, but in a regular one – for the first time in my life I was defined as average. I didn't like that.

Over the next three years I had my head down, the blips on the Attention Drawn to Robert Forster graph being my continued ability at cricket, a growth spurt in my fourteenth year that saw me reach six foot-plus, and my refusal to join the cadets (army, navy or air force) which in hindsight seems the most astonishing thing of all. How did I have the nerve to buck what was considered compulsory? Making friends was easy, and there was far less snobbery and bullying at the school than I'd expected. The education was liberal, and it was clear after the first year that what strengths I had ran to the humanities. Chemistry was incomprehensible formulas and explosions, physics the longwinded explanation of the bloody obvious, and maths deep water after multiplication. English was a slow courtship. There were few books at home, and so to encounter Charles Dickens' *A Tale of Two Cities* in first year was like a neophyte climber facing five hundred metres of sheer rock wall, an ascent not helped by 'Buster' Bevan, whose method of teaching amounted to eyeing slack-jawed boys and firing, 'On page 268, the coach arrives at a small village in rural France. The innkeeper has a dog. Dowling! What's the dog's name?'

I've never been back to Dickens. Far better was *The Great Gatsby* (it was also thinner); and *Catcher in the Rye*, read at the perfect age of fourteen, spoke straight to my heart. In third year came a book written by a former student of the school – David Malouf's *Johnno*, its milieu Brisbane of the Second World War, the time and place of my father's youth. I remember the shock and pleasure of recognition: Brisbane was subject matter.

*

Ken Bates had an acoustic guitar and suggested I should get one, and that's how I came to learn a musical instrument. My mother graciously taking me and my Suzuki nylon-string to the Academy of Music in inner-city Spring Hill for lessons after school. The academy was a rabbit warren of rooms beneath a music store, and it was here, in school uniform, that I first touched the Brisbane rock scene. My teacher, a long-haired local muso, taught me basic music theory and I progressed to the chords of 'Yesterday', 'I Walked The Line' and some Chuck Berry riffs, Brisbane being a big blues town. It was apparent that I wasn't going to be the next Eric Clapton, not that I wanted to be, happy as I was to strum along with Ken to his choice of America and Cat Stevens tunes.

Ken was one of four or five boys in my circle of friends at

school, and we had a casual approach to hobbies at fifteen: Phillip Tanner was into surfing, so some of us bought surfboards and surfed. Music was there from the start. My father prepared for work with the radio on, at a volume heard throughout the house. Local AM stations 4QR and 4KQ mixed news and songs, the impact of the sounds of 1962 mirrored in the ease of my recollection of ghost pop classics like 'I Can't Stop Loving You' by Ray Charles, 'Red Roses For A Blue Lady' by Andy Williams, 'Those Lazy-Hazy-Crazy Days Of Summer' by Nat King Cole', 'Wolverton Mountain' by Claude King, and 'Hello Mary Lou' by Ricky Nelson. Then The Beatles hitting, and the change on the radio to the jump of 'Love Me Do' and 'Please Please Me'. I had photos of the band on my wall and a white plastic Beatles guitar to thrash, my interest so great that I was taken across the road and shown the photo-splattered teenage bedroom of the Manchester-born Harrison daughters Cathy and Judy, their father, in these Beatles-obsessed times, a minor celebrity with a first name of George.

My hysteria peaked at seven. I don't remember the Beatles hits of the next couple of years. Perhaps my father changed stations, or my interest faded, like a signal, to pick up again for The Lovin' Spoonful's 'Daydream' and Donovan's 'Sunshine Superman'. Catching my eye were long Saturday-afternoon TV shows hosted by exuberant pop stars with shoulder-length, centre-parted hair and paisley shirts. I'd lie on my stomach, chin cupped in my hands, watching late-sixties Australian rock groups and lonely female singers mime their latest singles, a call from Andy or one of the other boys in the street enough for me to flick off the screen and run out to play.

My parents, marrying in the mid-fifties, in their late twenties, effectively missed the sixties – Al Jolson, whose career must have been waning at their birth, a singer they both admired. Further afield, I had no uncles into blues or jazz, or aunties who 'sang a little'; my doting grandmother and Grandpa Charlie had played piano and sang, but I never heard them perform. Many years later my mother told me, 'My father would have loved to do what you do.' I was of a generation not told to be a farmer or a priest. The musical void, as in many Australian households, was filled with sport. My mother had been a physical education teacher before marriage, and my father was famously (in family legend) on the tennis court at my birth. The Ashgrove Golf Club, where both my parents were members, was at the bottom of our street, and golf was added to cricket and soccer as sports I played. Reigning over all was the fate of the Australian cricket team, a place in the squad every boy's dream, and the sporting pages, shared with or wrenched from my father, were my earliest reading.

So the strand drawing me to music was thin, and it was at my request that a record player came into our home. My parents bought a blue, all-in-one Dansette-style player light enough to lift with a finger, and with a stack of old jukebox singles from a business partner of my father's, I now had music at my control – three scratched Creedence Clearwater Revival records my favourites, John Fogerty's powerful rasp the first voice to grab me and tell me that some men roared like lions at the world.

*

Sometime in the wilds of 1972 I was home sick, and my mother had skipped work to care for me. I was sitting in a loungeroom chair enjoying the luxury of listening to the radio by day and not a snatched half-hour at night, and the dust in the air from my mother's sweeping was creating a glittering storm effect when from the radio came, 'Didn't know what time it was the lights were low oh oh/ I leant back on my radio/ Some cat was layin' down some rock and roll/ Lotta soul, he said.'

Immediately there was something different about this record. It was *knowing*, and confidential, the voice pitched somewhere between male and female, no gruff Fogerty or Lennon this time. The verse exploded into a chorus of tower-high melody and romanticism purposefully built to stun a fourteen-year-old. 'There's a starman waiting in the sky.' Ah! I was gone. For the sensitive listener the starman was the singer. We'd been waiting for him – I'd been waiting for him, without knowing it – and now he was here. 'That was "Starman" by new English singer David Bowie and his album is called . . .' (here the DJ paused, perhaps to gather breath) *The Rise and Fall of Ziggy Stardust and the Spiders from Mars.* Every name in that sentence was perfect and a mystery had been solved. I'd been buying occasional, three-month-old copies of *Melody Maker* or *NME* – that's how long they took to reach Australia by sea – and so the arrival of the record matched the first press and photos I saw of Bowie. Sound and vision in step, and what was more attractive, the singer or his song? Bowie didn't make me question my sexuality, and I didn't rush out and copy his haircut, although a few boys at school went a bit spiky; it was significant, however, that the most beautiful pop star of the early seventies was a man. Across town in a boarding school, a boy a year younger than me was being teased for having a Bowie poster above his bed.

*

Nineteen seventy-two was not only the year of pretty Ziggy, it was also my grandparent's fiftieth wedding anniversary, celebrations held at Cranbrook. My grandmother, wilting at the chance of attention, had let a hairdresser spin her wispy locks into a Harpo Marx perm; beside her, my grandfather sat as men of his vintage did, quietly ticking like clocks. They were seated at the head of the table in high-backed chairs, before a spread of relatives, cakes and tea. In honour, I read them a poem, birthdays and family events having recently prompted me to put lines to the page. Poem read, Aunt Sibbie slipped to my side, asking if we could speak in private.

'Did you write that?' she asked me in the garden.

'Yes I did.'

'Have you heard of a poet called Samuel Taylor Coleridge?'

'Um . . . yes.'

'He wrote a poem called "Kubla Khan" and another one called "The Rime of the Ancient Mariner".'

To hear such words coming from my aunt.

She paused to give me a withering look of consideration, then pursing her lips she went on, 'Samuel Taylor Coleridge had a son and his name was Derwent. And *he* was a teacher. Before our family came out from England, Derwent Coleridge was our family tutor. He was a good man and our family liked him a great deal. So much that it was decided to name the eldest child of each generation after him.'

I am Robert Derwent Garth Forster. Destiny had tapped, a pat to encourage stirring feelings I had of being someone with a gift for words. And see what they had brought me – a confession from an aunt in a rose garden. To my shame, as I listened my adolescent mind, on a twin track, had quickly moved to the flaw in the story. My grandfather's name was Derwent, incurring the unfortunate shortened form Der, and he wasn't the eldest son, and by now I was wondering if my parents had noticed my absence.

We went back to the party in silence. I didn't quite know what to make of the tale. It seemed fantastic, a jewel sitting on the plain gold band of our family name. And why was it a secret? I made a note to check a Coleridge biography when I could. I did. Coleridge had two sons, Matthew and Derwent.

As study got more serious and decisions on directions in life and university places loomed, I got lighter. It had taken me a while to work out the school, but in my fourth year I cracked it. I was helped in this by being able to drop subjects, so the sciences went. I chose the easy maths, and topped it. English was my masterstroke. I wondered what, if one teacher was marking two hundred essays on the same topic, would happen if paper 163 was completely different, went off on a whole other tack.

I was brave enough to try. The subject was Wilde's *The Importance of Being Earnest*, and ignoring the set questions, I wrote a play, scenes that put Wilde in the audience watching a first-night production of his play. Either it was going to be a triumph or I'd be hauled before the head of English to explain. I got the highest grade of seven and attention in the average class, as only half a dozen boys in the smart classes got such a grade. Crucially, I was being rewarded for doing the unexpected, which set a thrilling and dangerous precedent.

During the final years of school, when grades and patches are handed out in a general sorting that never happens again, I was in the first XI cricket team and prefect material. (The school wisely withholding the latter position.) My confidence was restored and I was enjoying my new role as raffish, lanky lord of mischief, willing to endure censure or detention for the sake of a quip, liked by the younger teachers, an enigma to the ancient and stern with my high grades and attention-seeking behaviour. My English essays were now fierce, Burroughs-style free association and still garnering top marks: I liked being provocative and successful. And it was this person, to the surprise and pride of my mother and father, who strode across the City Hall stage on speech night to accept an academic award and join a clutch of clever boys from whom I'd been separated five years earlier.

My instinct after that was to run, perhaps sensing that I didn't know much about life, women or money and that I should. Surfing magazines and other youth-culture literature whispered that it was possible to live in a caravan park in northern New South Wales near a surf break, work part-time in a petrol station (the owner generous in letting you hunt waves when the swells were on) and have surf chicks make you raisin toast and tea, all to a soundtrack of Neil Young's *Harvest*.

This was the school lunchtime fantasy talk and our parents were having none of it. Gap years hadn't been invented then; I wanted one, and chafed at the hypocrisy of those who claimed that after twelve years of education the will to learn, the very nut of what had been taught, would drop like a stone as you walked through the school gates for the last time.

I had been accepted into law, to start first semester in February 1975, but a sign of trouble ahead came when a friend explained that some legal terms require ten definitions. That was enough for me to change to arts.

There was one profession that would have had me settled into the workforce. The alternative commercial life of Brisbane traded in the dark arcades that linked the main city streets and the unrelenting sunshine. (It was noted by some that broader ideas went with cooler temperatures.) Here another heart of the city beat; Elizabeth Arcade had the East Wind Bookshop at its entrance, where I'd bought my copy of *The Communist Manifesto* – to wave before my grandparents and get the required gasp of horror – and inside the arcade, on its sloping tiled floor, was the town's only vegetarian cafe, an anarchist bookshop, Discreet Records (filled with choice pre-punk records), and at the far end, opposite a Mexican restaurant, Willy Bach's hair salon. I'd spied the young kids with their glam cuts snipping hair. Roxy Music was on the stereo. With a supreme act of will I approached the bearded owner to ask if he would take me on as an apprentice. 'No,' he said, and no more.

Stunned, by my courage and the rejection, I retreated. I would have made a great hairdresser. Had *the* salon in Sydney, LA or

London. When I hold a hairdryer it's the only thing that feels as natural in my hands as a guitar.

That seesawing summer, I drove around in a second-hand Falcon my parents had bought me. I was looking at my city from the driver's seat, finding out where I was – a capital city, but not Paris or Rome, and it had a hayseed image, lacking the cosmopolitan groove of Sydney and Melbourne. The local media proudly called it a 'big country town': depressing for those of us who didn't want to live in a big country town. The landscape, though, was stunning, especially the line of western suburbs that ran out from the city centre on a ridge – Red Hill, Paddington, Bardon, Ashgrove – to end in the one-road-in, two-roads-out kingdom of The Gap. It was a slice of San Francisco in the town's flat, Los Angeles-like bake. Above us the skies were deep blue – popcorn clouds skirting the afternoon horizon. Storms came on Fridays, lightning-jutting beasts that pelted the city with an hour of tropical rain, washing it clean and giving to the vegetation an intensity of colour that was almost psychedelic. The University of Queensland was on my round, situated in St Lucia at a bend of the Brisbane River. The campus, girded with sandstone arches, acted as a sanctuary in a town such as this; it would buy me three years' escape from the nine-to-five world, I thought, and by then I might know what I wanted to do.

None of my schoolfriends were in my faculty. Phillip Tanner and Malcolm Kelly were studying engineering; Ken Bates, who I quickly lost close contact with, was sensibly doing law. I was looking for friends and connections as I weaved down the tight, ant-like corridors of the Michie Building, home of the humanities. The majority of the arts students were women: smart girls from private schools thinking of becoming high school teachers. I soon befriended Virginia Clarke and Marissa Trigger – the misfits had found each other. Virginia was like no one on campus. She lived in rough Inala, had gone to Oxley High, was into The New York Dolls, and Iggy and the Stooges, and in dress and demeanour eschewed the hippyish, home-on-the-prairies appearance of most of the student body. Her cool quotient was proved to be at ten when, seeking to impress her, I casually dropped the name of a band I was in, which was pinched from a one-off performance of a pop group in a sixties TV show.

'The Mosquitoes?' She smiled. 'Like on *Gilligan's Island*?' Virginia was clever and in my ear; she raved about a rock band formed by older boys from her school, inviting me to their gigs and telling me they were soon to record a single. They had just changed their name to The Saints. I listened and simmered in the belief, ridiculous even to myself, that no Brisbane band was going to be of any significance till I started it.

Around us, on noticeboards, in lectures, at rallies and meetings, there was revolution in the air. The Queensland government had been run long-term by a cunning, right-wing hillbilly dictator named Joh Bjelke-Petersen: a 'bible-bashing bastard', the prime minister Gough Whitlam had called him, the Whitlam government to be toppled in my second semester, Bjelke-Petersen at its throat. With the Brisbane press spineless, and the 'country town' myopia quelling any dissent from Business or Church, it was left to the university to voice fury and organise resistance to the cuts to civil liberties. As a seventeen-year-old fresh from the cloister of grammar school, I walked straight into Berkeley 1968. And there wasn't the comfort of hearing any anger echoed at home around the dinner table, my father a worker but not a union man, politics and social justice not of great interest. I wasn't born for the barricades, was bewildered at them, bobbing through my first year of tertiary education like a cork on stormy seas.

No refuge in the English department either. 'If you want to do creative writing you'll have to go somewhere else,' I was told by a tutor as she returned my work unmarked. My school method and its hitherto success vanishing in a stroke. Had I gone too far in adding photographs between the text of my assignment? (In the nineties I would come across the scrapbook-like work of renowned German author W.G. Sebald and think, *I used to do that.*) My problem was that literature instilled a creative impulse in me, not an academic one. Theme, comparison and textual analysis were not my passions, whereas the biographical data of the writer and the entertainment value of their work were – not good when English is a plank of your degree. And I was lazy, not willing to join the sprint to the library to snaffle the best books and hold them on long loans. I did go, to find sanctuary and works outside my reading lists.

My interest in the counterculture led me to Paul Goodman's *Growing Up Absurd*, and anything I could find on the Beats and commune history. I tried unsuccessfully to uncover more on my neighbour Noel Mitchell's death through back issues of the city newspaper, *The Courier-Mail*, and in the magazine section of the library I entered New York via *The Village Voice* – CBGB's

bills, off-Broadway reviews, loft prices, and an early photo of
Talking Heads: two men and a woman who hadn't assumed
a rock uniform when beginning a band. Interesting. With no
clock or surveillance on me, I spent days crisscrossing aisles as
one association triggered investigation into another; until the
task at hand was belatedly recalled in the late afternoon, to drag
me back to the bare shelves where I had begun.

University results were not mailed to students, or discreetly
placed on campus noticeboards. Instead they were printed at the
end of each semester in *The Courier-Mail*. There were no secrets
in this town. Of four subjects, I scraped through two; it was a
chilly morning at The Gap. I'd been apprehensive about getting my results, having come to realise that the borders I chafed
against at school suited my subversive temperament better than
the freedom I was given at university. To *feel* free, I need a system, a box to run my hand along. There was one shock, though:
the lowest mark of one for journalism after having done all the
assignments. Had I quivered too much as my professor leant on
my neck at the typewriter? Should I have joined him and other
young men at the university pool? Excuses I couldn't put to my
bewildered parents.

*

'Early one mornin' the sun was shinin'/ I was layin' in bed/
Wond'rin' if she'd changed at all/ If her hair was still red.' It all
depends on where you come in with Bob Dylan – for me he
was a pop star, not a prophet, *Greatest Hits Volume I* being the
first album of his I owned, and 'Knockin' On Heaven's Door'

sitting beside 'Ballroom Blitz' and 'Me And You And A Dog Named Boo' on my AM radio. By 1975 I'd caught up, in time to appreciate the excited and rejuvenated opening lines of *Blood on the Tracks*.

Music was still one in a field of interests I had, a horse on the inside rail soon to pull out and overtake everything else. I'd bought a decent record player from the proceeds of a summer job at Woolworths, and seen Roxy Music at Festival Hall, my first concert – Bryan Ferry, in a white tuxedo jacket, black hair glistening, gliding through the band to the microphone, making a big impression. I was reading the music press more often, and with money from a part-time job my father had organised at a brush-making factory I was buying albums. Not enough to fill a wall, but key records I'd play over and over again, like Bowie's *Diamond Dogs* and *Young Americans*. Important too was the forgotten sixties pop collected on *Nuggets*, and the first Velvet Underground album. My keen appreciation of the Velvets was based on a misunderstanding. I thought they could barely play, while marvelling at their songs; only later did I discover the avant-garde credentials of John Cale and the long-time rock'n'roll roots of Lou Reed and Sterling Morrison. It got me thinking: what would a band be like that was not traditionally proficient on their instruments, but astonished by having the best songs in town?

Nothing illustrates my perplexed state of mind at the start of second semester better than my results at the end of it. I try six subjects, withdraw quickly from two, pass two, and only do one English subject – EN103, Introduction to Literature B –

which is where I meet Grant. He is sitting two or three seats down from me in a room squared with white tables, where twenty students sit facing a tutor leading a revision of the weekly lecture and a discussion of the texts. The atmosphere is competitive, allowing the smarter and more confident students space to shine. Grant is one of them, but I can also see he is not protective of what he knows, which is a lot. He is leaning forward, listening, brown hair touching his collar. Pressed jeans, smart shirt. I am soon to learn he is a year younger than me, an anomaly in the school system allowing those born in January and February to start a year early, and maybe that fires his attention and gives his acne-traced moon face its touch of innocence.

By mid-semester we are talking as we leave class. There's an instant groove to our humour and a little more curiosity in our thinking than is usual in the corridor-to-lift, lift-to-front-door chat. He would have talked film, and told me that he worked part-time at the university cinema – the Schonell; I would have countered with music, that I owned an electric guitar and had just started a band. And we must have spoken of schools; he'd boarded at Church of England Grammar School ('Churchie') and had a room on campus at St John's College – so, a country boy used to living alone far from home, in contrast to my suburban family life. The boarder and the day boy. Big differences. Each of us would have noted the depth of the enthusiasms in the other; still, it was always a quick farewell with no plans made to meet up during the week, or during the holidays when the semester finished.

And it could have all ended there. Another interesting person you meet who walks out of your life. Instead: first week, first term of the following year. A different subject, and there he is. 'Hey, it's you,' we chorus. While the others in the room nervously peek at each other, Grant and I greet one another like long-lost friends – which, in a way we will never understand, we are.

We pull up chairs and begin.

Escaping the Vampires

Had Grant and I looked closer at our fellow pupils, we would have noticed that EN170, Drama 1A gathered the more eccentric and outgoing students in the English department. For me, though of interest, the subject had the reputation of being an easy pass; for Grant, sailing through his degree, it was an exotic choice but one linked to his passion for film. Unbeknown to ourselves we had landed in the perfect place to foster a friendship. Drama tutorials broke from the university, being held off campus in the Avalon Theatre – a small, timber and brick building not unlike a suburban house, five hundred metres from the entrance of the university on Sir Fred Schonell Drive. Here was a learning environment different from the swift shuffling in and out done in other subjects. Best of all, drama courses could be taken over two years – there was time to get to know one another.

Leading our class was Professor Harry Garlick – the first person you could say who held authority over Grant and me together, and we got lucky. Harry, in his forties, communicated his ideas with a manner so reserved and charming that I mistook him for an Englishman for the entire time I took the course. There was something of the schoolmaster about him too, but one willing to indulge the louder and more wayward members of the class. The general subject was the history of the theatre from the Elizabethan Age to the present, and as much as I enjoyed the early classes, it was when we reached the late-nineteenth-century plays (Ibsen, Strindberg, Chekhov) and beyond that things got interesting for me. The full rush coming with exposure to the work of Genet, Beckett, Ionesco, Brecht, Pinter and Pirandello – a strand of laugh-out-loud absurdist texts that could be read in an hour and contained an outrageous line in plot and jokey dialogue. These were the first things I encountered at university that spoke right to me, that hit with the freshness and punch of a favoured album or an episode of *Bewitched* or *Get Smart* – the cultural benchmarks of a television-watching child of the sixties.

If the first image I have of Grant is him sitting a few places down from me in class, the second has him standing at the bottom of the steep concrete stairs that lead up to the Avalon. He is waiting for Harry, chatting with a group of students as I arrive; under his arm are three records. This was typical of Grant, unabashed as he was in carrying film and rock magazines, novels and poetry books around campus. It was something I didn't do – the Velvet Underground records stayed at home – yet I admired him for it, and it helped me see what he had to offer.

The three albums were Ian Hunter's eponymous debut, *Paradise and Lunch* by Ry Cooder, and *Late for the Sky* by Jackson Browne. Hunter had been the lead singer and song-writer of Mott the Hoople, and his appearance is testament to Grant's love of British rock, especially the riffy glam kind. The record begins with Hunter intoning in uber-cockney brio, ''allo', a greeting Grant and I would sporadically drop on each other for the rest of our lives. Cooder, an FM radio and critics' favourite, was in the middle of a fine run of roots albums – long on feel, short on extended guitar solos, although he was a mas-ter guitarist. Both of these albums I also owned. As for Jackson Browne, he was Grant's preferred singer-songwriter of the time, his long, mournful songs appealing to those searching for some-thing literary or 'deeper' in rock. I thought he was a pretentious West Coast hippie, an opinion I hoped I held to myself. Perhaps it was just the quick-changing musical times that saw him fall further back in Grant's estimation.

Our taste in music was similar from the start, with no sense of having to convert the other to a position. If there was one generalisation that could be put to our exchanges, it was his championing of The Monkees to my Velvets and mid-sixties Dylan leanings. The breaking wave of punk we both welcomed, and our opinions on each new artist and group were generally in step.

The drama department didn't give acting lessons, although we read plays aloud and some scenes were staged. Grant and I liked to fossick in the costume trunks, through the medieval cloaks, the capes, the bowler hats, to get to the swords. Immediately it was Errol Flynn and Basil Rathbone between us. We would joust, our free arms bowed, our legs splayed, fighting in mock seriousness; and then, knowing that traffic was in gridlock on Sir Fred Schonell Drive, we would burst out of the doors of the Avalon to continue our duel down the long front stairs of the theatre. Our eyes locked as we alternated pinning the other to a wall or railing, only for the other to gallantly fight back. Drivers and passengers of the stalled cars sat open-mouthed or laughing as we came into view. Soon we were sword-fighting between the cars, with not a giveaway smirk, only the occasional roared 'You cad!' or 'Take that, you bastard!' And then just as quickly the fight would retreat up the stairs, like the rewinding of a film reel, and we'd disappear through the theatre doors.

These were the first Go-Betweens performances.

*

I visited Grant only once at St John's College before he moved with a group of university friends to a delightfully shabby house at 19 Golding Street, Toowong. Grant had a room at the front of the house; next to him was Andrew Wilson (a medical student and friend of his from north Queensland) and his girlfriend, Karen Byatt, who studied social work. In a third bedroom on the other side of the house, past the kitchen, lived Ian Lilley (an archaeology student and school acquaintance of mine) with his girlfriend Cathy, who worked a day job. The large lounge-room was in the centre, furnished with stuffed fifties chairs and a couch that faced a poster of Fellini's *Amarcord* big enough to be classed as wallpaper. A record player sat on top of a wooden cabinet that held shelves of Grant's albums and singles. The house was perfect in layout and feel, and there were trees shading it, so the rooms, even on the hottest days, were cool and musty. I would drop by often enough to be asked to contribute food money. Golding Street was special; it was the first share house I experienced, and I liked the easy coming and going lifestyle and the people who lived there.

But it was Grant I came to see, and I was received in a manner that varied little through the years. He would be lying on his neatly made single bed, a magazine propped on his chest, which he'd drop below his nose on my arrival to offer a dreamy greeting of 'Oh, hi Bobbie.' He was one of the few people to call me that. I might have had a morning lecture or come from a shift at the brush factory, and here – was Grant. Outside, the world was whirring, people were doing things, conducting business. *His* contribution: reclining in bed in the early afternoon, having been there since late morning, a glass of cold milk on a bedside table, reading the latest edition of *Film Comment*. The lesson from this, and perhaps the greatest one I ever got from him was – *it didn't matter*. Grant had none of my suburban, middle-class hang-ups about the proper appropriation of time and effort. He seemed remarkably unattached from the start; his connection to the world, I was to discover, was through the things he loved, even as they disconnected him further from the world around him.

The walls of his room were coated in movie posters, with

a predominance of Charlie Chaplin one-sheeters – Grant's cinematic passion du jour. 'Chaplin is a genius,' he said the first time I stepped through the door. On the floor, like towers spiking up through the floorboards, were stacks of *The New Yorker*, *Film Comment*, the *New York Review of Books*, and a rock pile consisting of *ZigZag*, *Rolling Stone* and *NME*. Long, low bookshelves against one wall were filled with contemporary American fiction – big on McGuane, Barthelme and Cheever – plus a history-of-cinema section and poetry books. Prior conversations had hinted at what could be here. To see it all stacked at his fingertips stunned me.

What would he have seen at my place? A single bed, a record player, fifty albums, a few paperbacks, and a guitar case *all messed up*.

Besides being impressed with what I saw, I suspected I was the first person to really understand what was on display in his room, and he knew that. This in turn relates to how I perceived myself at the time, because although I was failing half my courses and was a tall, goofy kind of guy, unsure of myself and with absolutely no idea of what I wanted to do, I thought I was the smartest person at the university. Yes, really. It just didn't show up in my grades. How could it? When what I valued, a messy mixture of high and low culture, wasn't being taught on campus. I knew I had something no one else had, but what?

Meeting Grant didn't dissolve all these dilemmas in a day; he was, though, the first person I'd met who was entirely on my wavelength, who I soon came to regard as an equal – a huge admission from me, knee-deep as I was in nothingness and the mud. Vitally, too, he was keeping his options open. Speaking in dreams, uttering 'New York' and 'Paris' not as honeymoon destinations, but as cities to one day walk through and work in. To conquer. Little of this or its consequence was running through my head as I bowled in and out of Golding Street on my way to and from university. But magic hands, belonging to whom we never knew, had lit the candle.

His bedroom told one other story. Boarding school. This explained the neatness and the sense of protectiveness that went with what he'd collected. I was to learn that he lent little – 'Read it here' – and when he did lend an item it was expected to come back in as good, if not better, condition as when it left.

We delved seldom into each other's pasts. At eighteen is there really any need? Plus we were uptight, itchy boys. But details did pop out. His middle name was William and he was born in Rockhampton. His father was a doctor, who died when Grant was six. (This remained very tender territory, never explored in subsequent conversations.) He was an eldest son, like me, with two younger siblings, Lachlan and Sally. After his father's passing, Grant's mother Wendy had taken the family north to her hometown of Cairns. The late 1960s in this tropical town – with holiday visits to the hinterland farm of Wendy's sister Gillian, her husband Gerry and their two children Nicola and Bram – was a golden time after a bruising beginning. And it was from this idyll, at the age of eleven turning twelve, that Grant was sent sixteen hundred kilometres south to board in Brisbane at 'Churchie'. A country boy without a dad, scared, you would have to think, of being teased and tested.

He responded with academic success, ability at sport – cricket in particular – and the side of him that was increasingly drawn to music, film and books. Lonely boarding-house hours allowing an almost fanatical focus to be given these passions. As self-protection, and as the rewards of school and his interests flamed, an arrogance must have crept in – never too much to dissuade me, but it was there when we met, the twisted smile when correcting my mispronunciations, a sleepy-eyed superiority when supplying pop culture facts. Two weeks after his seventeenth birthday he was at university passing every subject. The impression he made, and this was certainly perceived by others too, was Grant as boy wonder.

His great love was film, and working part-time at the Schonell in the flush of new Hollywood and European art cinema was a dream job for him. He also wrote film reviews for the student paper, and articles for the nationally distributed *Cinema Papers*, surely making him their youngest contributor. He burnt for the screen and wanted to be a reviewer or director, or both, like his heroes François Truffaut and Jean-Luc Godard. He knew he couldn't do this from Brisbane, and the arts degree was a sensible career foundation that also bought him time: you had to be twenty or twenty-one to apply for entry into the country's leading film school at the National Institute of Dramatic Arts (NIDA) in Sydney. That was his future.

My idea of a good movie was *The Sting*. And I was to jokingly hold a populist, reverse-snob attitude to film all the while Grant led me to fall under its luminescent spell. Soon I too was talking Italian neorealism, film noir, and the genius of Orson

Welles, my nose in the history of cinema and back issues of *Film Comment*. I discovered a world as quirky and wild as rock'n'roll. It set us off on adventures – talking our way into a university French class to see Louis Malle's *Zazie dans le Métro*, taking a lift to the twenty-third floor of a city building to watch the films of Kenneth Anger, presented by the great man himself to a film society of thirty people, all of whom were at least twenty years older than us. There were also movies at home – skipping a lecture on Grant's instruction to indulgently curl up before the midday movie on TV, to not only watch a rare showing of Truffaut's *Stolen Kisses*, but, in the jargon of the day, read it too.

*

While Grant was in shared-house bohemia, I was out in the suburbs going through some of the messiest years of my life. My parents resisted me leaving home. The student houses of Bardon and Toowong were unknown to them and yet regarded as corrupting (perhaps they knew their son all too well), and being financially unable to move I stayed put. After the harmony and accomplishments of my school years, university opened the cracks, or the generation gap, to be more precise – I was being educated out of my parents' viewpoints. It was a sting to education they didn't see coming, and one I didn't communicate, moody and sullen as I was. I knew the suburbs were a trap. The image I had in my head was *living with vampires*: one bite of the neck and I'd have a local girlfriend, be going to teenage parties, and it would all be over by the time I was twenty.

To ward this away I had my set of essentials – a car, some cash, and a guitar. Sounds like a Springsteen song, doesn't it? Music was about to come and save me.

The Suzuki nylon-string had been superseded by a black Ibanez Les Paul, the kind of lairy electric guitar you walk out of a music shop with the first time. I wanted to start a real band – The Mosquitoes was me on guitar jamming with non-instrument-playing mates – and with schoolfriend Malcolm Kelly on bass, and a schoolboy drummer named Dave found through an ad, we began rehearsing halfway through my first year at university, in 1975. This was the group I'd told Grant about. We practised at various places that were usually associated with my father's work. As extraordinary as this sounds – and in hindsight it comes to me as a truly heroic action – we would meet at an engineering works in the middle of an industrial estate by the airport on a Sunday morning, let ourselves in with the key I'd been given and unload our gear onto the factory floor, clearing a space amidst the lathes and welding equipment to plug in and play.

Our repertoire, like our practice location, ran counter to the prevailing music scene in Brisbane. We didn't play heavy metal or progressive rock, and we never could work up the required three hours of tightly rehearsed material needed to break into the suburban-hall dance scene – the only gigs in town. We played a mixture of short, fast-paced songs from The Beatles ('I Feel Fine', 'One After 909'), The Beach Boys ('Help Me, Rhonda', 'I Get Around', 'Sloop John B') and The Doors ('Love Me Two Times', 'Riders On The Storm'), plus odd pieces of fancy such as 'To Sir With Love' by Lulu, 'Rebel Rebel' by

Bowie, and 'You Sexy Thing' by Hot Chocolate. None of them done with the right amount of cabaret professionalism essential to secure regular, or irregular, gigs. It was fun, and I wasn't to know I was learning how songs were constructed.

Another problem halting the band's progress was our inability to find a lead guitarist. Someone who could weave melodic lines with any sensitivity around my rhythm guitar and the vocals of Mal and me – many Ritchie Blackmore/Jimmy Page sound- and look-alikes tried. One thing did come from the auditions: when we asked these lightning-fingered virtuosos to play a riff or a song of theirs, it was evident that the primitive songs I'd just begun writing were better than anything they showed us.

My frustration with this auditioning process was accompanied by a drifting away from the band through the influence of punk. The Ramones' first album, which I bought on import in April '76, was the moment everybody else in rock suddenly sounded flabby and old, and it led to a turn in my thinking. If a musician couldn't be found, a friend could be taught. It then followed that a group could be cast like a play or a movie. This solution may have been partly inspired by a story floating through the music press about the beginnings of a group out of New York called Television. They had yet to release their debut album and meisterwerk *Marquee Moon*, but a single, 'Little Johnny Jewel', was on rotation at Golding Street, as was the myth of the band's foundation. Exasperated at finding no musicians capable and compatible enough for the material he was composing, singer-songwriter Tom Verlaine had taught his best friend Richard Hell to play bass.

Grant and I could sing together, our renditions of 'Daydream Believer' in lofty, tipsy voices as I drove him home from end-of-semester parties at the Avalon solid proof of that. If the sword fights were one intimation of our future, the blending of our voices was another, and in the march to music there were trips to Brisbane's three import record shops, where we authoritatively flicked through the racks in search of the singles and albums we were reading about in *NME*, *The Village Voice* and *New York Rocker*, the last a fantastic, short-lived fanzine that took us into rehearsal rooms and lofts, the dream locations of our favoured New York bands.

In early '77 I asked Grant if he'd form a band with me. 'No,' was his blunt reply. His NIDA dream was still very much alive. I backed off and kept trying to shape my group. We'd played one gig, a sparsely attended dance at Dave's high school, and at the end of '77 came the opportunity to play *two* shows. The second was an end-of-term party at Dave's home, and my last performance with the group; the first was of greater importance, being an opening round of a Battle of the Bands competition, held in a downstairs room with a stage at the Academy of Music. The group had sharpened over the previous months. We were now a three-piece, the idea of a second guitarist abandoned, and we had a name, The Godots – filched from my drama studies. It came with a jokey slogan swimming in my head, which was never used: 'The band everyone's been waiting for.'

My songwriting had also improved, taking a lion-sized leap with the completion of a simple, predominantly two-chorded number, a paean to the female librarians at the university – helpful, distant women I idealised – that swelled and built over three verses and choruses to end in a shouted climax of the song's title, 'Karen'.

I had pretty much fallen into songwriting, my eye and ego having been on other forms of self-expression: a movie-maker with an eight-millimetre camera, writing fiction or plays, or should I become Brisbane's Robert De Niro out at the Avalon? All the while, I'd been chugging along compos-ing songs, 'Transatlantic Airways' and other sub-Bowie/Ziggy things that bore little relation to my life, until one good song, 'I'm The Doll', changed all that, zeroing in as it did on my stranded predicament. It also had the best tune I'd written so far. I was listening intently to the first Jonathan Richman and the Modern Lovers album and *Ramones* while taking broader lessons from songwriters and authors I admired. Write what you know: that came to me. I'd never rewrite 'Starman' or 'A Hard Rain's A-Gonna Fall', but then Bowie and Dylan hadn't grown up in The Gap, looked for golf balls in the tall grass behind the fifth hole at Ashgrove Golf club, or driven the rollercoaster hills in a beat-up Ford aching for a girlfriend. I'd had a breakthrough in my approach with 'Doll', and 'Karen' was the next good song I wrote, getting me very excited indeed.

I brought it to our final rehearsal, wanting to play the song at the Academy. After showing Malcolm the chords and explaining the feel and structure, we had a first run-through in his parents' garage. (Yes, the glories of garage rock.) The hair on my arms was prickling and my head helium-light as I strummed and sang the ascending and descending steps the song took. At its banged conclusion there was a spooked silence between us. For two years we had been chasing the history of rock'n'roll; 'Karen' sounded as if it could be part of it.

Each of the four groups in the Battle of the Bands heat had twenty minutes. Our set consisted of one cover, 'Sweet Jane' by the Velvets, and four of my originals. The other groups, in long hair and denim, did tight facsimiles – 'cover version' is too loose a description – of early-seventies hard rock numbers. Two things stick in my mind from those twenty minutes. My Iggy Pop impersonation as the guitarless lead singer on 'Sweet Jane', which had the audience more bending in laughter than cowering in fear, and performing 'Karen' for the first time. Writing and rehearsing it was one thing, playing it live to an audience another.

An attentive silence came over the room as we began the song, brought on by the hypnotic beat of the long introduction; I was sensing a power I'd never known as I stepped to the microphone to deliver the opening lines: 'I just want some affection/ I just want some affection/ I don't want no hoochie-coochie mama/ No back door woman/ No Queen Street sex thing.'

I'd been waiting a long time to say that. Here was a declaration from a twenty-year-old, anti-rock'n'roll in its dismissal of sex clichés, and with a local reference thrown in. It went on: 'Helps me find Hemingway/ Helps me find Genet/ Helps me find Brecht/ Helps me find Chandler/ Helps me find James Joyce/ She always makes the right choice.'

The audience was unused to this kind of language coming off a Brisbane rock stage. Even nonbelievers – those hostile to how plain we looked in our white shirts and black trousers, and to the rawness of our playing – were aware that something special was happening. We had a few supporters in the crowd – my brother, who had mimed on bass while Mal played guitar on 'Sweet Jane'; Mal's girlfriend, who I could see was following the song's story and laughing on certain lines; and sitting halfway back at the end of a row of seats was Grant.

We didn't win the heat. Later I learnt that The Saints had entered the same competition years before and they didn't win their opening round either. It didn't matter; a few realisations came from our performance. You didn't need much instrumentation if you were throwing interesting lyrics over hooky chord changes; if anything, 'noise' got in the way. And we had been billed, through a misunderstanding – Beckett not travelling far or well out of academia – as The Go Dots. I liked the change.

By now, Grant was finishing his degree with the intention of heading north for Christmas and New Year. I was about to lose him. His mother had recently remarried and was living with her new husband on a cattle property five hours west of Cairns called Oak Park. In early December, days after a cancelled Blondie show we were to attend, Grant was preparing to leave. I had to try one more time. I now thought of myself as a songwriter, having followed 'Karen' with a flood of new material including 'Lee Remick' and 'Eight Pictures', *and* as a salesman. I approached Grant again with the idea of starting a band.

He surprised me with a plan.

I should come over to Golding Street, play my new songs into his cassette player; he would then take the tape up to Oak Park, where he would listen, think on my proposal, and send me his answer by mail. Has an audition for a band ever been more bizarre? But then, if Grant and I were starting it, how normal was it ever going to be?

A postcard arrived at The Gap just after Christmas bearing the image of an idyllic remote beach ringed by rainforest and blue water, and the words 'Greetings from north Queensland'. It read, 'Dear Rob, I hope your practice is going okay. I've been listening to the tape – boy, there's something there for the future. I've seen the new Blondie dates and I was depressed. Anyway. Grant.'

Grant, I was learning, could be cautious. But I knew him well enough by now to know that this was a yes.

That Striped Sunlight Sound

We were driving across the Grey Street Bridge, Grant in the passenger seat, when he turned to ask, 'Have you thought of a name for the group?'

I knew I had the right name, but I also realised that the band, however long it lasted, would be a contest and configuration of our wills. And be the stronger for it. I drew breath and as evenly as I could said, 'The Go-Betweens.'

He waited a few seconds, letting the name ring in his head.

'Good,' he said.

Thirty-two years later and five hundred metres downriver, I would open the Go Between Bridge, the first new bridge to span the centre of Brisbane in forty years.

I'd had a plan B back then, but it wasn't really a contender: The Hepburns. Named after Katharine of course. I liked the sound of it – the 'hep' and the 'burns' had a rock'n'roll feel to it, although it's hard to imagine anyone less rock'n'roll than Katharine Hepburn. And that appealed to me too. But with a name like that and a song called 'Lee Remick', we'd be backing ourselves into a corner. And the Hepburn Bridge . . .?

If someone had snuck up the front stairs of 19 Golding Street in early 1978, to peer through a slit in a set of curtains drawn to shut out the fierce midsummer sun, they would have seen two young men with guitars slung around their shoulders, micro-phones at their mouths, belting out an assortment of primitive pop numbers. We were a two-piece band, rehearsing the songs I'd played into the cassette player. Grant was already pushing me. 'When are we going to learn "Karen"?' I was holding that back as a prize for early progress. I needn't have bothered. Anything he put his mind to was going to get his best; all the focus and inten-sity that had gone into film was transferred to music, to the bass guitar. A two- or three-day gap in rehearsing and I'd return to see he'd made another leap, his fingers raw – he probably hadn't left his room.

The instruction I imparted to him was simple. I explained that we must play corresponding notes on our guitars, and while showing him where they sat on the bass, and the scales that moved around them, a wonderful thing became apparent: Grant was musical. Here was our first piece of luck. He could have fumbled, and only maintained a crude rhythm to my gui-tar chords – this had been the way when most musicians had taught a friend, a reason for Richard Hell subsequently being sacked from Television by Verlaine. Instead, Grant had the root notes covered immediately, and in the weeks and months after-wards was adding the attractive melodies that were to become a feature of his music.

The intensity we put into the group was helped by the fact that neither of us had a girlfriend. Grant was involved with a woman, but she was also the girlfriend of Steve Hadden, a funny, handsome friend of his from St John's College. Here was a warning: Grant could be flirty with other guys' partners. As for myself, having grown up without a sister, gone to a boys' school, and arrived at university without ever speaking to a girl for longer than twenty minutes, there must have been waves of uncertainty and strangeness coming off me that were detectable to the few young women I did meet. (Virginia Clarke's leather skirt and full figure were so overpowering as to disembody me.) This dilemma was fuelling my songs, and would do so for the next eighteen months.

*

In one respect, Brisbane in 1978 was like London in '77 or New York in '76 – the year that punk rock broke. Miraculously, Brisbane had a chapter in the short history of this new musi-cal movement. The Saints, after self-releasing their debut single '(I'm) Stranded' in 1976, followed it up with two albums, and in '78 they released their third and best, *Prehistoric Sounds*, and broke up.

The Saints and their myth haunted the town's nascent punk scene. It was still possible to visit, as Grant and I did, a bombed-out terrace house in inner-city Petrie Terrace and gingerly walk over splintered floors to the site of the group's debut album cover shot. Damn that we weren't photographed there. Important also was the manner of their departure from Brisbane. The steps were glass-clear and majestic – record a classic first single, send it off overseas, and get signed to a London label for a multi-album worldwide deal. Voila! For a band of dreamers, which The Go-Betweens were, here was our shining path.

At the end of February, a number of bands were billed to play at Baroona Hall in Caxton Street, Paddington. There were four hundred people in the high-staged, country-style hall when Grant and I arrived, an early show of strength from the town's punk 'community'. We knew no one in the room, and after watching two bands play, something prodded my pride and I asked Grant whether, if I could get us a chance to play between groups, he would perform. He agreed. I found a woman involved in running the gig, Anne Jones, and after explaining that I was in a newly formed band, I asked if we could play. 'We'd be quick,' I added. She said she'd find out, and returned to say, 'Two songs, after this group. Their drummer will back you.' And so it was with punk.

Ronnie Rebbit and the Toadettes were comic hippies, and in a matter of weeks bands like them were no longer on bills. Their drummer Gerard Lee was a published short-story writer of some notoriety, and he sat behind the drums with a wry smile as he listened to me give instructions for our songs. Before us, the crowd, some of whom were hellbent on replicating the violence they'd read about at London gigs, murmured and growled. 'The first song is fast,' I told him while adjusting my guitar strap.

'I'll count it in and we'll just go.'

He nodded. 'What's it called?'

'"Lee Remick".'

Another smile.

Full marks to Grant. He'd never played with a drummer before and he'd been learning bass for under two months. I was spitting out the song's opening lines, 'She comes from Ireland/ She's very beautiful/ I come from Brisbane I'm quite plain,' knowing a killer chorus would arrive in ten seconds. The crowd stood open-mouthed in wonder. We *were* playing the best pop song to be written in town since '(I'm) Stranded'. The hall cheered as we finished, and I turned my back on the appreciative audience to impart further ideas to Gerard. 'This song doesn't have any drums except in the middle, when you play a solo and then stop.' Given the success of the last song, he was willing to follow this crazy notion. The second song was 'Eight Pictures', a raw, waltz-time ballad – 'I shot you with my Kodak/ Caught you making love with him' – as startlingly different from punk orthodoxies as cheeky 'Lee Remick'.

At the stairs that led offstage, people were waiting to meet us. An image that attaches itself to this moment is of a debutant, long hidden and groomed, entering a ballroom and suddenly meeting everybody. We were no longer two anonymous university students, we were The Go-Betweens. It had taken ten minutes and was to change our lives. Amidst those proffering handshakes and introductions were five guys in black suits who looked like a 1964 beat group. They were the headlining band, The Numbers, and their bass player, a cherub-faced, blond-haired young man named Robert Vickers, was one of a few people there that night who would re-enter our story.

This had always been the run of the night's events in my memory. So it was a surprise when, in 2013, a photo surfaced on Facebook which on close inspection proved to be of this first show. The photographer, Paul O'Brien, had in the space of two songs snapped an image. It's our 1957 Woolton Fete shot – John Lennon and a skiffle band on the back of a truck – and in it, Grant and I are playing our *own* guitars. We must have come with the intention of asking to perform. And with the evidence of the photo, I faintly recalled that we did bring them along. It also explains my spur-of-the-moment courage in asking to play. When Anne Jones said we could, we dashed off to the car. The opening of our career, then, not as romantic as I'd wished to remember.

The following week we got a call from The Numbers asking us to play at their next gig, in the Queensland University refectory. There we did 'Lee Remick' and 'Karen' with their drummer Dennis Cantwell, again playing with no rehearsal. There were fewer people at this show, but one of them was the most important person I'd met since Grant.

*

The Toowong Village in the late seventies was a tree-lined street of single-storey shops. In our minds, Greenwich Village. One shopfront had a large, fishbowl-like glass window: the Toowong Music Centre. It wasn't your average suburban record store, thanks to its owner, Damian Nelson. He was in his mid-twenties and had opened the shop in early 1976, stocking it with a broad selection of records that pleased his taste. It had a passing trade that included shaggy-haired, shoulder-bag-carrying students of both sexes on their way to and from university. Three blocks back was Golding Street. Grant was a customer, impressing Damian with his boy-wonder shine.

Soon Grant was doing a two-hour lunch shift in the shop, allowing Damian to drive his metal-grey Peugeot back home to his parents' house in Bardon for lunch and a round of tennis on the family court, then return for the afternoon shift. The three of us quickly became friends, and although Damian had the car and the shop and a circle of vivacious women vying for his attention (in appearance he was a very seventies mix of Edward Kennedy and Robert Redford), he wasn't an egocentric businessman. The store was a meeting place, its owner by turns intrigued, amused and supportive of his fast-talking friends and their decision to form a rock band.

I was at Golding Street, listening to music or reading from Grant's library, or both, while eating an inch-thick peanut butter sandwich probably, when he returned from his shift at the shop to tell me that he and Damian wanted to start a record label. And finance the recording of a single by us.

I was stunned, and grateful. Two gigs, no drummer, and now our first record – it sounded just right. We'd come to The Go-Betweens as romantics, me teaching my best friend bass, doing our first show after six weeks, and neither of us having served any kind of standard rock'n'roll apprenticeship in pubs and clubs. Always interested in short cuts, and believers in the

Hollywood version of stardom – quick and lucky – at times we barely thought of ourselves as musicians, but as conductors of a whole set of ideas and influences that got their best expression through a pop band. The Monkees on their TV show never played regular gigs or loaded gear. They hung around a house, were up for madcap adventures, freezing the action to play a brilliant song. And that was Golding Street too. We knew it wasn't going to last, that the hard work and disappointment would come, but the dreamy flight of our early years never really left Grant and me, or our vision of the band.

We formed the Able Label with Damian and he set about finding a recording studio, booking Bruce Window Studios, where The Saints had recorded their first single and album, out of the phone book. Days before the session, Grant and I had our first ever rehearsal with a drummer, Dennis Cantwell, in the Golding Street loungeroom. The choice of songs was important; this could be the only record we ever made. Our models were the Velvets, The Doors, and Roxy Music, groups capable of pop and arty adventure. 'Lee Remick' and 'Karen' covered that.

We arrived at the studio at nine a.m. in mid-May, to find that the engineer allocated to us was a tall, thin hippie named John Davies who not only took our music seriously, but recorded us with punch and clarity. And he was quick. At one p.m. we were out in the car park, dazed, with a master tape under our arm.

If recording in Brisbane was possible, manufacturing a record was not. The tape had to be sent to a pressing plant in Sydney, and we waited anxious weeks for our order of five hundred singles to arrive. Phone calls brought little news, and more worryingly, on occasions there was no knowledge of the where-abouts of our tape. In mid-July Grant and I decided to make what would be the only long car trip we ever did together. It was a thousand-odd kilometres each way from Brisbane to Sydney, and we set off with the intention of visiting the pressing plant and seeing the first city either of us had been to that was bigger than Brisbane.

Our first stop was a newsagent two hours south of Brisbane at Coolangatta, a coastal town on the Queensland–New South Wales border. I watched from the car as Grant ran out of the shop jubilantly waving a copy of *Playboy*. The publication was banned in Queensland, and we had known about this particular issue for months; in it, Bob Dylan had given his first full-length interview in three years. Grant leaped into the passenger seat. 'Got it.'

If a film of *Grant & I* is ever made, it could start here. We are twenty and twenty-one years old and driving off to rescue our first single. It's early afternoon and on one side of the road runs the Tweed River, while on the other sugarcane fields come up to the kerb. In the distance on our right is a low mountain range capped by one angular peak – Mount Warning (cue thunder-crack). We pass Murwillumbah, the first town after the border, its outer ring of wooden houses perched high on riverbanks. Creedence Clearwater Revival country. Grant opens *Playboy*.

There's a tradition between us that involves reading to each other. Certain lines from a magazine, a key passage in a book. Grant will read me his mother's letters as they arrive – dry, fact-filled pages detailing the minutiae of country life. And Dylan interviews, especially those crazy confrontations between the straight press and the dandy Dylan of 1965–66. 'How would you describe yourself'? 'As a song and dance man.' We pore over them for laughs and attitude lessons, and Bob gives good interview; he only does a few and he seems to take them more seriously than other singer-songwriters, or perhaps the lightning of the man's mind just makes them better. So we are excited to have the latest instalment.

But . . . things have changed. We are now recording artists too and it's no longer 1975. Does he know about Richard Hell and the Voidoids? Will he namecheck any of the new New York bands? We know he's aware of Patti Smith because they've been photographed together. But how much has Dylan's recent move to LA blunted his knowledge of the real world? There are new yardsticks to measure the man by.

The interview is of course brilliant. It's also long, and the kilometres tick by, and the afternoon gets darker as Grant reads each question and answer while I eyeball the highway. We enthuse at some points, but we are waiting for a big-bang moment, a passage where Dylan will burst through the maga-zine and talk straight to us. The interviewer asks him about the instrumentation on his albums. Grant reads Dylan's reply with growing excitement. '"The closest I ever got to the sound I hear in my mind was on individual bands in the *Blonde on Blonde* album. It's that thin, that wild mercury sound. It's metallic and bright gold, with whatever that conjures up."' Grant and I know *exactly* what that conjures up. I bang the steering wheel. 'He's done it! Every journalist of the last ten years has tried to describe the albums he made in the mid-sixties and who does it best?

Dylan himself. Genius! That wild mercury sound . . .'

This got me thinking of descriptions for our music. A few weeks later I came up with 'that striped sunlight sound'. It was a Brisbane thing, to do with sun slanting in through windows onto objects in a room, and the feelings that evoked. Years before, I'd taken photos of the Suzuki leaning against a wall with the sun on its honey-coloured body, and somehow this fitted the music The Go-Betweens made. We stuck this description on the sleeve of our single as an answer to an imagined interview. The phrase endured, and became a term for a bright, poppy Brisbane sound with winsome or witty lyrics attached, which our first single helped to inspire.

We found the pressing plant and were reassured that our record would soon be done and sent to Brisbane. Not knowing Sydney, we'd driven straight to a boarding house in the harbour-side suburb of Manly, to approach the city centre by ferry. Crossing the Harbour Bridge by car was too dangerous for two innocent Queensland boys. We didn't see any gigs and made no connection with the music scene. Perhaps there was nothing on midweek. We did visit White Light record shop and scored the second piece of treasure for the trip. All the latest English and American import records we had, but in one rack we found a much sought-after item – a second-hand copy of the fourth Monkees album, *Pisces, Aquarius, Capricorn & Jones Ltd*. We put it beside the copy of *Playboy* on the back seat and drove back to Brisbane satisfied.

*

The day after I turned twenty-one I moved into Golding Street. On a night not long after that, Grant and a few friends left for the cinema; I chose to stay in the house alone. It was a time when songwriting was almost a public act to me, my corner bedroom like a stage above Brisbane. I'd pull up a chair, cradle the guitar, and start the search for a song with a feeling that a major work was possible. It was a highly romanticised view of songwriting and my abilities, and yet it was why I'd opted to stay behind. In a swoop came the music for 'People Say', which I immediately recognised as a breakthrough melody. There was a classicism to the tune, with its switch between major and minor chords, and a repeated chorus that flew out of the verses. There was relief too – I was capable of crafting a song, another single, without relying on the hyper-raw blend of Velvets and Modern Lovers influences that had fuelled my songs so far. The words I laboured on, writing some of them in university classes. If I didn't have a girlfriend, I imagined one, and she was impressive: 'The clouds lie on their backs/ And rain on everyone/ But you always stay dry/ You've got your own private sun.'

In September I walked into the Toowong Music Centre to have Damian present me with a copy of our single. (This was another special moment, Damian's smile acknowledging the significance of the exchange. And already there was a box of singles on the counter.) The black vinyl in my hand, solid and real as a Greek tablet or a book, seemed an outrageous achievement when neither the songs nor the band had existed a year back. All kinds of emotions flashed through my head – gratitude to Grant and Damian, naturally, and the strength of my attachment to the songs that chronicled my late teenage years not with anger, but with a certain wit and naivety. You *do* feel about your first record like you feel for no other – if only because it could be the only one you make. And if that were to be the case, I knew it was good enough to survive.

Built into the frame of the band was the idea of having a woman as a third member. If Grant had wanted to play drums, we would have had to find a female bass player. We didn't want men only – too rigid and predictable, and every book or movie we liked had female characters. The Go-Betweens were intent on reflecting life. Attached to this was the beauty and utility we saw in the configuration of a trio, the way three people of both sexes moved around each other, as they did in *Jules and Jim,* and one of our favourite TV shows, *Mod Squad.* And it wasn't important if the woman could play drums – like Grant, she could learn while in the band.

Casting. I'd approached a woman we'd seen at shows who we thought looked like Patti Smith's kid sister – intense, with hacked hair – but she turned us down. Lissa Ross, a young Natalie Wood look-alike into horses and drums, joined us for a few weeks, long enough to be part of our first photo session, and then returned to horses. With the release of the single imminent and a drummer not magically falling into place as other things had, we found Timachen Mustafa through an ad in a local paper. Tim was outside the punk scene, which was fine with us, and we liked his crisp, poppy drumming that chimed with the direction our music was taking, the year after punk.

We mailed our record to the Australian and overseas rock press, where it was widely and positively reviewed, and to a select group of people who were important to us, including Lee Remick, Roger McGuinn of The Byrds, and Lenny Kaye, a rock journalist and guitarist for Patti Smith. We also targeted a list of record companies, one of which, Beserkley UK, the London-based home of Jonathan Richman and the Modern Lovers, overwhelmed us by offering a worldwide multi-album deal. (The Saints plan was working!) As a further ego boost, Beserkley wanted to release both 'Lee Remick' and 'Karen' as A-side singles, and asked us to provide B sides. We enlisted Peter Walsh, a free-floating guitarist around town and fellow *Highway 61 Revisited*-era Dylan devotee, to enlarge our sound for the recordings and a series of gigs we were promised in Europe. Walsh was enigmatic. The first in what would be a long line of people to present himself to us flowered in appealing mannerisms – the theatrical flourish of hands in conversation, the precise ritual of extracting a cigarette (Dunhill Reds) and lighting it, the knee slap as he laughed.

For a few weeks we walked around like kings. The complications with Beserkley began when we asked to be repaid for the B-side recording costs – communication from the label stopped. The deal was off, as was our fast track to stardom; we were getting a crash course in the music business and the cruel, cruel world outside the environs of Toowong. Maybe it was going to be harder to stay on a record label than we thought.

*

When I'd been showing Grant the rudiments of the bass, I knew I was teaching a songwriter. Hey, I couldn't expect to invite the most dynamic and creative person I'd ever encountered into an artistic adventure, to have him turn off the very features I found attractive in the first place. Grant was going to write songs; it wasn't in his personality to ask me if that was permissible, and it wasn't in my nature or best interests to deny him. These were the unspoken terms of our commitment to working with each other.

It was back in March, just after our first performance, that he'd played me a bass riff and asked, 'Can you make this into a song?' We did – it was called 'Big Sleeping City' and it stayed in our repertoire for two years. Another melodic bass line begat 'Don't Let Him Come Back', which would be the B side to 'People Say' – our first recorded co-write. Soon he had bought an acoustic guitar and I showed him some chords: he raced off again, in time creating a songwriting style, different to mine, that combined the single-note melodicism of his bass-playing with chord structures. I'd lie in bed at night listening to him play – getting better every day.

Life at Golding Street the months after I moved in was simple yet filled with purpose. I was now studying part-time, still working at the brush factory, and considering not finishing my degree. The open-minded approach I'd taken to studying had seen me come away with something solid – The Go-Betweens. My parents had been in despair of their wayward son. Back in March I'd fallen asleep at the wheel when driving home late one night from Grant's; the car crossed to the other side of the street, climbed an embankment and flipped. I had to be dragged out through the windscreen and was taken to hospital miraculously unscathed. So they were happy to have me dedicated to *something*, even a rock band. And we were a three-piece again: with the collapse of the Beserkley deal, Peter Walsh had left to form The Apartments with another talented songwriter, Michael O'Connell. Grant and I would clock their songs, as we did a few other good bands around town – The Poles, The Patients, The Riptides. A strong new number from any of them had us burning to get home, pull out the guitars and play.

We were gigging too, and as Brisbane had little music industry infrastructure or anyone hip over the age of twenty-five – they'd all left town – shows could pop up anywhere, in pubs, hippie cafes and loungerooms, on campuses, at pool parties. It was a no-airs-and-graces scene: stardom wasn't on offer but freedom and idea-incubating isolation were; you could play five ordinary new songs at a show and it wouldn't destroy your career. On the flipside, five great songs wouldn't make one. Every band was aware that, with their apprenticeship done, they had to skip town.

Until then, the punk scene was mostly tucked into houses and flats in the inner suburbs, and although the people who went to local shows might have numbered only a thousand, bands from each pocket of town came with their own look and style. Toowong had bohemian pop, Grant and I in our long-sleeved business shirts and jeans, black school shoes or sneakers, hair unfashionably over the collar – a touch of the Lovin' Spoonful, having never sweltered in leather and chains in the heat of punk or Brisbane as we followed our two elder brothers of style and songwriting, Talking Heads' David Byrne and Television's Tom Verlaine. Verlaine a rock'n'roll romantic despite his icy demeanour, and Byrne twitchy and smart, playing music that pushed into the future. Talking Heads at Festival Hall in 1979 was a monumental event, bringing the daring and wonder of New York to the 4000-capacity venue with about a quarter of the equipment other groups had previously burdened us with – a lesson in minimalism, with a message: You can do this.

Across town in New Farm was where the art kids lived, with a level of pretension similar to Grant's and mine but differently expressed – polaroids pegged to their clothing, asymmetrical home-dyed haircuts, the music of The Residents and Eno. The houseband was Zero, once a fierce feminist group, whose core members, keyboardist/singer Irena Luckus and drummer Lindy Morrison, had taken in bassist John Willsteed to steer the band in a post-punk direction, incorporating covers of Gang of Four, Wire, and XTC. Zero were also on the circuit, and the capture of my heart by their tall, attractive drummer can be dated to the day I changed the last lines of 'People Say' (a day before recording, again with John Davies) from 'So pack your bags your saxophone/ I'm gonna take you to Rome' to 'So pack your bags your drums/ I'm gonna take you till the kingdom comes.'

There hadn't been many women around the scene and those there were usually had boyfriends in bands. Grant and I, by swerving away from university and full-time employment, had been taken out of the currents where young men and women mingled. Plus we weren't hunters, high-charged heterosexuals confident about coming on to women, and in this regard we'd perhaps gone too far the other way, being regarded as too odd or eccentric to be reliable partners for sensible girls. I'd hoped that writing songs about librarians and movie stars might have made me a candidate for a perceptive girl, but I was wrong. Lindy was the first woman I'd met who'd gotten to me, spun my head, and maybe part of the attraction between us was our differences: she was six years older than me, far more outgoing, politically engaged, and our bands were a world apart. I seemed to fascinate her as much as she fascinated me, so with no small testing steps to learn from, and no control over myself anyway, I took a leap and tried to court the most dynamic woman in the city.

She was living at Wellington Street, Petrie Terrace, in a free-wheeling timber house filled with actors, jugglers, ex-prisoners, architects and beauty queens – there was no place like it in Brisbane, it was almost *too* bohemian. And this became a world I gradually moved into, the third house of my life. It was a punk residence, but its roots were in the early-seventies counter-culture and the two co-existed; and with us becoming a couple, Lindy joined a number of women around the scene in their late twenties, Irena included, who left hippie boyfriends to take up with younger men in new wave bands.

For Grant, the shock must have been not so much that I had a girlfriend, but that she was someone as different and unexpected as Lindy. Still, whoever had come along and become a partner to either of us was going to affect a friendship that had bloomed into a shared artistic endeavour. And being in

the first throes of sexual life, and with the relief and joy of having a girlfriend, I would not have been overly sensitive to the
threat Lindy might pose, nor to Grant's concerns or, at times,
his feelings. He handled it remarkably well, as he would other
unanticipated moments of mine over the next few years. But my
commitment to Grant and The Go-Betweens didn't waver, even
as I began to spend nights away from Golding Street.

*

Starting in 1977, Grant would fly north each year at the end
of June for the Oak Park Races. The family property was large
enough to hold a racetrack, and friends and families from the
region would gather with tents, provisions and alcohol for the
annual meeting. It was difficult to gauge Grant's feelings about
'the land'. He had been sent away from it, to fashion himself as a
city intellectual – no rural affectations hung on him, and yet the
country was a skin he couldn't, or didn't want to, shed. There was
a tug, the reality of which was evident when his brother Lauchie
and cousin Bram visited Golding Street. I was in shock. Here
were two big-hearted teenage boys in pressed jeans, cowboy
hats, western shirts and boots, up for fun in the city, and as they
roamed the student digs, Grant's worlds collided. One eye took
in the familiar ribbing and tales of family and farm, the other
was clocking my surprise.

He returned from Oak Park in mid-'79 with a driver's
licence. 'It says you can drive a manual and an automatic,' I said
when he showed me.

'That's right.'

'You can drive a manual?' He'd been away a week.

An innocence poked through. 'The local policeman asked if I wanted to drive one of them too.'

Soon a car arrived, a white second-hand Corolla – a gift from his mother. It was strange to see Grant behind the wheel, it just didn't seem right for him to have so much hands-on engagement with the world; stranger still to be a passenger as he drove me through the western suburbs. We were close to Golding Street one afternoon, not long after the car's delivery, when the engine began to splutter. Grant managed to guide the vehicle into a ditch. A look at the dashboard showed the problem. No petrol. He didn't know you had to put it in. He probably thought you could drive the car forever.

We walked home, and with my car in repair we had to hitch-hike that night, appropriately enough, to a beatnik-themed Tom Waits show at the university. The next morning we returned with a can of petrol to find the Corolla gone. Stolen. Grant never drove again. His life one tank of gas.

Don't think, though, that any of those days were accompanied by portents of doom or unease. They weren't. We were living lives of zero responsibility: anxiety was waiting on a Magazine album release date; stress was a car dash to the Schonell, Grant angry that we might miss the credits. Damian was in on all the adventures, the third musketeer, and The Go-Betweens, if anyone was looking, could be seen in the Peugeot being driven through the tight, hilly curves from Toowong to Bardon, for an Able Label production meeting at the Nelson residence. Damian, wise Damian, had baked scones earlier in the day, and with bowls of jam and cream and a large pot of Earl Grey tea (Grant's and my introduction to the brew) they were brought on a tray to a table in the downstairs den. I had an idea for the label. We'd write a song and record it with local swimming sensation Tracey Wickham on lead vocals. There would have to be ten thousand people in Brisbane who'd buy that. Dreamy Mrs Nelson in her morning coat sat nearby tinkling the piano. She'd played on the radio in the fifties. Damian's fifteen-year-old sister Theresa was about to arrive home from school, dump her bag at the front door and come down for a last scone and scrape of jam. Life was that tough.

*

Our long-held wish to go to London (New York looked hard; there was a reason everyone in a band there was thin and bug-eyed – no food) was cemented after Tim left the band in August, before the release of 'People Say'. The success of 'Lee Remick' had pushed us to press seven hundred and fifty records (copies of either now fetch a thousand dollars), and with drummer Bruce Anthon stepping in, we played some local shows. There was no organisation in place to play Sydney or Melbourne: you had to move there. I was conflicted about leaving, the dream of escaping Australia with Grant, two drifters off to see the world – and there was a lot of world to see – severely shaken by my relationship with Lindy. Things being further complicated when I joined Zero as a stand-in guitarist.

My time in that band, from September until November, was a carousel ride of cover songs to learn, lunchtime liquor sessions, the surreal humour of bass player John, the European sorrow-fulness of Irena, all spun to a blur by those first months with Lindy. And it was the Zero crew, crammed into a car – arms and legs waving out of windows like a thirties cartoon, puffs of grey smoke from the exhaust pipe – who to the shock of my parents and the dismay of Grant, given how close to take-off I'd left it, delivered me to the airport.

There was heartbreak leaving Lindy; my parents thought they'd never see me again. Mad months were behind me, of earning travel money, saying goodbyes, being in bands with the two most significant people in my life. A time so frantic I carried it onto the plane. Only when the wheels touched down at Heathrow did the kick-in-the-stomach feeling come that I'd actually done this, I was in England, and Brisbane was no more.

Athens and Tear Gas

The American writer Elizabeth Hardwick once wrote, 'When you travel your first discovery is that you do not exist.' I've always liked this line without knowing exactly what it means. Some things are like that with me, pieces of lyrics, poetry or prose that ring true although I don't fully comprehend them, couldn't explain them lucidly to another person. Grant and I didn't disappear when we travelled to England; the situations we encountered, though, tended to come at us as one, and be experienced as one. The diversions of the previous months shrank as we regained the exclusive company of each other, processing our surroundings together, convinced of our destiny.

On arrival, he and I and a Brisbane friend, Gerry Teekman, who had travelled with us and was to leave a few weeks later, headed to a house near Clapham Common. It belonged to the

Holleymans, a couple my parents had met on their first and only trip to Europe in the mid-fifties. From beds in their attic we ventured out excitedly each morning to see another slice of the city, usually Soho, to return in light rain and bewilderment to tea, toast, and television that finished well before midnight.

A few things were immediately clear. Most of London looked like the shabbier parts of Brisbane and moreover lacked an otherness that we thought foreign travel would entail. We knew there would be no sunshine; the shock, though, of coming from a New World city with a skyscrapered CBD, radial suburbs and vantage points to a flat, never-ending maze-like village was immense. In this nest was a music scene we'd been following from afar – being among it gave us an excitement that burnt for a few weeks. We bought *NME* on the day it came out, and that shrinking of time and sense of being at the centre of the action was thrilling. It was also what made one other thing spectacularly apparent – The Go-Betweens were going to get nowhere in London. The scene was too big, the walls too high, and we knew no one in the music business. We'd travelled sixteen thousand kilometres to advance the career of the band without bringing one telephone number.

The group had been rolling on serendipity and luck in Brisbane, and we thought it would miraculously continue here; that by wandering down Old Compton Street, there'd be someone, a Brian Epstein or an Albert Grossman, who would divine by our look, our stance, our holding of an Only Ones album, our reading of a Billy Wilder biography in a bookstore, that here were two young geniuses in need of money, a place to stay, and a five-album deal with Warner Brothers. As ridiculous as this sounds, the plan that Grant and I brought to London, never articulated to one another, was not much more developed than that.

There were now two options. We could either dig in, get jobs and accommodation, find a drummer, and start the slow consolidation of the band with shitty gigs and demos, or flip our journey over to a tourist trip, learn what we could, and sneak back to Brisbane with nothing in hand career-wise. Maybe it was time to give up music and turn to film. We were leaning to the tourist option just after Christmas, when I set off to Paris by train while Grant flew to Cairo and Greece with the intention of joining me a few weeks later.

Lindy and Irena had both been in Paris in the early to mid-seventies, and held romantic notions of the city. I had them too. And my schoolboy French, which didn't enable me to engage with the local populace much beyond ordering a baguette and a café au lait, was at last being put to some use. I was staying in a sparse single room – no phone, television or bathroom – on the top floor of a slum hotel on the Left Bank. My home was the streets, which I walked relentlessly in the bitter cold. Yet I was happy, and part of the joy came from being in a non-English-speaking land at last. These were also the first days of my life that I'd spent alone, which I managed to survive and appreciate. A channel for my thoughts were letters back home, especially to Lindy, who I missed dreadfully, and whose presence hovered in Paris. Being an adventurer and socially confident, she'd stayed at the Shakespeare and Company bookstore, where a tradition existed, for those game enough to apply, of stacking books in exchange for a bed on the floor of the shop. I preferred the solitude of a single room, even though it drained the little money I had.

When Grant arrived he took the room next to mine. He told me of playing Creedence Clearwater Revival songs with people he'd met in Athens on New Year's Eve, while I recounted how I'd been teargassed in a group of midnight revellers on the Boulevard Saint-Michel, then chased by riot police through the side streets to my hotel. This is how we started the eighties. I also mentioned a groovy record store I'd found a few blocks deeper into the Left Bank, festooned with black-and-white-check merchandise and other bits of Ska Revival paraphernalia that was fashionable in the UK at that moment. On visits we tried to connect with the staff, in an echo of the Toowong Music Centre, but the language and cultural barrier was too wide. We did leave an advertisement on the noticeboard – a carefully drafted call-out, dripping with music and film references, for a female drummer, *une femme batteur*, with our hotel address attached. No one replied. We were hoping a gamin-faced, stripe-shirted young woman would answer and lead us to her family and friends while completing a three-piece band that would startle France. This pop dream went the same way as the Soho plan, and after another week of coffee and baguettes we retreated to London.

I was now broke, my savings having lasted all of two months. Grant's financial situation was another topic that went undiscussed, and I could only assume he was being supported by his mother. As he drifted through the city by day, I worked as an X-ray clerk at St Mary's Hospital in Paddington, a job organised by an employment agency. My office was a basement room with floor-to-ceiling shelves holding thousands of alpha-betically filed manila folders of X-rays. Nurses and orderlies would bring me patients' names and wait as I sorted through the shelves to hand over the required envelopes. One name took me to the RO section – Robertson, perhaps – where my eye caught ROEG, Nicolas. There could be only one such person in London: the film director of Schonell favourites *The Man Who Fell to Earth* and *Walkabout*. I opened his file. He had a bad knee. On my last day of work there I snuck out a rogue Roeg X-ray under my coat. It's as close as Grant and I ever got to the British film industry.

We were in a hotel by now, which mirrored the cell-like dimensions of my work, and in turn our London experience. It was an oval-shaped building with a vine-like spiral feature outside that housed toilets and bathrooms. The rooms were dormitory-sized with rows of single beds. My wage covered my rent and cheap cafe meals, meat and two veg, over which Grant would revisit the sights of his day (my holiday being done by proxy) and we'd despondently consider our predicament, wondering just how long we could put up with this before crawling back to Brisbane, tails glued between our legs.

The few remaining pounds in my pocket went on concerts, and here we got lucky. Cult English groups didn't tour Australia with any regularity until the early nineties, and in these win-ter months Grant and I saw what would have taken us years to see back home. Amidst many concerts there were Gang of Four, The Raincoats, and Scritti Politti at the Electric Ballroom, The Cramps and The Fall there too. The Cure and later The Pretenders – 'Brass In Pocket' was number one that week – were at the Marquee. And we saw Echo and the Bunnymen, Teardrop Explodes, and A Certain Ratio on one bill at the Lyceum. It was an impressive run of groups and although we were being tossed about on the choppy waters of post-punk London, there wasn't a band that looked or sounded like us. In our insecurity we didn't know if this was a good or a bad thing.

We also saw films, Grant up on the repertory cinemas, and had just settled into our seats at a weekend showing of the Charles Laughton-directed noir classic *The Night of the Hunter*, when The Birthday Party walked in. We'd seen them on late-night Australian TV doing 'Shivers', and some members of the group had walked past us at The Cure gig. Unfortunately on both occasions we were too shy to introduce ourselves.

There was *one* slender connection we had to the music scene. Judy Crighton was a Queensland-born woman who'd begun working at the Rough Trade record shop in Ladbroke Grove in 1977. Her husband Ross had visited his hometown of Brisbane the following year, where he met us and bought a box of 'Lee Remick' singles. Our first two records had been reviewed in the UK press, and John Peel had played 'Lee Remick' and 'Karen' on his BBC radio show – there was a very faint hum on the band. To put that into perspective, the biggest break we got was when Judy put the sleeve of 'Lee Remick' on the shop's wall, which was covered with well-known independent records from around the world. She also got us an appointment with Geoff Travis, the head of Rough Trade records, who worked out of an office at the back of the store.

Geoff was already the John Hammond of indie rock – someone with a golden ear and the ability to spot trends and find big artists before they became stars. In the future he would sign The Smiths, Everything But The Girl, The Jesus and Mary Chain, and The Strokes, but now he was a tall skinny guy with an afro looking at me as I nervously handed him a copy of 'People Say'. The dub reggae that was pulsing from the office sound system was taken off and the bright, clipped, organ-and-guitar pop tones of our single rang out. It was one of those world-turning-on-its axis moments, where everything was afforded a new view. Our record sounded *w-a-y* out of time; it could have been recorded the day after Buddy Holly cut 'Peggy Sue', or in March 1966, or in Boston 1972 at the end of a Modern Lovers session. It didn't relate to anything going on in London in late 1979. Geoff shook his head. 'It's too poppy,' he said. I thanked him and left, our one chance gone.

*

Knowing that the Rough Trade shop was an essential stop-over for any indie record buyer or band coming to the city, three Scotsmen down from Glasgow with copies of their debut single in hand walked into the store two months later. They were Edwyn Collins and David McClymont, members of a group with a truly revolutionary name for post-punk times: Orange Juice. With them was Alan Horne, the group's manager and co-owner of their label, Postcard Records. While acquainting themselves with the shop and trying to hustle up business for their single, they spotted the 'Lee Remick' sleeve on the wall. Edwyn and Alan, who knew and liked the record from John Peel, pondered aloud the fate of the Australian group. Judy Crighton told them.

'Three strange-looking men came asking for you today,' said the receptionist at our hotel. 'They wanted to give you a package. I let them go up to your room. I hope that was all right?' We assured him it was and raced up the stairs. A brown envelope lay on Grant's bed. We opened it to find a single, a set of photographs of the group responsible for it, and a handwritten letter inviting The Go-Betweens to come to Glasgow to record a single on Postcard Records.

A cry of 'We've been saved!' should have arisen in the room, but the unexpectedness of the offer, added to the fact that the label and Orange Juice were completely unknown to us, meant that our response was a little more muted. Maybe I was starting to catch some of Grant's caution. We looked at the photos, hunting for clues. They showed three young men with unfashionable fringes wearing op shop clothes, denoting a band 'look', confidently posing with what would later become known as vintage guitars. They didn't resemble any of the bands or people we'd seen in London. We could immediately detect the playfulness of the poses, and the detail of the presentation alerted us to a group already consumed with their own myth – *this* we understood. The record burnt in our hands. If only we had a record player.

The Supports had one. They were friends of ours from Brisbane who had come to London and done all the sensible things to establish a band base that we should have. Grant and I often visited them in their Highgate flat, sheepishly bunking nights between the Holleymans and hotels. One evening I'd written a song in their kitchen called 'I Need Two Heads', its lyric an ultra-cryptic, even to me, attempt to articulate a reaction to the rush and roar of London: 'I look at you and I wonder why/ Animals extinct and I'm beginning to cry/ Give me your bank book and sometimes I think I need two heads.' (Grant would one day ask if the 'bank book' was his – it wasn't.) On the first Saturday after receiving the envelope from Orange Juice, Grant and I arrived at Highgate with their single, 'Falling And Laughing', in our hands.

That record was the first of four consecutive genius singles the band released over the next year and a half. The sound, look and overall aesthetic (steel-souled yet fey) of Orange Juice helped define indie rock. We of course didn't know this as we placed the single on the turntable and stood back to assess our new label mates. Three minutes later, as the last note rang out, the response in the room was bafflement. The record didn't sound like an indie single of the time, particularly those from London, which tended to be drilled and tight. This was not *that* – there was a demo-ish quality to the recording as the band shifted through an unusual set of influences, including funky bass lines and country and western guitars. Riding high in the mix was the singer, his heartfelt croon pushing the boundary usually held between listener and vocalist, and a lyric that added a new word to the rock lexicon, 'consequently'. We did like the Byrds-y sting of the guitars and melodic sections of the song, and the single did in a way match the playful, odd appearance of the band in the photographs. There was no question we wouldn't go to Glasgow, and letters and calls started between ourselves and the label to get us there.

We were picked up at Glasgow Central Station by David McClymont on the first of April 1980 and taken to 185 West Princes Street, the home of Postcard and Alan Horne. After an hour in the city and the two introductions, impressions were already forming. Grant and I had walked in on a 'scene', and allied to the excitement of this was the feeling that we'd left the holiday trail behind: sitting in Alan's kitchen, bags at our feet, having the Postcard manifesto declaimed to us, was outside the tourist experience. Also apparent was the manner of our new friends – flippant, whip-smart, with a biting camp turn of humour. Everyone in Brisbane suddenly seemed dipped-in-honey slow. The quality of a band's songs, and their career, were the burning centre of existence here, and not, as they were back home, one part of a subtropical lifestyle. And so, with the welcome and the outrageously engaging Horne cosmology settling in our heads – 'Orange Juice are the greatest band in the world', 'Postcard is an antidote to the hippie betrayal of punk' – David asked if we wanted to visit the band's singer and lead songwriter, Edwyn Collins.

Glasgow immediately felt right. The quaintness of the city glimpsed on our quick cab ride to Alan's, and now the wide streets of West End, with their rows of three- and four-storey sandstone Victorian terraces. David was our guide, as he would be throughout our stay. We entered an apartment block similar to Alan's and made our way upstairs to Edwyn's room. As we went down the hall the rising volume of John Fogerty's 'Almost Saturday Night' could be heard in a far bedroom. David knocked then opened the door, and there on his knees with his ear to a speaker was a tall, thin young man dressed in the manner of a 1950s student actor, with a waterfall of hair tumbling into his eyes. He turned to us from his position on the floor and without introduction asked if we thought the second guitar on the track was a Telecaster or a Rickenbacker. Grant and I stood there gobsmacked. To have zeroed in on a musician taking a record like this – a beautiful piece of early-seventies rock/pop that we knew and liked – seriously, at a time when pop singer-songwriters were not in vogue, was a wonder. A Stanley-meets-Livingstone moment, except it involved two sets of musicians. Edwyn was the band's leader, we saw that, the pied piper that David and the other members were following, and around whom Alan was building his label. As Grant and I stood chatting with and appraising our Postcard comrades, a lead singer/guitarist and a bass player, there was a feeling we might have just met our match.

Preparations for us had been made. Grant moved into a spare room at Edwyn's, while I was billeted around the corner in yet another spacious, bay-windowed apartment (how these places amazed us after the cupboard-sized rooms of London) with Anne Hogarth and Robbie Kelly, art-school friends of David's. There must have been people like them in West Berlin or the Lower West Side at the time, warm-hearted and hip, Anne in bright red lipstick and fifties dresses, Robbie, James Chance-like, in a box suit. They were early Orange Juice fans and a lovely couple, taking me in and making life comfortable for the first time in months.

Alan had our career in gear, with a lunchtime show at the Glasgow School of Art booked before our arrival. Thrilling as this was (a beautiful turn to The Go-Betweens story, now back on and brilliant), if there was one downside to being with Postcard it was that it caught us a little on the hop. Our idea of where the band stood musically was in flux, and untried as we travelled. Suddenly the spotlight blinked on and there we were, performing to passing students, some of whom stayed to watch, while our attention was more focused on those against the back wall: Alan, members of Orange Juice, and a few others in the growing Postcard coterie there to assess the new group on the label. On drums and moral support was Orange Juice's Steven Daly; he was not only musically compatible with us, putting a new beat, clipped and percussive, under a heavily scrutinised set of our songs, but also the most worldly person we met in Glasgow, with an eyebrow in permanent arch at the politics and intrigue of his band and label.

Two of the numbers, 'I Need Two Heads' and 'Stop Before You Say It', were judged suitable for our single. The latter, along with another song of mine, 'Careless', had to do with Lindy ('Clumsy me, clumsy you/ Fell in love/ and we don't know what to do'), and were written before I left Brisbane. These were songs that broke or extended the mould of 'People Say', ushering in

another phase in my songwriting – more fragmented and jagged, a letting go of older rock influences in the need to keep
pushing the band's music forward.

The next show, days later, was in Edinburgh, the prim
daughter to Glasgow's sooty maid, and the hometown of the
third band on the label, Josef K, or Josey K as they were known
in Glasgow. Primed on Alan's heated tales, we were expecting to
meet four drug-addled nihilist malcontents, but instead found
friendly guys in suits up for a chat about Television, and Richard
Hell and the Voidoids. Josef K were on the bill with us, as was
Orange Juice, and whether it was a stand-off over who should
headline or in deference to us as the new group, we played last.

That show remains the most nerve-racking performance of
my life, because as good as Josef K were, this was the night that
Orange Juice bared their milky teeth. There was a Beatles '62
thing about them. Own humour. Own dress style. Own songs
and sound in the heart of a city. Grant and I had heard snippets
of their music in the practice room; we'd also heard arguments –
band tension new to us. Onstage in Edinburgh we got the
full show, and it was astonishing. The best forty minutes of
rock'n'roll I'd seen. And it *was* rock'n'roll. The group would
quickly be overtaken by their image and labelled 'wimpy' – for
now this was in check and they played with amped-up ferocity
and power. Immediately obvious, too, was their superiority to
the bands we'd seen in London, drowning as many of them
were in reverb and effects. Orange Juice had clarity, which made
their stinging songs and each member's contribution all the
more powerful. 'Falling And Laughing' sounded much better

live – like a classic, in fact, but they had at least half a dozen of them. Grant and I, five metres back from the stage, were counting. Edwyn, as leader of the group, was another revelation, one pertinent to me: you could be funny onstage without it being detrimental to the seriousness of the band.

We were also gathered in Edinburgh to record. Castle Sound at the edge of the city was our introduction to eighties recording – shiny, spacey, sparkling, helping to mark the sonic shift from 'People Say' that 'I Need Two Heads' represented. On that single Grant and I improved as musicians, each of us having a guitar solo, and the two songs were more elusive than anything we'd done before, meaning we had a very competitive record at the dawn of the decade. It was done in hours; the studio was tag-teamed to a waiting Orange Juice, and we watched them record 'Blue Boy' and 'Lovesick'. It was clear that something special was happening. Their debut record, as charming as it was, was a dry run for the focus and drive they put into these new powerful songs from Edwyn. It was whiplash pop, miles away from the doom of the Joy Division imitators or the rumble of The Fall. Orange Juice had cut a major record that, given any kind of chance – and the media eye was already zeroing in on West Princes street – would break the band and take Postcard and all those who sailed in it along with them.

Which makes our decision to leave in late May all the harder to explain. Why go when we had a single recorded for a fast-rising label and were living in a city we dug? I was missing Lindy – that was the nub of it. First love had bitten hard. It was six months since I'd seen her, and six months seemed to be the length of time I could endure without her. She was generous in her letters, but there was no guarantee she'd wait. Grant and I had come to the end of our first phase in Glasgow – I was penniless, and we'd need to find permanent accommodation and a drummer, among other things. To Grant's credit, when I told him I wanted to go back to Brisbane he didn't try to talk me out of it, though a certain resignation fell on him, indicating his disappointment. Making the best of the situation, he said he'd return home via New York.

I'd put my personal life before the band and made a decision that could have skittled our immediate future. I thought guiltily on my actions for years, and it was only when we went to Europe at the invitation of another label – and, without wishing to be cruel, when the promise of Postcard had faded – that I thought the ledger may have been evened up.

Goodbyes in Glasgow were tough. A sign of how attached we were to our friends and the city came when James Kirk, the quiet lead guitarist and second songwriter of Orange Juice, and the one the band vowed was the most eccentric member – a badge worn high at Postcard – presented me with a battered blue, home-painted Burns Nu-Sonic guitar as a parting gift. This was the guitar we'd seen in the hotel photographs, the instrument that the pre-Orange Juice group The Nu-Sonics had named themselves after.

I returned to Australia with strange bounty: a guitar in a pillow case, an X-ray of a famous film director's knee, a cassette of our third single, and a bruised heart. My parents paid for the flight.

Deconstruction Time

The Gap was as I'd left it – green and ever-growing. There would be occasions down the track when I felt happy to be back: when I was wrung out from being on tour and in need of shelter, days of sleep, a full fridge, laundry done by Mum, and a round of golf with the family. At those times, home acted as the washer to the face before being sent out for another round in the rock'n'roll ring. Now was not one of those times. Now I didn't want to be under the concerned eye of my parents, defeated and disorientated as I was, wondering how, and if, I could get Lindy back (we hadn't immediately restarted our relationship) and re-kick the band.

It all seemed daunting, and showed Grant to be the guiding star he was in my life. I missed his companionship dreadfully, and our shared mission, which kept me making good artistic decisions. This was the drudge I'd have been in without him. My solace was recalling Glasgow and listening to our single – these things I believed in, and if I'd been smarter I would have waited for our record's release, but I didn't.

David Tyro was a musician who'd been drifting around the Brisbane scene for a few years. I must have contacted him in my search for a job, because he subsequently found me one, working beside him packing books at University of Queensland Press. He must also have shown me the guitar synthesiser that he played in a Keith Levene from Public Image fashion, and with The Go-Betweens' sound shifting I was intrigued enough to contact Clare McKenna, a drummer and member of the Zero gang, to arrange rehearsals with them both, she in turn having a flat in New Farm for me to move into, following which a gig was offered to us at, of all places, Baroona Hall. I was in effect laying trails of gunpowder that would blow up in my face and burn some unfortunate people standing near me.

Grant, who I'd been keeping informed on some of these fast-moving developments, arrived back home bewildered and irritated, to take up the bass with new faces in the practice room. The gig was a brave failure, a glimpse of where we were headed but one that didn't work, and Grant wasn't happy; his frustration with me for putting a line-up of the band together without fully consulting him was as close as he ever came to boiling over. To add one final act to the drama, Lindy and I were now back together, and when I went to tell Clare the new band was no more, I got a rueful smile from her – she knew what was going to happen next. I had to tell David too, and it was now very uncomfortable at the warehouse. So uncomfortable I left. No doubt about it, I'd fucked up.

Apart from having to accommodate my missteps, Grant had returned from New York in fantastic spirits. His entree to Manhattan was Robert Vickers and his groovy American girl-friend Janie Heath. Robert, having set off from Brisbane in early '79 in search of Graham Greene adventures in Mexico, had ended up in New York playing bass for a power-pop band called The Colors. They were on the Downtown circuit, including CBGB's, and had the patronage of Blondie drummer Clem Burke as producer. It was the tail end of the no wave scene; giants from mid-seventies bands still walked the Bowery, and the streets were buzzing and dangerous. Grant had hit another world after Glasgow, one that could have been built for him – everything close, open all hours, with bars, apartments, and a swirl of people living far into the night. The backdrop was the glittering city we'd both dreamt of, stuffed with inspirational figures, from a young Brando at the Actors Studio in the forties to whoever was putting out a great record, film or book Downtown that week. It was the pages of *The Village Voice* and *New York Rocker* flapping to life, and Grant had gotten to it first and it was in his eyes when we met on his return.

Physically he'd changed too. Maybe it was the disorientation from the months away, and my not having seen him for six weeks, but the baby fat was gone and his hair was cut short. He came back transformed, and moved into a one-bedroom flat – no more shared houses – in a set of Art Deco apartments in inner-city Spring Hill called Dahrl Court. It housed the town's eccentrics: bachelors in their sixties who grandly went to the races on Saturday by taxi, to limp home on foot. The landlord was known as the Man with the Movable Wig, who upon discovering you were a musician would insist on playing you *Switched-on Bach*. Grant also returned with treasures to add to his Golding Street collection: obscure New York records ('Lost Is Found' by The Erasers' Susan Springfield a favourite), magazines and books, plus the movies he'd seen to cross off Schonell wish lists. Although we were on our arses, back where we began and without a drummer, we had experienced bigger brighter worlds.

I went to make the Big Ask; what else could I do? It was the obvious next step, and with the turn my songwriting had taken it was musically compatible as well, but still, I was shaking when I asked Grant if Lindy could join the band. He didn't blurt out a yes, that not being his style, and I was asking a lot – to bring my girlfriend into something as precious as our group – and I was coming in on the back of a few bad decisions. Grant was gracious with his approval, realising by now that the volatility and naivety that forged my songs spilled into my life and would inevitably be brought into the band. In my defence, it really was time for us, in our early twenties, to be forming outside emotional attachments; mine happened to be with a female drummer.

The traffic wasn't all one-way – Lindy was not only joining The Go-Betweens, she was leaving Zero. A band that was like a family, the core of an outsider art clique, her move seen as a kind of defection. She was finely juggling her feelings for me, and the joy we had in making music, with the ambition she saw in Grant and me as singer-songwriters and her desperation to leave town. With her joining, the original idea for the band was fulfilled – we had our female drummer. That she was nearing thirty, had graduated from the University of Queensland as a social worker, changed to acting in agitprop theatre and then taken up drums fitted the group's unorthodox story. Visually, too, we were a great band.

She and I moved into a flat on St Pauls Terrace, around the corner from Grant, and with none of us having a car, Lindy, who was tenacious in tracking down practice rooms, found an empty floor in a nearby office building. So began our routine, and like a trail of miners going off at night, we'd walk down to the city's edge, open up the room, unpack our instruments, tune up, and get down to the business of constructing a working relationship between the three of us, and a sound. Any illusions Grant and I had of being a pair of students bunking off in a band were now gone. Travel had intensified our feelings about the group, and we were on our third single, wishing to make a defining album. Our uni friends were now qualified, and on the long, even road that having jobs guaranteed. A rock band was the path away – a tunnel, in fact – the clattering, fractured music we wrote and practised the appropriate soundtrack as we headed further underground into poverty and hard work.

Lindy and I were on the dole, and the ducking and weaving around that began, our income supplemented by occasional lunchtime work from the ever generous Damian, who was soon to change. He sold the shop, returned to university to gain a teaching degree, married, got a job and started a family. The late seventies in Toowong was like Kenya in the twenties or Paris in the 1890s, another faded golden epoch.

*

All of Alan Horne's dreams and schemes were coming true. Letters from him and Edwyn had been giddyingly chronicling the rise of Postcard, and with the release of the Orange Juice and Josef K singles it all burst forth – the Sound of Young Scotland, no less, atop the indie charts at a time when this meant serious record sales and cultural impact. Grant and I read the two-page spreads in the UK rock press, recognising the clothes, fringes, guitars and jokes we'd seen and heard months before. We were happy for our friends, and a little jealous; there was agony in following their success from such a distance.

In October 'I Need Two Heads' was released in the UK, and it too got single-of-the-week reviews and chart action. This was gratifying, and the moment to be in Glasgow or London, but no one had the money. There was a consolation prize, however. The myth of the band was very much enhanced – how had The Go-Betweens jumped from Brisbane to Glasgow to land on the hippest record label in the world? – and so Missing Link, a Melbourne-based record company working out of a record store, offered to put out our single in Australia. A show, our first with Lindy, came with the deal. We were to play the Paris Theatre in Sydney on 28 November 1980 with two other bands on the label, The Birthday Party, and Laughing Clowns.

Air travel being expensive, we came down by train and

went straight from the station to the venue. The front doors of the theatre were open, and not knowing anyone to report to, we went through the foyer and sat in the darkened stall seats at the back, in time to watch The Birthday Party soundcheck. They looked fantastic in their black suits and ties and jagged art-school haircuts, all the while puffing dramatically on endless rounds of cigarettes. They were playing melodic rock songs; sure, there was wild guitar noise from Rowland Howard, the band was dangerous, and Nick Cave was screaming and gesturing at the ceiling, yet these unreleased numbers were identifiable from their strong, song-title choruses – 'Cry', 'Zoo-Music Girl'. It was impressive music with a big visual whack, and in the darkness I sank in my chair. But maybe everything wasn't lost. The next band mightn't be so good, and with us playing first, there was still a chance to shine. I was reassuring myself as the members of Laughing Clowns, led by their enigmatic frontman, ex-Saints guitarist and songwriter Ed Kuepper, took their positions. There were horn players setting up, a keyboardist, and a drummer who even by his first touches of the kit was like no drummer I'd ever heard. As they were poised to start, I remembered the first time I'd seen Ed play.

When The Saints put on a show at Queensland University my excuses to Virginia for not going to their gigs ran out. She and I arrived to find fifty people scattered along the walls of a low-ceilinged room and the band already playing. My impressions of them were hard to coordinate as I'd seen little live music, going to out-of-the-way halls to hear bands play Uriah Heep covers not being my thing, and this was pre-punk. The Saints were loud and their guitarist was bent over his red Gibson SG in a defiant slouch that became his trademark. The singer, curled black hair in his eyes, a troublesome youth, sat intermittently in a chair in front of the small wooden stage with his back to the audience, only going to the microphone to sing. I thought that was cool. We left after half an hour. Outside, Virginia asked me what I thought, and considering the slow tempos of the long songs we'd heard, I said rather feebly that they reminded me of Roxy Music. She huffed. That wasn't the right answer, and soon after she told me they'd recorded a single.

A few months later, with The Gap pin-drop quiet at ten o'clock, having watched an episode of *Callan* with Dad perhaps, I was lying in bed with my transistor radio on the windowsill, listening to the smooth West Coast tones of 4ZZZ's American disc jockey Bill Riner. He'd already played a round of songs, and I was drifting off to sleep after two or three more numbers when a murderously effective guitar riff came thundering out of the speaker. A song was on, taken very fast, with breakneck sections crashing out of one another. All topped by a vocal that didn't bother enunciating any of the lyrics except for 'I'm straaaanded on my own. I'm straaaaanded far from home.'

I was immediately bug-eyed. I was Frankenstein on the slab with electricity crackling out of my feet. My body vibrated on the bed as I lay in a catatonic state, listening and absorbing. And then, like a wind gust, it was gone. I waited for the back announcement. 'That was "Kashmir" off Led Zeppelin's double set *Physical Graffiti*. Before that we heard "Roll Um Easy" and "On Your Way Down" from Little Feat's fine, *fine* album *Dixie*

Chicken. And before that with "(I'm) Stranded" was The Saints. They're a Brisbane band, and their single, just out, is available at Discreet Music in town.' My mind tuned out. I couldn't fucking believe it. I thought of Virginia and cursed myself for not believing her. I got the single, released on the band's Fatal label, the next day, and I wish I'd bought twenty and was now selling them slowly on eBay.

After *Prehistoric Sounds*, Kuepper had relocated to Sydney and started the Clowns. Singer Chris Bailey kept The Saints' band name and the London address. Kuepper was beginning again from scratch. Could he do anything as good, and how long would it take to tell? About thirty seconds.

My eyes were now two ping-pong balls just above chair level. The songs the band were soundchecking were long, built on propulsive rhythms with explosive instrumentation stabbing out melodies and arrangements. Ed's guitar was a magic wand, sending forth riffs and heavy chord wattage. He was conducting the band. They'd play a couple of verses and choruses and then launch into extended instrumental passages that ventured further and further away from the initial tunes and structure, till you thought that all was lost and gone, the world had ended, and then a teasing refrain from the horns or the drums would start, and the entire band came crashing back with Ed leading the charge on vocals. It was breathtaking, and if The Birthday Party had a hint of London in what they did, no one anywhere in the world was playing music like Laughing Clowns.

A voice bellowing from the pit broke my reverie. 'Are The Go-Betweens here yet?' It was pure Broadway. We walked out

of the stalls, down the sloping aisle of the theatre to the biggest stage we'd ever seen, and introduced ourselves to our new
friends.

That night, as in Scotland, we played with two groups who
had arrived at a confident musical style. And as in Scotland we
got by, our fragile, stark melodicism appreciated and in contrast
to the power and blast of the other groups. There was cultural
significance here too – each band, whether by intention or not,
from a different east coast city, showcasing a new music that
had ignited out of the ashes of punk. Offstage, there was camaraderie and powerful personalities. Ed Kuepper and Clowns
drummer Jeffrey Wegener – ice and fire. Ed, who everyone
had enormous respect for, led a group that was like a set of
dusty characters in a Western posse. The Birthday Party were
a tighter band, onstage an explosion, offstage approachable,
friendly and charismatic.

*

In early 1981 I read a book that influenced my thinking on the
band. My love of biography had been initially triggered by Don
McLean's *American Pie* – the first non-greatest hits album I'd
bought, and an important record in that it alerted its listeners,
impressionable thirteen-year-olds like myself, to inspirational
figures outside or at the edge of current rock'n'roll. In this case,
Vincent van Gogh, Wild Bill Hickok and Buddy Holly. That
sent me to the Ashgrove Library to find van Gogh's letters to
his brother, and Dave Laing's account of Holly's life. I discovered there was valuable information to be learnt about artists

and famous people that was not in their work, yet illuminated it. And if I wanted to become famous, to follow ambitions I couldn't name, I had to know the paths, especially that poignant phase, which would become my favourite, when an artist is about to achieve their breakthrough. Those spine-tingling days or months when they know they're going to make the jump to fame and fortune that will change their lives forever.

I was still frequenting libraries when the pitch of what I was reading hit the high note of Richard Ellmann's *James Joyce*. Here was the art of a writer complemented by the art of a biographer. Joyce, committed to his work and vision, leaves his hometown Dublin for a life of travel, exile, money struggles, and the slow recognition of the greatness of his work. This immediately sounded familiar to me. The story of The Go-Betweens wasn't going to be mirrored in rock biographies, in the life of The Rolling Stones or Pink Floyd, with their flush starts and fame. Our path would follow another model, 'the wrong road' as Grant would one day sing – progress made in zigzag shape, foreign cities seen in poverty, all nerves tested. I recognised this in our fourth year as a band, when making our strangest music, with potential hit singles 'Lee Remick' and 'People Say' not having been picked up and covered by other bands. It was a feeling I had that we just weren't top-forty people. We knew too much and this wasn't the sixties, when adventurous people (Lennon, Jim Morrison, Grace Slick) got their music into the charts. The pertinent question was: Joyce reached *Ulysses* and Paris; where would we get to?

The majority of the band's better songs and musical ideas

were now coming from Grant. His role was no longer restricted to bass playing and harmony singing; he was a songwriter singing more of his own songs, with his wiry, melodic bass lines at the centre of our sound. A challenge eagerly taken up by Lindy's wildly inventive, percussive drums. Drums and bass were undergoing a re-evaluation and prominence in rock music, post-punk in particular – The Pop Group, Joy Division, Siouxsie and the Banshees. Guitars were scratchy and off to the side. Singers screeched and yelped, as if the tips of swords were being prodded into their bodies. I had to adjust everything, my guitar playing, my singing, my position in the group – I certainly hadn't picked two ten-pound weaklings – as Grant flew off on a three-year burst of first songs.

The changes were heard on our next single, 'Your Turn, My Turn', recorded in Sydney at Trafalgar Studios in April '81. (Singles were of supreme importance, like a report card of a band. Groups were conscious that everything they wanted to show to the world, including how far they'd progressed since their previous record, had to be compacted into a single's release.) The bones and hook of 'Your Turn' was a great bouncy bass riff of Grant's, with the feel coming from Lindy's cracking snare and punching bass drum, far more rhythmic than anything we'd done before. Our engineer was Tony Cohen, who had started in the pop world working with producer Ian 'Molly' Meldrum on chart records such as The Ferrets' 'Don't Fall In Love', to quickly find his metier in the underworld, having recently engineered The Birthday Party's *Prayers on Fire*. Tony was completely idiosyncratic, with a mad scientist's demeanour and a round-eyed delight in finding 'interesting sounds'. Beside him in the studio, the veteran of many a session, stretching back to his time in sixties bands and a role in the original Australian production of *Hair*, was the head of Missing Link, the urbane Keith Glass. He offered us the chance to make an LP.

Normally a band gets to draw on years of material when recording their debut album. Our abandonment of sixties- and seventies-flavoured songwriting, and the transition represented by 'I Need Two Heads', had not yet led us to a confident new style. We had to forge it, a sound to suit songs, songs to suit a sound. It was a two-way thing, and time-consuming. Playing few gigs, few being available, we became in essence a practice-room band, and in this four-nights-a-week schedule, riffs and chord structures were gravel to the mixer – thrown in, rolled around and often rejected as we kept searching for suitable material. So as the July recording date loomed, we weren't finessing two- or three-year-old numbers, we were writing an album from scratch in a town we had picked dry and loathed. After the Spring of Punk, Brisbane had adjusted to the newer, darker edges of music by reverting to its darker and harder self. The Bjelke-Petersen government was now in its third ruinous decade – the police cruising Spring Hill for suspicious-looking young people while a visible prostitution and drug trade operated around the corner.

Another problem was my songwriting; I was suffering a crisis of confidence. I'd seen Edwyn up close, Grant was blossoming, Ed and The Birthday Party were both on fire, and listening to recent albums like *Colossal Youth* by Young Marble

Giants was inspiring, but showed me no way forward with my limited guitar technique. I laboured for hours each day on atonal guitar riffs and stabbed chords, trying to piece something together. The carefree days of songwriting, when a few turn turn turns of a Byrds album or the Velvets' live *1969* had me stroking chords and writing attractive songs at will, were over. Back in mid-1979, The Go-Betweens would have made a great album. A simple-sounding, naive pop masterpiece, out of synch with the scene, admittedly, the success of which would have changed our lives, and the bombing of which would have made it difficult for us to reinvent ourselves. Now the music I composed robbed me of the ability to write coherent words, and I ended up with songs like 'Midnight To Neon' and 'Arrow In A Bow', which, through constant rehearsal, might have sounded tight and attacking but were too oblique for even the most dedicated lyric decipherer to understand.

On warm nights I'd walk down to confer with Grant. His one-bedroom apartment a bohemian paradise. Dark polished floors, a gas cooker, a loungeroom edged with stacked books and records, a few movie posters up of course, and a bathroom with forties fittings; Robert Mitchum could have opened the door. Also in view was a typewriter on a table, typed pages piled by its side. With the band settled and Grant in a new home, old ambitions had returned. Poems. A story that might bloom into a novel. Set in north Queensland, he'd hinted. We drank, smoked, played guitar and listened to records. A favourite, reducing us to tears of laughter, was *The Palladium,* a twenty-minute routine from early-sixties comedian Lenny Bruce chronicling the ambitions of a deluded, 'hip' American comic as he tries to convince his sceptical manager to book him at the prestigious London Theatre on a bill filled with wily old-school performers. It remains the most devastating and funny deconstruction of show business in existence, and resonated at this low ebb of our career.

Another visitor at Grant's, cynical about showbusiness yet enthralled by its tropes and mores, was Peter Walsh. He had broken up The Apartments, and like us set off on a voyage of sonic discovery with his new group Out of Nowhere. He and Grant would play guitar into the night, jamming on chord sequences or riffs. This was something I couldn't do, needing as I did a fixed thing to accomplish. A song. A box to run my hand along. It exposed a difference between Grant and me: behind the formal greeting at his door, and the fifteen minutes of banter it would take to warm him up – his face to the world a sleepy, distant gaze – a great generosity of spirit prevailed, in music-making and with his friends. I was more calculating, in life and art. The Strategist, Grant would much later call me. My nature was a reversal of his: an easier approach, a more guarded heart.

*

After the Paris Theatre show we'd done gigs in Melbourne, some in support of The Birthday Party, others on our own. I know we were there on 8 December 1980, the day John Lennon died. In freezing July of the following year we returned to record our debut album, Tony Cohen having booked us into night sessions at Richmond Recorders, to take over from a Melbourne pub rock band who we thought were going nowhere called Men at Work. Tony had a signature sound – big and ultra-dynamic – he didn't have a producer's instincts, though; bands had to choose their best songs and arrange them themselves. Our selection had Keith decrying, 'Where are all the songs from your May demos?' We were moving too fast, spinning material on our quest, and the features of the resulting album are its forceful instrumental sounds and the attack of our playing, more than the things we'd been noted for in the past and would be in the future – attractive melodies, literate lyrics and a chiming sound. Raw bones jut out, as they do on many records from that year, the songs being of varying quality (Grant's 'Hold Your Horses' and 'One Thing Can Hold Us' strong, 'People Know' my best) and from different places. 'Eight Pictures' is from 1977, 'Your Turn, My Turn' was brought in to start the album. There was one key track whose importance we recognised, and placed last as a promise of things to come. Grant's 'It Could Be Anyone' is a spiky two-chord verse giving way to a chorus of gorgeous cascading chords, cherry-topped with a great guitar solo from him. Here was the balance between tunefulness and attack, between what we loved from the past and what had been absorbed from the present.

So, no classic first album; *Send Me a Lullaby* is not *Marquee Moon*. But a band has to keep thinking they are writing their own story, and not be tied up comparing themselves to other groups. This was *our* way. We received the automatic career fillip that comes from making an album, and it was well reviewed. The secret that we could do better was perhaps ours. With more concentrated preparation, stronger songs, and possibly a producer, we could make that masterpiece.

One of the best features of the album is the cover. Jenny Watson and her husband John Nixon had moved into Dahrl Court. They were artists from Melbourne, where they'd been involved in the punk and post-punk scenes and also taught at various art colleges – one of Jenny's students was Nick Cave. Coming to Brisbane, where John had taken up the position of director of the Institute of Modern Art, was a jolt. We became friends and there were some enjoyable beer-soaked nights where we locked horns, The Go-Betweens in the novel position, given the modernity of our music, of being old-world defenders. John and Jenny, John especially, were adamant that art and time began in 1915. Mention Matisse and a red tone came to his face. We'd never run across this kind of thinking before, and it was refreshing. John's work on canvas was conceptual and geometric, while Jenny's was figurative and naive; recent work of hers scattered in their flat caught our eye, and we asked if she would paint our portraits for the cover. She got the three of us with precision, placing us on the album with the touch of a master psychologist. I'm in one square, linked to Grant and Lindy, who don't connect. My eyes shoot off in deference to Lindy, but go past her. She stares out confident and defiant, while Grant, in the bottom panel, looks down, knotted with the greatest concentration of colour. The remaining square is the band name in simple painted script.

An era was being documented. The inside gatefold had photographs of our two apartments. A video for 'Your Turn, My Turn', our first, was shot in Grant's flat. That about wrapped it up. It was time to go, even if we didn't have the money to leave. Our album was out and a third year in Brisbane could not be faced.

'Melbourne Town'

Two sides of the river, didn't know I had to choose
Two sides of the river, didn't know I had to choose
One was offering a new dance aesthetic, while the other
    was trying to reinvent the Memphis blues.

Women with cleavage, didn't think I'd see it in my time
Women with cleavage, didn't think I'd see it in my time
I was prepared for anything, but I'd forgotten about the
    plunging neckline.

Two sides of the river, one up one down
Two sides of the river, one up one down
We were children in the garden, and the King he'd left town.

Red ribbons, red ribbons as far as I could see

The women wore red ribbons, red ribbons as far as I could see

The men were all dressed in black, where did that leave me?

Everybody was drinking, that's where both sides could agree

Both sides were drinking, that's where everyone could agree

Some people went on and became famous, while others just

lingered in obscurity.

I wrote this song in Italy in the late nineties, and what made me think from my perch high in the hills above Rimini of the six months The Go-Betweens lived in Melbourne, from December '81 to May '82, is a mystery to me. Perhaps it's to do with the music of the song, which is blues – a style I'd never used before and haven't since – and how this musical form, with its rhythm and grit, its language of redemption, loss, carnality and casual violence, found a place in the Melbourne scene, especially in St Kilda, the side of the river The Go-Betweens grew to know best.

We arrived in early December, another leap at the year's end. Lindy and I found a small terrace house in North Carlton and immediately a great thing happened. I wrote a good song. 'By Chance' was a hard-fought-for number that I had been making my way towards for the past two years. In it I managed to combine the spindly notes of a riff with fractured chords and make it stick and flow, while giving myself just enough room to say something that made some kind of sense – 'My head fits/ Into my hands/ I roll it around/ And nothing comes out' – very 1981.

I was away again, my songwriting driven by the simple logic that if I could write one strong song, I could write another.

Grant, who had a knack of finding apartments as Lindy did practice rooms, moved into a funky Deco bachelor pad in East Melbourne. The Go-Betweens were spreading out – in the eyes of those we knew, however, our places of abode implied a decision that disappointed one group of people. Unbeknown to us, during our visits to the city the previous year we had hooked up with two scenes of musicians, and their circles, who viewed each other with great mistrust and suspicion. It was a situation alien to us, as Brisbane was one inner-city pool of people – the town not big enough to sustain opposing sides. Through The Birthday Party we'd connected to St Kilda, south of the river, to the Crystal Ballroom set and the wild-living bands and people who fanned out from it. Through Missing Link, and connections Grant had made, we also got to meet members and friends of Equal Local and Tsk Tsk Tsk, who lived with poise and conceptual thinking on 'new pop' and dance music in Northcote and Fitzroy, north of the river. Drop some St Kilda name to them and there'd be an intake of breath or a sad, wry smile; mention northern names down on Acland Street and we'd get banged tables and an exasperated 'What are you doing hanging around with those people?' The first few weeks in town for the appropriately named Go-Betweens were spent gingerly trying to please everyone, as we alternated social activities between the north and south sides of the Yarra.

The city was to be our finishing school – our Hamburg. Here we could play to good crowds in St Kilda, the city, Collingwood, and it was like playing three different towns. Given the dark theatricality of the scene and its bands, we soon realised we needed to put on more of a show, hard as that was for an intense, instrument-gazing three-piece. We didn't have to don make-up or scramble up PA stacks, but we could no longer just stand onstage and strum. We buffed up our act as best we could, added one or two moves (did anyone notice?) and worked on our ability to say something witty between songs – I was channelling Edwyn.

We weren't the only newly arrived band in town; The Birthday Party had come home from London before Christmas, to tour and prepare songs for their upcoming album, *Junkyard*. Melbourne in general, and St Kilda in particular, went into a kind of torpor when the group was away, and their return upped the dynamic considerably. And with it came a new aesthetic; the feathered haircuts and the dolled-up art-school clothes were gone, replaced by T-shirts, leather pants, tattoos on upper arms, and a demented take on Stooges-like rock'n'roll. The change shuddered through the music scene. Favoured albums from previous years by The Pop Group, Pere Ubu, and Magazine sold en masse to thrift shops. The Birthday Party were *the* Melbourne band, and being around them was an energy charge. Nick, grinning in the back of a taxi: 'We've got a new song. "Hamlet (Pow Pow Pow)".' Their influence and a few weeks of gigs were evident when we went into the studio with Tony to record our fifth single.

'Hammer The Hammer' is Grant's first great pop tune. An urgent, melodic verse, a foot-to-the-floor chorus – its lyric the repeated title. Perfect. From his earliest songs I found his lyrics surprisingly oblique and melancholic. This was the second revelation, after the contents of his Golding Street bedroom. For as soon as he began putting words to melodies, there was a conflicted tone to his work that caught me off balance. Songwriters aren't necessarily their songs, and in person he was barrel-chested – stocky, even – capable, you would think, of carrying the world on his shoulders. His material, though, was never light; nothing I can remember was as transparent or silly as what I wrote. No 'I'm An Architect' with its 'I've got plans on you.' Or 'Summer's Melting My Mind' or 'Lee Remick'. He would have been wanting to cut his own cloth, but that wasn't the whole story. There was a sadness, expressed often through the prism of 'love' songs, that made me realise I had in a way misread him, or not been privy to a set of feelings he chose to communicate only through music. Therefore, 'Hammer The Hammer' begins with 'You can say what you like when you're alone/ Knock down the walls, swallow the phone/ When you're all alone, it won't change.' Nothing too dragging, but it built on 'Your pride's my pride/ You're on your side/ I stand tongue-tied with my lies' from 'One Thing Can Hold Us', to add to 'Under blue sky, under your eye, under clouds so dark they make you cry' from 'Hold Your Horses'. It became a persistent line of ache, song to song, the magic mix of his songwriting – melancholia and exquisite melody – there from the start.

Who these songs were aimed at or written for I didn't know. Women were glimpsed – a face at a show, or someone departing Dahrl Court mid-morning. There must have been something going on, as he was a good-looking guy in a band with a house full of books and of independent means. He did like the role of eligible bachelor and he played it well, with presumably enough interested women passing through for him to have some kind of sexual or romantic life and song subject matter – his lack of commitment, I assumed, the matter. The pool of women swelled considerably in Melbourne, yet he remained as he wanted to be, a single man. He kept me guessing, as his operating method was cards hugged to the chest, his emotional side always in check. This didn't bother me, but for Lindy, who lived on raw nerves and confession, it fanned a growing frustration she had with him. And he with her.

The B side to 'Hammer' was 'By Chance'. And with Tony at his favoured Armstrong Studios, recording our lean instrumentation with power, we had swerved back on track.

*

The finishing school of Melbourne also included lessons offstage. We were in a city of far greater sophistication and swagger than our hometown, and we met and moved amidst people who embodied and flaunted these attributes. There were many of them on both sides of the river – one, though, can be pulled from their ranks; he's actually waving us over, personifying the qualities of the rest.

We'd met Pierre on our first trip to Melbourne, in late 1980, when supporting The Birthday Party. Our procuring of this show caused consternation among a number of local bands close to the headliners, including Pierre and the Fabulous Marquises.

Their ruffled feathers were smoothed somewhat when Rowland Howard endorsed us, saying we weren't still the group of 'Lee Remick' and 'Karen'. Our image from that first single hadn't been entirely shaken, linked as we were to Brisbane. In an inversion of the US north–south divide, coming from Queensland was the equivalent of coming out of Mississippi, which, given the appreciation for the Southern trash aesthetic on the south side of the Yarra, almost made us hip again.

We were welcomed there as innocents, unhardened by the furious local rock'n'roll lifestyle and the strand of cynicism that went with it. We did some catching up, but after the sleepy streets of Toowong and Spring Hill, St Kilda was akin to walking onto the set of *West Side Story*. The boys with their knives and greased hair brewing trouble in one corner, while the girls with their porcelain skin, black ruffles and curls sat demurely together waiting for an approach. A shock after life up north, where the tropical heat and the utility of clothing needed to withstand it tended to blur boys and girls together. Brisbane was never sexy; it had feminism and op-shop unisex chic, while Melbourne was a silver rocket trip back to the fifties, all the guys wanting to look like Elvis – in Memphis, in the army, in leather for the Comeback Special, or in his dying days, it didn't matter. The girls were witchy, flirty and confident, with a twisted, nineteenth-century doll-like quality that at times could be quite unnerving. Lindy and I had a monogamous relationship and I had no desire to stray, but giving Grant and me frontline reportage was Pierre.

He was everything we weren't – a flamboyant womaniser,

hetero-camp, annoyingly self-assured, unreliable, and a rogue. We adored him. Women were frequently a game; old-fashioned seduction was 'on', which to our astonishment often worked, and when it didn't there was little apparent emotional damage, only arms around the boys at the bar. He staggered us with his aren't-I-so-handsome duplicity and he did possess a killer smile that got him in and out of a thousand bedrooms and punch-ups, and charmed us too. He'd been in punk bands and was a friend of Nick and Rowland's in their palling days, when they encountered a hail of influences and moved through the city like wolves – already a gone golden age. He told us a history of Melbourne that began with his first band, Teenage Radio Stars, and proceeded to fill in with precision the movements of every important musician in town, up to the formation of his current group, which was in its fading days, as was Pierre's musical career. 'I want to be a rock star, but I don't want to do the work' – his own frank assessment of the situation. People who didn't know him wondered what we saw in him, and at times we didn't know ourselves. Pierre was an attitude installer and we needed that – an upwards tilt of the chin; the bowlegged swagger when walking down a street, denoting it was yours; and lessons on how to enter a rock club, knowing your presence upped the star quality of the room. Little things – we didn't take them quite to Pierre's level, and we didn't have to, enough rubbed off – a thin coat of rock star varnish for wherever our erratic, city-to-city career was taking us.

The release of *Send Me a Lullaby* and our single allowed us to play Sydney and Brisbane, our first Australian tour with

Pierre as tour manager. Melbourne, though, was starting to feel like a town we had to leave if career momentum and health were to be sustained. Keith had told us he couldn't finance a second album and was shopping *Send Me a Lullaby* overseas. The coming Melbourne winter and the idea of foreign labels judging the band on songwriting from last July didn't lift our mood.

Then a miracle. Some view our career as essentially luckless, acknowledging the quality of the music yet noting its failure to produce the gold bars of rock'n'roll success: hit singles and stadium tours. There *was* good fortune, we would have crumbled after a year or two if there hadn't been any, and archangel Geoff Travis at this moment agreeing to license our album and single to Rough Trade Records while extending an invitation for us to move to London and record a follow-up LP was solid proof of that.

St Charles Square

In the two and a half years since my last visit to Geoff's office, the independent music scene had grown out of its chaos and frenzy to where a few bigger companies were releasing records into a large market running on the various strands of post-punk rock. Indie rock had become a business, and in the process the Rough Trade shop and label had split, the record company moving to a warehouse-sized building on nearby Blenheim Crescent. After being on a series of one-man labels, we arrived in London in May '82 to find what was for us a Hollywood studio set-up, with all a band needed – booking agent, press department, radio plugger, accountant, and A&R man Geoff, under one roof. Things would never be so simple again.

While our record company was bigger, we missed the sense of community we'd experienced with the bands on our previous labels. To our surprise we turned out to be one of Rough Trade's few London-based groups. The Fall, and Blue Orchids were in Manchester; Weekend, and The Gist, who had splintered out of Young Marble Giants, were in the country, leaving in London The Raincoats, who lived around Notting Hill Gate, and Scritti Politti. The latter had changed drastically since Grant and I saw them play at the Electric Ballroom in early 1980. They'd gone new-pop, which some of the punk-era bands were doing, convinced they were top-forty bands after all. When we arrived, the push and the money (signalling 'prioritisation of a group' – controversially so inside Rough Trade, which prided itself on its democratic principles) was aimed at breaking the former skank-pop, postmodern-theory-toting Scritti Politti into the charts. Green Gartside, their lead singer and songwriter, could be seen walking through the label's offices strumming an acoustic guitar, a genius-in-residence sign flashing over his head. To be fair, the group's latest single, 'The Sweetest Girl', was very good, and the label held its collective breath as the song hovered outside the new grail that was the top forty.

We were hanging around the offices too, when we got a tip on accommodation ten minutes away at St Charles Square, off Ladbroke Grove. The owner of the terrace house was a woman with connections to Rough Trade, who was happy to offer the band the empty floors above her basement flat for nominal rent until the house came up for sale in September. It was fairytale stuff – three musicians run away from home, break into a deserted mansion, and are allowed to stay for one magical summer. We slept and worked by curtainless windows that looked out over gardens and rooftops, the moon within arm's reach above our sleeping heads. Each morning Grant and I would pick a floor to play guitar and write, to meet up and swap songs and spin arrangement ideas. 'Do we need another guitar riff for the intro?' 'Should the second chorus be repeated?' A process was set in train that continued on every album, whereby he and I would finesse the material we each had before rehearsal began as a group. Lindy would be in another room industrious on her drum pad, joining us to add her rhythms – completing the sound. This routine went on for months, crafting and preparing songs for an album we knew had to be brilliant.

We talked to Geoff about producers; some, given our modest budget, were fanciful – Robbie Robertson from The Band, or Lindsey Buckingham from Fleetwood Mac, a favourite of Pierre's. 'You've *got* to get Lindsey!' The person we settled on at Geoff's recommendation was less grand but would prove a fine decision: John Brand, an engineer who'd been working with new wave acts XTC and Magazine for Virgin Records and was wanting to make the career leap, as many engineers do, to producer. The first band Geoff had given him was Aztec Camera, and with them he'd made a great single, 'Pillar To Post', and he was about to start recording their debut album, *High Land, Hard Rain*, at ICC Studios at Eastbourne, on the coast south of London. We were up next.

Aztec Camera had followed us onto Postcard, and were led by a seventeen-year-old songwriting genius called Roddy Frame. Our first exposure to them was their single 'Just Like Gold'/'We Could Send Letters', which we'd bought in Sydney while recording 'Your Turn, My Turn'. The A side was strong, the B side stunning – a deceptively fast-paced ballad with gorgeous melodic sections and a brave lyric: 'I found some blood I wasn't meant to find/ I found some feelings that we'd left behind/ But then some blood won't mean that much to me/ When I've been smothered in the sympathy you bleed.' Everyone was wild about Roddy, and Geoff probably thought he had an artist capable of cutting a career to the shape of Neil Young's or Van Morrison's. We met him and fellow Aztec Camera member, bass player Campbell Owens, at Rough Trade. They were starry-eyed, but with a cheeky confidence that came from knowing they had a bag of good songs.

Also down from Glasgow was Orange Juice. Steven Daly and James Kirk had left the band under mysterious circumstances, to be replaced by Malcolm Ross from the disbanded Josef K and Zeke Manyika on drums. Postcard had cracked like an egg on the first waves of money and acclaim. Orange Juice were now on a major label, and we met them at the Columbia Hotel bar in the company of members of ABC, another smart group with their songs in the top forty. Orange Juice would eventually get there, charting with the wonderful 'Rip It Up', and while our friendship with them stayed strong, a slicker, funkier direction with an eye on the *Top of the Pops* prize was not where our music was taking us.

*

ICC Studios was the kind of middle-priced analogue-recording facility that today no longer exists, squeezed out of business by digital home recording. There was a 24-track recording desk, a two-inch tape machine, some good outboard gear and microphones, and a recording room big enough to fit a three- or four-piece band – all that was ever needed to make a great Go-Betweens record. John, after putting us through our paces in rehearsal – our first major drill, having someone break down song structures and instrumentation, to tighten and enhance them when reassembling – was looking for precision in the recording process, and like many English producers, he favoured a careful layering of instrumentation. It's a method that can lead to a sterility of sound, but John got the balance between live recording and a coating of overdubs just right. In the process he did a wonderful thing to our music – he rained colour through it. Where *Send Me a Lullaby* was like a great recording of us in the practice room, and powerful for that, *Before Hollywood* was a production – the band brightened, the tunefulness brought forward, the quirky riffs and time signatures kept – yet, through John's engineering skills, clear and punchy.

With the help of John's friend, keyboardist Bernie Clarke, a member of early-seventies Sydney glam-rock big band Kush, we formulated a sound that was not fashionable at the time: live drums, electric and acoustic guitar, Hammond organ and piano. 'Rock is dead,' we had been told by London 'rock' journalists on our arrival, the future of music Kid Creole and the Coconuts, and the latest Spandau Ballet twelve-inch. And we weren't going for easy rock'n'roll revivalism either; helping to pull the band away from that was Grant's guitar playing and Lindy's drumming. Her drum kit sounded fantastic and she rode every queer-timed riff and rolled on every chorus we put to her. *Before Hollywood* is a master class in creative rock drumming; hers is the distinguishing instrument.

The songs were certainly the best bunch of material Grant and I had written. They had come in a gold rush over a warm English summer, and reflected our particular obsessions yet were similar in musical intent – an aligning of the swift turns and aggression of post-punk with pop songwriting, something John had picked up on, and the reason, perhaps, Geoff had signed us. Not many other bands were doing that, and if they were it wasn't with an attractive sound.

My songs were mostly built out of 'By Chance'. I was writing better guitar riffs, and they were the foundations for 'Before Hollywood' (the LP's title track) and 'On My Block', the former the history of Hollywood cinema before the invention of sound; the latter ('The main gate to the mansion is locked/ It's on my street and it's on my block') had me luxuriating in outsider status, a role I'd keep coming back to for more songs. 'As Long As That' was an ode to Lindy ('Think of someone and double it/ That's what I did'), 'Ask' a mighty guitar crunch, and 'By Chance' – I'd run out of puff, no new fifth song – meant my contribution to the record, my half of the painting, in my opinion was pretty bloody good.

Then came Grant. Getting to know someone or their work can be like looking down a camera lens, each click bringing what was blurred into relief, until what's before the eye is clear, bigger. The songs Grant delivered were the final click, and they were enormous. 'A Bad Debt Follows You', 'That Way' and 'Two

Steps Step Out' ramping up the push-and-pull stratagem of 'It Could Be Anyone' and 'Hammer The Hammer' into an exciting set of pop songs built on his greatest strength – melody, which he could spin by the yard. He had become a riff merchant on guitar, a legacy of his bass playing that allowed him to string notes together as a musical entity, and, to his further credit, commit them to memory and play them evenly in rotation. They sounded fantastic under my songs, and I would watch him construct them under his own as I strummed back his chord sequences – this was a part of our songwriting process.

His best riff, however, I missed. My defence being that as we sat chair to chair playing our songs, there were so many attractive scraps of music coming from Grant that I didn't at first catch the quality of the bones to 'Cattle And Cane'. It proved difficult to put chords to, so I doubled his part; then Lindy arrived with her drumsticks and announced that the song was in some incredible time count (remember, Grant wasn't a traditional rock musician), 13/8 or something, which theoretically only Charlie Parker could play, and to her credit she didn't try to straighten it, only preserved its oddness, in turn making one of the most distinctive beats in rock.

Grant knocked the song further into shape, to shine in the practice room, the killer moment – the unpacking of the masterpiece from the crate – coming when he sang the opening lines: 'I recall a schoolboy coming home/ Through fields of cane/ To a house of tin and timber/ And in the sky/ A rain of falling cinders/ From time to time the waste/ Memory wastes.'

My god, the beauty of that, and here he was in song, the person I'd known since university.

A companion piece was 'Dusty In Here', directed to the ghost of his father. A gorgeous slow tune, it was a surprise to Lindy and me, and choking, too, to hear him address his father so directly. 'And twenty years, and six feet down I'm told/ I know your face, I share your name.' The music climbs: 'You won't write, no you won't write/ That's all I ask, that you just write/ And you say no, that you can't speak/ You lost your voice, you let it go.' I was stunned at the confession, and as a song-writer amazed and a little envious at his inventiveness. With both songs, he'd opened up a new topic – childhood. Why hadn't I thought of that? And it passed my test – Dylan and Bowie hadn't written about theirs. Furthermore the album, at Grant's suggestion, was dedicated in an extraordinarily anti-rock'n'roll gesture 'to our parents'. It joined another inscription, etched onto the run-out grooves during the making of the vinyl mastering lacquer – short, cryptic messages left there by bands wishing to impart one last whisper. Ours read 'two wimps and a witch', the description of us by Helen Glass, wife of Keith, which in our ebullient mood we were happy to share with the world.

In the final days of recording Geoff came down to hear the album. He was hard to impress, not being the clichéd, over-enthusiastic, arm-waving record executive, his demeanour more the young university don whom the brighter students strove to impress. The record clearly surprised him, and whatever estima-tion he had of us as a band, and hopes he held for the record, had been exceeded. Hearing *Before Hollywood* sequenced for the first time with our record company manager and producer present was a wonderful experience, and when we got back to Rough Trade, word was definitely out – The Go-Betweens had cut a classic.

*

Grant and I had signed our first publishing contract shortly before the recording of the album. We'd been in at Rough Trade on one of our regular scavenging missions for cash, as an advance against record sales, when Geoff said, 'Why don't you go sign a publishing deal and get an advance that way?' He even gave us the address – Cherry Red Publishing off Westbourne Grove. The publisher there, exuding old-world music-business bon-homie, was Theo Chalmers. Our songs, from *Before Hollywood* onwards, were to be credited as Forster/McLennan, the order of names a nod to the better known Liverpool songwriting team. Also at this time, Grant and I made a verbal agreement that each of us would have an equal number of songs on every album. It was casually said and done, and in the moment the agree-ment was made neither of us was to know how much easier this would make the assembling of records in the future, when the stakes got higher and the pressure on us was much greater.

The house at St Charles Square had been sold, and through friends of Theo we got a three-bedroom flat on Fulham Palace Road. Grant, Lindy and I moved in, and the third bedroom went to a Brisbane friend of ours with punk rock heritage, Clinton Walker. He was a gentle bear of a man – much growl, little bite – who had gone to the same high school as The Saints, founded two punk fanzines, done a radio show in Melbourne, and written the first book on the Australian 'new music' scene, *Inner City Sound*. We'd met him on our travels, although his name, in a comic twist, was familiar to me from long ago: Virginia had once asked me ('because you have a way with words', a lovely thing to hear when you're eighteen) to write suitable endearments on a birthday card to a 'sweet boy' she had a crush on. It was Clinton.

The four of us hadn't been there long when the chance to reciprocate Melbourne hospitality came knocking. Nick and his girlfriend Anita Lane, and Birthday Party bassist Tracy Pew with partner Kate Jarrett, needing a place to crash after a Berlin recording session, bunked on the loungeroom floor. Winter was approaching, money scarce, and life in the crowded house became nocturnal. The only person up early was Clinton, who after passing a rock history test set for prospective employees, was working at the Notting Hill Record & Tape Exchange. He'd return each night with an armful of records to peruse, and a playlist emerged. These albums mark the time. Billy Swan's *I Can Help*, The Beach Boys' *Surf's Up*, which we followed to sequence *Before Hollywood*, The Gun Club's *Miami*. Also James Brown's 'King Heroin' single, and a track that flattened us all, Van Morrison's 'TB Sheets' – a two-chord, nine-minute groove describing in scat-sung images a harrowing visit to a sick friend in hospital. I'd listen, lost in admiration, willing myself to simplify my songwriting. There were two other records that got a spin. Nick and Tracy had a test pressing of their Berlin recordings, *The Bad Seed EP*, with four very strong songs on it. This would have intimidated me in the past, being perhaps the most powerfully concise thing they ever did, but our album was strong enough to follow it.

Given the amount of guitar Grant had played on *Before Hollywood*, and his frustration at still being on bass after five years, it was an obvious next step for him to move to guitar and for us to get a new bass player. Two guitars, bass and drums – the classic rock band line-up – allowing us to present the album's colours in concert. Tim Mustafa excepted, we had never taken someone into the band from an advertisement, preferring friends to join. The group was so idiosyncratic and strange even to ourselves that we thought people needed to know us to be able to play the music. Peter Walsh, who'd moved to New York (and was the subject of Grant's 'That Way': 'In search of a new voice/ You burnt all your lyrics/ Moved to a new town'), had been sent a pre-release cassette of our new album along with word that we were looking for a bass player: Robert Vickers, with the career of The Colors cooling, approached us and in late January took over Clinton's bedroom in the house of darkness and wonder to become the fourth member of the group.

We gained more than a bass player. The triangle became a square and I could breathe again. It was hard being in a three-piece with my girlfriend and closest male friend. The music and the band image had gained a cohesion from these relationships, but it meant that Lindy and I could never walk away from the group and clear our heads. It was all-consuming, from waking, to the breakfast table, to the practice room, to record company meetings, gigs, social engagements, the bedroom, and it went on seven days a week – I hadn't realised how tightly it had wound my nerves till Robert joined. He was fresh air on past disagreements and an added perspective on everything that came our way, his shrugged 'Let's carry on' response to any adversity a blessing. And he was another piece on the chessboard between Grant and Lindy, who got on most of the time, more so in public, but had differences that were irreconcilable. These were primarily due to their contrasting temperaments and social manners. Grant was emotionally contained and had to be approached respectfully, tiny steps over a bridge, while Lindy was a verbal flood, who due to a dose of late-sixties/early-seventies 'truth-telling' had less regard for personal borders. Both were highly intelligent, a quality they acknowledged in each other, and both had doctors as fathers. One of the few other things they had in common was me, and how I came to appeal to such disparate people was a conundrum I'd been turning over in my mind in the rare moments of sanity I had.

We knew that if we could get through the winter, the last icy pass to freedom, the album and its first single, 'Cattle And Cane', would significantly reposition our career. These were my favourite pages of a biography come to life, but they proved harder to live than to read. The months dragged on a cabin-fever diet of brussels sprouts – the vegetable, like the work of Dickens, another thing I can never go back to. Lindy, desperate for money and the dignity it confers, was having to work as a cleaner, one job taking her to the house of a Pink Floyd member. A moment of brightness for me was writing the music to 'Part Company', the strummed folkie chords setting up the possibility of telling a story, not a fragment. The act of writing a good song I find to be like taking a photograph – a flare is set off at the moment of composition that permits me to recall my surroundings far better than the normal workings of memory allow. So, I see our bed in the house on Fulham Palace Road, feel my toes in the thick, caramel-coloured carpet, notice the window on the cream wall facing the busy street, and inhale the trapped air of a bedroom and an apartment furnished for nine-to-five workers to return to – not for itinerant musicians to maintain. A phone bill climbing into hundreds of pounds will never be paid. Nick and Anita have to be asked to leave so we can walk through our loungeroom to the kitchen of a morning. Tracy and Kate come and go; in the end there isn't the money to keep our home, The Go-Betweens fleeing one weekend into a cold February night, unpaid debts the engulfing flames, never to live under one roof again.

I don't remember how Lindy and I found the squat in West Hampstead, but it made cramped apartment living with members of The Birthday Party and a gonzo Australian rock journalist seem the very picture of normalcy. The house was a three-storey terrace, not dissimilar to St Charles Square, but in a posher part of town. On the ground floor in a large front bedroom was a gang of politicised Canadian lesbians; under them in the basement lived an acid casualty who slept in a coffin-shaped bed surrounded by hundreds of stinking empty milk cartons. On the second floor, beside the house's bare communal kitchen, was the bedroom of an ivory-skinned, pre-Raphaelite beauty with whom Grant had a brief affair. She was the sister of the acid casualty – there's a song title. Each day she'd walk her brother in his zombie state to the shops for a little food and another carton of milk. On the top floor, in the attic, lived perhaps the most upstanding folks on the premises, Rowland Howard and his elfin, fine-featured girlfriend Genevieve McGuckin. It was quite a household.

In our makeshift bedroom in a room behind the lesbians we were awoken one morning by screams: 'You're on the radio! You're on the radio!' We stumbled into the front room to hear the tail end of 'Cattle And Cane' being played on the BBC 1 breakfast show. '"That's Cattle And Cane",' announced an over-bright voice that I hadn't heard anywhere near our music before, 'by a group called The Go-Betweens. We know absolutely nothing about them, but we think it's a rather m-a-h-r-vellous record.' There was cheering in the room and Lindy and I looked at each other in bemused disbelief. I did wonder what kind of record company sent a record to a radio station with no information, but that was just as quickly lost in the euphoria. Later that day we strolled into Rough Trade as heroes; indie bands only got played on the evening programs, including John Peel's, the high-rating breakfast show being the much sought-after turf of Culture Club, Duran Duran, and Wham – probably not even Scritti Politti had been broadcast there.

The radio play was the first lick of magic our records would bring. The change in the band's fortunes was quick, due to the power of the three UK rock weeklies, whose reviews of both album and single ranged from extremely positive to ecstatic. They noted our sound – a fresh arrangement of traditional rock instrumentation with songs to match – and that we were Australian only added to the exoticism of the music. We watched the band's profile rise like a flood before our eyes, bringing with it the greatest thing that can befall a group – the ability to say no. In the beginning it's always yes, as you knock on doors, ache for a break, push to a place you know exists, where famous bands graze, fielding offers, picking and choosing what they want to do. Now that was us in a month. Requests came for radio sessions, large press features – our Able Label singles, Postcard, and debut album no longer the sum of our story, but neatly spaced stepping stones to the launch of our career – and tours. Suddenly we had to be everywhere at once, with dates at first through the UK and Europe, and then an offer from Australia, to start in Sydney in late May.

I went into Rough Trade on the day before we flew off, in the rush picking up a single by a new group on the label, to throw into my suitcase that night. With just a few pre-release promo copies in the office, I can confidently say that I brought the first Smiths record to Australia. We'd be away for two months, and there'd be changes while we were gone.

Geoff had a new love.

Playin' in a Travellin' Band

Sydney had been glimpsed. We'd performed there a few times, never staying long, only picking up the impressions you get when on tour. A stroll around one part of the town during the day, a quick, alcohol-affected sample of the nightlife after the show. As with Melbourne, the dash of the city was impressive. The people I'd met were mostly early-seventies Brisbane friends of Lindy's. Robyn Stacey was a photographer. John Hoey an ultra-handsome, toy-collecting pop culture freak. Jim Dickson the bass player for The New Christs, fronted by former Radio Birdman lead singer Rob Younger. They all lived in a funky terrace in Paddington. Down in Elizabeth Bay, on the top floor of a spectacular block of flats known as Gotham City, was an actor with an elastic body and face, Geoffrey Rush. I always enjoyed meeting Lindy's friends, not only for who they were, but for the effect they had on her. In their company she reverted to the relationship she had with them in the past, in essence to the person she once was – an outgoing social-work student entranced by her talented artistic friends. She was gentler and warmer in their presence, and a certain frustration that she claimed came from always being around younger people vanished.

We had been brought to Australia at the optimum moment. Album and single out for two months, and here we suddenly were with dates booked. The local reviews resembled the overseas response but had a louder echo, given the smaller chamber of the Australian music scene. Added to this was a mystery for the press to proudly unfold: nervy three-piece leaves Australia to return a year later as roaring-lion four-piece with classic LP and single in tow. The tour promoter was Clive Miller, not your average Aussie booking agent, being honest, sharp-minded and gay. We liked him and he us, especially Lindy, whose charisma and larger than life manner appealed to many gay men. Clive had been tracking our London progress, getting his bid in early to bring us back at the right time to strike.

Although neither 'Before Hollywood' or 'Cattle And Cane' went near the charts, their impact was considerable. Audiences were much larger than we'd played to before and the touring schedule longer, encompassing both city and suburban venues and taking the band to Adelaide and Perth. Supporting us were groups like The Triffids and The Moodists, who represented a coming wave of bands out of punk aligned to a similar set of influences to our own. And in a further crowning typical of what 'Cattle And Cane' achieved, we got to play *Countdown* – the one-night-a-week, watched-by-everyone pop television show. There we were on a studio set built to suggest an outback shearing shed, shades of Oak Park, playing a song that in the program's context, and amid the latest videos of Culture Club and Human League, became even more undefinable and beautiful. We all got our cameos – Robert in tight suit and fringe looking like a member of The Byrds circa '66, Lindy intense over the high hat, me weighing eight stone and projecting with all my might haughty rock star allure, and Grant out front, earnest before the camera in a black hat. Having played guitar for just four and a half years, he was singing his song to the nation, a song that, like the set but more successfully done, twinned the beat of the city with country childhood visions. Thirty years later, the song was number nineteen on APRA's top thirty Australian songs of all time. The boy wonder had struck.

When not out on the road we roamed inner-city Sydney – oh that the world championship of rock groups, with an attendant music press keeping score, was being played out here. It was a carefree cafe life in Darlinghurst, beginning with a late breakfast of amphetamine-strength cappuccino and Kent cigarettes, followed by a stroll up to Victoria Street, where Nicholas Pounder's bookshop and Didgeridoo Records (a Laughing Clowns hangout with Albert Ayler or a Factory twelve-inch on the stereo) sat amidst another row of coffee houses. On the street, coming out of terrace houses or red-brick apartment blocks, would be Clinton, Andrew Wilson from enigmatic pop combo Frontier Scouts, photographer Marjorie McIntosh – hip enough to own a Talking Heads bootleg – and members of various bands good and bad. I'd sit at a table in the winter sun, alone or with the band or friends, watching the passing parade and appreciating the ease of life.

Too easy? The complaint we heard from the groups we played with was one we knew – too few record labels and not enough money, plus there were just so many times you could play Sydney and Melbourne. As I bit on my toasted focaccia and sipped my frothy coffee, the *Sydney Morning Herald* on my lap, the bargain struck by the band seemed right. We'd have to leave this life but we'd take as much succour from it as we could, before returning to face the harsh, contradictory condition London presented: day-to-day uncertainty sitting right next to golden opportunity.

*

Lindy and I arrived home in West Hampstead to find that bailiffs had pasted an eviction order to the front door of the squat. We'd been given a month to get out, with a court date provided should there be grounds for objection. Considering we were living illegally in someone else's house, I couldn't think of any. A few of the squat-living veterans claimed that by appearing at the hearing a valuable extra month could be granted, but it was Lindy and I who travelled to the Strand to find the courthouse. Amidst much polished wood and wigs, the judge sat high in his tall chamber as we awaited the call for our address. He glanced up when it came and we raised our hands, hopeful for the mercy of an additional month. There was mumbling from the bench and the signing of papers, then the anvil came down with the verdict. 'Two months.'

A not too dissimilar sentence had been brought down on our career.

London is a music business town, and you cannot leave it for longer than a week and expect anything to be the same as when you left. I'd played The Smiths' single in Sydney, and through the sniffy dismissals from friends I could hear in 'Hand In Glove' and 'Handsome Devil' two very melodic rock songs. The leaning, naked man with his marble arse on the cover could be a problem for marketing, but there was a rallying call in the lyrics, which is always attractive, and the band sounded robust in a non-indie-rock kind of way. Rough Trade was a place of high attrition, and no doubt when we joined the label one or two groups had fallen from Geoff's gaze and the reach of recording budgets – the quickness of the turnover, however, was astonishing. We'd been feted in March; by August we were on thin ice. Our cause wasn't helped by making two mistakes. The first was supporting The Smiths on our first show back in London, and the second was botching the recording of a new single.

Before we'd left for Australia, Rough Trade suggested we record a new song as a momentum-maintaining move, to be released on our return in July. It's always hard for a group to turn down the chance to record, and John Brand and Eastbourne were on offer again. 'Part Company' was my best new song, but not a single; Grant, having hit the highs of the previous year, had yet to write a solid batch of new material. That should have been reason to pause; instead we pushed on. 'Man O'Sand To Girl O'Sea' was a rock number of mine, containing an arrangement kink no one in the studio could solve, and in Australia we decided to re-record the song when back in England. Bands dither, hypersensitive to what the public will hear. In August, to Rough Trade's fury, John took us to an expensive residential studio in Surrey, the bill for the three-day session approaching the cost of our album. Add this to our demotion, which being support act for The Smiths, who'd released just one single, assuredly was, and we were in trouble. 'How was it?' Morrissey asked from the wings, gladioli in hand. 'Terrible,' I could only reply. He sighed.

Internal London drama aside, 'Before Hollywood' and 'Cattle And Cane', still only months old, were beguiling people elsewhere.

*

In the late nineties the English group Suede put out a song called 'Europe Is Our Playground', and when I saw the title, I thought, That's how it was for us. Moving to the UK had implied playing Europe – unlike many English groups we met in the eighties, just becoming popular and tripping around the UK was never going to be enough for us. Europe proved easy: for our first trip, back in August '82, Mike Hinc from Rough Trade Booking got the dates, we hired a driver and a van, and off we went to Sweden. To play a rock festival in the woods outside Stockholm, waking up in the promoter's house by a lake, is one of the things you join a rock band to do. That encounter, with its large dose of hospitality and care, set the style for all subsequent visits.

Badgering Mike, we returned to Europe in March and April of the following year, and now, in October, we had three weeks of concerts taking in Scandinavia, the Netherlands and Germany. Rough Trade Germany was very supportive of our music – seeds were sown that made the country in time our biggest audience. The rock press in each of these places were curious about us too, and Grant and I were happy to expand upon any cultural or historical questions thrown at the group, which on this trip came from journalists trying to pin the coordinates of a 'new Australian sound' to the films of Peter Weir.

Spirits restored, we returned to London to greet Clive Miller, now our manager. We'd waited a long time before taking someone on: the right person hadn't appeared. As with the arrival of Robert, Clive loosened tensions, allowing us to leave the study of budgets and focus on music. For him it was a jump from Sydney tour promoting to the fingerwork of dealing with a band full-time, and the muscle needed to do business on behalf of the group. In this respect Rough Trade were difficult: there was the strain of the past months, and the label could be prickly with band managers, preferring to work directly with musicians. Fine for a three-piece band from Hackney, trickier when you're four Australians hustling tours, recording budgets, shelter and wages by yourselves.

*

It was night in the days before Christmas, and I remember the cab pulling up out of the darkness at the end of the tunnel into the mythic yellow glow of Manhattan. I was like a little boy on

his first fairground ride, lightheaded and open-mouthed, craning to see the sights and blending them with images already
stored in my mind – the lights of the late-night delicatessens,
the boxy yellow cabs, the vertical fall of buildings to the pave-
ment – while a noise familiar from movies, car horns and a
hum that I couldn't place, pitched the volume of the city at an
excitement level like no other. I took every bounce of the cab
as encouragement, wishing to be in Greenwich Village, Central
Park, Tiffany's, Broadway, the Chelsea Hotel and 4th Street
simultaneously. We reached the downtown hotel, and really all
I wanted to do was stand on the street and scream to the sky,
'I'm here.'

Our records had not come out in the US, a market Rough
Trade had yet to crack. Here it was word of mouth, among
hipsters who read the English music press and bought import
copies of albums. We had one champion: long-time *Village
Voice* rock critic Robert Christgau, who gave *Before Hollywood*
a score of B-plus on his fabled rating system. For the band,
that meant America was effectively done. We had approached
the country with no notions of conquering it – the places
we were playing, New York, Boston and Philadelphia, being
in rock'n'roll terms almost the next three gigs you did after
Dublin.

Of our few New York shows, a set at CBGB's was the highlight, and one of the best performances the band ever gave,
inspired as we were to be playing a room where a number of
our favourite groups had launched their careers, albeit with, it
has to be said, the worst toilets I'd ever seen. To celebrate and

strengthen my ultra-romantic connection with the city, I had put out word that I wanted to try a Quaalude, that most New York of drugs, after the gig. Some eat haggis in Glasgow, others suck oysters in Paris. I remember taking the tablet surreptitiously out of Bill Arning's hand – he was a friend of Robert and Janie's; had been in The Student Teachers, a hip, late-seventies Downtown band, and was now studying to be a museum curator – and washing it down with a sip of Schlitz beer at CB's bar, and that was my last memory for twelve hours.

I woke the next afternoon on the floor of Bill's bedroom, disorientated and groggy, wondering how I could get my life back in order. 'Well, it's Gay Pride Day and I'm marching uptown, which is in the direction of your hotel,' said Bill. So I joined thousands of gay men and women walking slowly up Fifth Avenue. There were many things I'd imagined doing on my first visit to New York – this, as pleasant as it was, hadn't been one of them. Bill was charming company. He was a tall man with a fringe that he'd whip back on every quip. I was bracing myself against the freezing weather and the expected displeasure of Lindy as I returned waves to supportive onlookers.

At the hotel she was understandably angry at my disappearance. Clive, at her shoulder, couldn't quite keep the smile off his face.

*

The booth, the lighting and – I'll say it, although it certainly didn't feel like it at the time – the comedy of what happened next took place at an uptown diner not dissimilar to the one in

Seinfeld. Geoff Travis was in town, as were The Smiths on their first American trip. We bunched around the booth, the band, Clive and Geoff, who had not brought good news. He told us there was no money for us to make another album. We were no longer on the label. It was a hammer blow. Among the whims, madness and inequity dished out by the music business, we'd thought the quality of our album and singles – they were on many best-of-1983 lists as we spoke – would guarantee us a follow-up album on Rough Trade. Geoff was remorseful, and somewhere in our glum disbelief we knew we owed him and the company a debt for plucking us out of Melbourne. *Still.* We were crushed. By our reading of the situation, all Rough Trade chips were being pushed to the square marked The Smiths. We had seen other bands go; now we were being shown the door.

The Year of Living Generously

Throughout that year in which the band made the leap to professional rock group – when the focus and passion we put into our music was matched by the amount of work and travel it demanded of us – I saw more of Grant yet knew him less. As our dreams for the group came true, as we sat side by side on tour buses and aeroplanes, now Forster/McLennan the songwriting team and two internationally known rock musicians, except for the rare moments when both of us registered the gaining of a particular goal and there was an acknowledging smile or glance between us, important events went by largely in an uncredited blur. Perhaps a time would come when everything would be reviewed; for now we were enjoying ourselves, alive to the victories and defeats, entranced by the music, our heads turned by praise. We were cocky, and like most rock bands, no matter how clean their image, were drinking and partying when we could, while pushing on to a prize we knew we had enough talent to win. So Grant, like Robert and Clive, came to be one more person to be dropped off from a van, usually late at night, at the end of a gig or tour or recording session, to meet up with again a few days later to start fulfilling another dream on the list that had been drawn up in the ever-receding days of our beginning.

We were back in London at the start of 1984. I temporarily lose the order of where Lindy and I and the other band members lived that year – songs, as ever, help illuminate the way. I remember a small terrace house in a street of small terrace houses in Wandsworth; Lindy and I were briefly there with Clive, and Grant was sometimes there too, though more likely visiting. With Clive at work, the three of us rented *Texas Chainsaw Massacre* from a video shop, and after thirty minutes of blind terror expelled it back there, *in daylight*. The flash from writing 'Rare Breed' (a future B side) not only brightens the couch we were sitting on, but the television in the large front room facing the street. A far better song, 'Draining The Pool For You', was written weeks later, when Lindy and I were living at the Barons Hotel, a poky bed-and-breakfast off Queensway in Bayswater. We were about to go out, and being old enough to know not to hurry a woman applying her make-up, I picked up the guitar and strummed a chord sequence that became the verses to the song. The flare this sets off allows me to see the white plastered walls, one lamp on, Lindy in the bathroom, door open, thin carpet, dead curtains facing the

134

street; and for all its 1940s drabness, this picture remains in my memory as cosy.

*

The band weren't label-less for long. Geoff having the ear of Seymour Stein, the head of Sire Records – the home of Talking Heads, The Ramones, and a new signing, Madonna. Seymour was a New York record man from the sixties, appreciative of Geoff's A&R ability, having just signed The Smiths to Sire for the US. With the label opening a European branch in London, we were signed on Geoff's recommendation, gaining what could be considered a promotion from the man who'd let us go. A key to the deal was the advance we received against record sales – a sizable pot of money enabling us for the first time to live and plan beyond a month. Clive had a budget, putting the group on a basic wage, the first for Grant and me after six years in the band, and allotting portions for prudent use, such as recording our next album in a French villa about an hour back from the Riviera. Studio Miraval was owned by Jacques Loussier, a pianist and composer, famous for his jazz-style interpretations of Bach. The studio was in a large hall and had a control room with a recording desk du jour – an SSL. On offer was an experience enjoying a heyday in the boom years of the music industry – a secluded luxury location with state-of-the-art recording facilities.

We were picked up at Nice airport and driven in true European style – at breakneck speed through single-lane curves, death by oncoming traffic a possibility at any moment – to a large terracotta-coloured estate ringed by vineyards. We were allocated bungalows. We met the cook. We strolled around the farm buildings admiring the burnt-hill views, before being escorted through the studio.

There was at one end of the large recording room an oval-shaped window with a multicoloured swirl like a mural painted upon it.

'Who did that?' I asked Jacques Hermet, the in-house engineer.

'Jon Anderson. You know him? Lead singer of the group Yes.'

I would, for the next six weeks, be singing and playing guitar under a piece of art made by the lead singer of Yes. Oh no. Wham had recently recorded here too – another piece of information given to us with not a flicker of irony. (Later we were shown photos in pop magazines of George and Andrew reclining in beds and barns that looked very familiar.) There was nothing to do but settle in, not hard after London poverty, with a cook and red wine from the Loussier grapes at hand.

John Brand, whose manager had booked the studio on a deal, was now in surroundings that corresponded to his time at Virgin. He also came with an approach that harked back to those days.

'Now we are going to make a proper record,' he said.

It wasn't meant badly but my heart sank. I thought *Before Hollywood* was a proper record, and like Grant and Lindy I was very proud of it. What constituted such a record in John's eyes became apparent when, instead of miking the band's instruments and starting to record, we spent three days getting a bass drum sound. Then started the dreaded discussion of live versus programmed drums and suddenly we were face to face with eighties recording hell. Little was getting done as John manoeuvred Lindy into accepting the use of drum machines. The rest of the band were trapped, literally, in Miraval as the clock ticked and things nosedived towards disaster.

The era of the obsession with time-keeping was upon us, automated recording and mixing desks and synthesisers forcing the requirement of absolute accuracy in the drums; no 'feel' was allowed. It came down to what kind of music you wanted to make – modern pop or music with an old-time feeling. And that led to what kind of band we were in April 1984. We weren't an underground noise group with no immediate chart prospects. We weren't Lubricated Goat or Einstürzende Neubauten. We had pop songs and one of them, 'Bachelor Kisses', written by Grant, sounded to John and Sire like a hit single. Wouldn't a hit single make our lives a thousand times easier in London? But this wasn't a decade when pop hits were recorded live in the studio. Now they were intricate constructions, taking days or weeks to build, and the first thing to go was the drummer. A rhythm machine was programmed and the other members of the band took turns in fitting their part to a giant gyre of sound so complicated that a pair of hands couldn't hope to mix it.

All rock bands with any commercial aspect to their music were faced with this process. In the past, for a non-mainstream band to have a hit single was to sell out; now, in the eighties, the issue for us was getting the fucking thing recorded.

The methods of recording forced an existential crisis on The Go-Betweens that was never resolved over the following years. Instead we took a zigzag approach album to album, single to single, confusing record companies, managers, our audience, and at times ourselves.

Another matter was the nature of the songs Grant and I brought to the album; they weren't as unified as those on our previous record. 'Bachelor Kisses' was a beautiful ballad, again exploring the terms of romantic commitment. Grant positioned himself as wise counsel to an attractive woman tentatively commencing a relationship: 'Don't believe what you've heard/ Faithful's not a bad word,' to then dissuade her in the last chorus: 'Don't be slave to Bachelor Kisses now/ They'll break their vow.' (In a weird and wonderful echo of the song's sentiment, thirty years later Miraval was sold to Angelina Jolie and Brad Pitt, who exchanged their wedding vows there.) Grant's other songs were a mixed lot. There were no more love songs; instead 'Unkind and Unwise' was a pop number in the vein of 'Cattle And Cane': 'The salt in the wind moves over the mudflats/ Sticks to your skin and rusts up the lights.' And 'Five Words' was a gorgeous folk strum recorded on a day when John was away. Lindy is on brushes – the album breathes. The surprise of the record, especially in view of Grant being perceived as the more commercially minded songwriter of the band, was his jettisoning of two great melodic rock songs we'd demoed in November, 'Attraction' and 'Emperor's Courtesan', for the dry funk of 'Slow Slow Music' and the feedback-driven, spoken-word sprawl of 'River Of Money'.

Both benefited from the sheer sonic punch John could pull from the desk, a feature of the album that also serviced my songs, the most important of which were 'Part Company' and 'Draining The Pool For You'. These songs, numbers I still play today, were the beginning of a more mature writing style where I fused the strumming of my late-seventies tunes to the curves and kinks of the past few years. Add experience and time and I had grown-up songs with better lyrics. 'Part Company' was a break-up song, although Lindy and I hadn't split. The situation had been flagged in the opening lines of 'Man O'Sand': 'Feel so sure of our love/ I'll write a song about us breaking up.' 'Draining' was the blending of the band's fate to mine, defiant and proud: 'I got hired, but I got tired, of draining the pool for you.' The tempo was 'TB Sheets'.

We left Miraval a little bewildered and bruised. The isolation imposed by any recording studio was amplified by the distance of this one from the world; factor in its luxury surroundings, which we didn't leave in six weeks, and you have in part the reason for the reserved estimation the group had for the album. Was it a 'proper' record? We didn't know, and no one from the record company flew in to enlighten us. Grant, Lindy and I travelled back to London together in a harmony we could still find. Grant must have had the album title in his head for some time, and this was the moment for its offering. *Spring Hill Fair.* Beautiful.

*

Sire had its offices in the Warner Brothers building in Soho. We were striding into corporate rock'n'roll, passing the desks and doors of big decision-making and million-selling records. The weekly pop charts were the operator's manual here – who was in the top ten, the top forty, the top seventy-five, and who in the tumbleweed-blowing oblivion that was any number lower than that. The fate of a single or a band's career could hang on the ability of a radio plugger to get a golf date with a BBC producer or DJ. Meanwhile, journalists waited in corridors to do interviews for glossy pop magazines, and photographers nervously gave their contact sheets to sharp-eyed publicists who scrutinised them for blemishes. Occasionally a pop star was glimpsed – was that Howard Jones? – or a new group of brushed-haired boys being patted and prompted by their manager before a meeting with a young, excited A&R guy who probably didn't have the power to sign them anyway.

This was the scene as we made our way to the Sire desk. Yes, desk. The label's expansion into Europe was staffed by one person working three days a week, with any decision of consequence, or one relating to money, involving phone calls to New York for approval. We were operating in two time zones, mirroring a weird major-label existence, one where every bill was paid.

For the album cover, Sheila Rock photographed us in an ornate Richmond theatre. A band's cover shot is a good read of a group, their current mood and hopes for the album included, and there we are, intense and suspicious, framed in a theatre box by gold-flecked, old-world showbiz glamour. In more crossed signals between band and label, Sire insisted we re-record 'Bachelor Kisses' for a better shot at the charts. And so to new producers, more days on the bass drum – how long did the

Stones spend on that for 'Brown Sugar'? – and a version of the song of no great variance to the Miraval take.

The single wasn't a hit, and it's hard to see how it could have been, with one person working the campaign. Grant, more vulnerable than I to issues of fairness, in and out of the music industry, and with his song on the line, would have taken this to heart. He was a believer of promises, holding people to them, and the single was definitely worthy of more than it got. My default position, a cynicism if you like, was that while happy to push our singles, I still couldn't see the crown being given to us, no matter how good 'Bachelor Kisses' was or how many times we recorded it. In recompense, our concerns for the album were allayed when it came out to positive reviews; the gains of *Before Hollywood* held. We played a few headlining shows on its release and then, on the sails of our single, went off on a fifteen-date UK theatre tour supporting Aztec Camera.

I was walking down a hill in Liverpool early in the tour when I came across an op shop. On a shelf was Christopher Isherwood's *Goodbye to Berlin*. The book was a revelation. Highly readable, well written, and shining through every paragraph a humour never overplayed, a sense of insight never ponderously given. The Berlin of the late twenties grabbed me, as did the life of the narrator, drifting, unattached, in and out of bars and cafes with a circle of high- and low-life friends. Nothing much happened in terms of plot and I liked that too, there was no arching story or contrived twists, and certainly no pounded moral outlook – 'I am a camera with its shutter open, quite passive, recording, not thinking' reads the famous line from the second paragraph. What was recorded was the detail I would have picked from the landscape. I knew nervous men in bars, and loud and serious people unaware of their volume; I'd also known wild girls like Sally Bowles, and I wished I had the easy and teasing way Isherwood had with them – later learning that he was gay helped explain that.

I bought more of his books, *Mr Norris Changes Trains* (my favourite), *Down There on a Visit*, *A Single Man*, and his magnificent autobiography *Christopher and His Kind* (a band name – Robert and His Kind?). Also in his favour was that Grant, still the keeper at the gate of literary taste, didn't know him well, and that Isherwood wasn't in the 'big boy' league; no bullfighting, blood or murder, and certainly no wife-swapping. That world had been redefined by Raymond Carver, whom many I knew read – Pierre, Walsh, Clinton, Grant – and other Americans writing clean prose about devastated lives. I admired Carver, while measuring the annoyance I caused by dismissing the work of his imitators as barbed-wire writing. Through Isherwood I was led to a group of novelists whose profiles were lifted in the eighties with reissues by Gay Men's Press – books such as *The Firewalkers* by Francis King or *The Wrong People* by Robin Maugham, which chronicled wry outsiders in foreign cities experiencing the comic and tragic turns of life from the margins of their new homes.

I watched Aztec Camera most nights. They were promoting their new album, *Knife*, on Warners, the follow-up to their debut classic *High Land, Hard Rain*. Roddy Frame was the most accomplished guitarist I'd seen. He would sit opposite you and dazzle. Fingers swooping up and down the guitar neck picking out single notes, to freeze in a tangle-fingered chord that I would squint to decode. The tonal tinge that made his songwriting so distinctive came from these jazz-like chords that he would strum with a wrist-snapping flourish. One of which, the major seventh, is recognisable as the 'Burt Bacharach chord', a sophisticated-sounding bling of notes that instantly evokes hits such as 'Walk On By' or 'This Guy's In Love With You'. It's a chord that wasn't in my songwriting repertoire until a night in Birmingham, when I was wandering about onstage after the show, guitar in hand. I played an E-flat major seventh, slid down to B-flat major seventh, passed through F and G major, ending on a C. It sounded wonderful and unlike anything I'd ever written. This was the bones of 'Twin Layers Of Lightning', the first song of a trio that included 'Spirit' and 'Darlinghurst Nights' and which saw the mysterious, comet-like reappearance of the Roddy chord over the following decades. (In 2002 he released *Surf*, to my reckoning his best album, with just himself on acoustic guitar.)

After the tour we went to Europe, with our biggest shows in Germany, including a TV appearance miming to 'Bachelor Kisses' in a cobblestone square. A first visit to Italy, and then to Paris, the capital of the country that Grant and I thought, before we first went overseas, would probably understand us the best. We were supporting a local group with a name that couldn't be any more rock or French – Marquis de Sade. The venue was a small cinema-like complex with curved seating and carpeted floor, in Les Halles. Our hopes were high; Grant had the history of French cinema in his head, ready to unload on any journalist, and we were playing the best of our last two albums – and we bombed. To steal from Lenny Bruce, 'It was an oil painting out there.' 'Rembrandt,' Grant said backstage. 'Vermeer,' I laughed. The 300-strong audience, sympathetic in appearance, were stone-faced between songs except for a little chatter among friends in the front row. It wasn't hostility – that we could handle – it was studied indifference and that was worse. At the show's end, in a fit of petulance, disappointment really, I gave the audience the finger; it barely caused a ripple.

Curious, I stood side of stage for Marquis de Sade's opening number. They played an agreeable variant of post-punk. I turned to the crowd – they were going nuts. France was going to be harder than I thought.

*

Record companies write into their contracts option clauses, which allow them to either keep an artist under contract following an album's release or let them go, depending on the album's success and the long-term faith in the artist. Sire let us go after ten months, not even releasing our album in the US.

Disheartenment aside, being dropped was starting to have a serious impact on our career. If we were to make a fourth album, it would be financed by a fourth record company. A sideways glance at our competition, those spotted near us at the starting line sharing a broad set of influences and of similar talent and age, had Echo and the Bunnymen on Warners, The Smiths on Rough Trade, REM with IRS, and U2 on Island –

all were locked into long-term deals, guaranteeing successive recording and promotional budgets. This gave a consistency to their careers, while we had to continually reintroduce ourselves to those working for us and to our audience – in effect, forever being dragged back to the starting line. Add the recently formed Nick Cave and the Bad Seeds on Mute (the same label as The Birthday Party) to this list, and all but The Bunnymen had a lead singer prowling the stage.

This was something else The Go-Betweens didn't have. We were two singer-songwriters chained to guitars. Neither of us could put our instrument down to sing our own songs, to then drag the spotlight offstage for one of us to become the media face of the group, which was the strategy the music business ran on to sharpen a band's profile. Bono. Stipe. Morrissey. A strategy with rewards, for as the clubs and concert halls got bigger, so the benefits of having a lead singer free to work the crowd pushed these bands' careers ever higher. We had songs, our coin from the start, and two singer-songwriters who could have fronted their own bands: when their songwriting and chemistry were combined, a unique and very powerful thing was created. Some got it. But how to present that? Was this why record companies were letting us go?

With the carpet pulled from under our feet yet again, we were about to leave for a long Australian tour and our first Christmas home in four years. Just days before we went, Geoff called Lindy, tipping us to a gig at the Ambulance Station on Old Kent Road that, he said, 'could be worth a visit'. He was on the scent of a new group. The district was rough, but no security was on the door as we walked into a bare set of rooms. Beer was being sold out of ice-filled garbage bins by people who looked like they lived in a squat. Actually this *was* a squat, and yet with no advertising four hundred people, representing a sub-group I'd never seen before – short back-combed hair and thin leather jackets – were milling around waiting for something to happen. I followed the rock'n'roll scent to a far room where a five-piece band with a trumpet player were set up on a low stage ready to play. 'Hi, we're The Kinks,' said the lead singer as they burst into their first song. I had to smile; this was the cheekiest thing I'd seen on a London stage in ages, and they were playing music that in late '84 was out of style, or not yet in vogue. No bass-heavy indie funk or gothy, reverb-laden rock – they were doing the sixties trimmed with a punk aesthetic and something of their own. They were called The June Brides.

At the break, I was surprised when some members of the band approached me, professing an admiration for The Go-Betweens. They knew the group, from 'Karen' to the smoother contours of *Spring Hill Fair*, my qualifications about the latter brushed away. I was touched; as unlikely as it sounds, this was my first encounter with simpatico London musicians since our arrival in town two and a half years before. They were younger, and this was another breakthrough of sorts, an indication that our music was appreciated by a coming generation of musicians and fans. You can forget that's possible. London, with its class system and last drinks and Tube rides for the poor, was doing its best to keep like-minded souls apart. But then where else were you going to see a bill as good as this, with headliners

The Jesus and Mary Chain doing one of their first shows?

There was already a 'new Sex Pistols' tag on them, and a small amount of fighting and over-exuberant, front-row-to-band interaction gave their performance an early punk aura. The effect, though, was a little contrived, as if people on and off stage were acting less out of compulsion and more in accordance with rock history. It wasn't Baroona Hall 1978. The group didn't knock me out, the white noise and the frequent interruptions to their thirty-minute set blocking the songs and whatever pop qualities they had. But in the studio they would shine, joining The Smiths as one of a few bands I clocked record to record. And the sense of a scene gathering was undeniable, and one I understood, the tight black clothes, Chelsea boots and foggy attitudes straight out of Dylan's *Don't Look Back*. London was changing.

Going to Write a Classic, Going to Write It in an Attic

Australia too. Although Missing Link no longer existed, a plethora of labels had emerged and in each capital city there was a set of bands making records. The independent music networks that would bloom in the early nineties into alternate rock and the mega-tour Big Day Out were slowly locking into a mass. For Clive, burnt out after a year and a half overseas, the solution was clear. We should stay in Australia, either Sydney or Melbourne, get a local recording deal and reverse the touring cycle, leaving from the comfort of home for strategic forays into Europe and the US. We had seen this approach in action – Australian groups parked in luxury-to-us Soho flats, playing one or two dodgy gigs, then flying home thinking they'd made progress, or realising they hadn't, but unwilling to start from scratch in a new country. The UK demanded commitment; you had to be there, ready to pick up any break that came your way.

In response to Clive's eminently sensible suggestion, the band were united at the end of the Australian tour in wanting to return to London. Even though we'd have no manager, record company or money to return to, it was one of our finest moments. For in our hearts we knew the job was not yet done, that our best music was ahead of us, and perhaps with it would come the lift in fame and recognition we so desperately craved. To put it another way, for the lengthy entry in the Rock Encyclopedia that we felt the group deserved, there was still a way to go.

While no longer our manager, Clive had bequeathed Lindy and me something of great value. An attic flat at 20 Highbury Grange, in the village-like ambience of Highbury Barn, North London. And so it was to an address which for the first time felt like a home that we returned, and to the eccentric collection of long-term residents who lived there. Sue with a stall at Camden markets. Fred a crumpled-faced, flat-capped odd-job man in his sixties. And in the basement a bald, serial-killer type in a blue suit who looked like Philip Larkin. Fred had inquired about my profession soon after our arrival. 'Oh, you're not the first musician who's lived here, you know,' he said. Who had come before? 'Val Doonican,' he replied. 'He lived here in the early fifties when he came over from Ireland.' Cardigan-wearing crooner by a fireplace. I took this as a good omen.

Grant and Robert lived nearby, in an enclave of Australian and UK friends in Hackney. Grant shared a flat with Jack Davidson, a laconic, chain-smoking (non-filter, forgotten the brand) Scottish artist who I once unthinkingly asked if he'd done any portraits lately. For him to reply, 'Nah. You written any symphonies *lately?*' We'd met him through Clinton when they both worked at the Notting Hill Record & Tape Exchange. Jack was in a band called Hackney Five-O. A few doors down was Peter Walsh, back as The Apartments and signed to a rejuvenated Rough Trade. The band released their debut album, *The Evening Visits . . . and Stays for Years,* later in the year. Great songs, strong opening lines: 'Day comes up sicker than a cat' (from 'Mr Somewhere', later covered by This Mortal Coil). Walsh was a doomsday philosopher: 'Waiting is better than any event.' And there were other Australian groups about too. The Triffids were in town ready to make their best album, *Born Sandy Devotional.* And Nick Cave and the Bad Seeds had started their turn to traditional songwriting with the massive 'Tupelo'. The biggest competition came from those we knew.

Highbury and Hackney weren't far apart, but winding bus routes and crossed Tube routes placed them at a greater distance than they were. I could have lived in Hackney if we'd ultimately had to, but being a person of extreme sensitivity to violence – cowards run in my family – I found it difficult enough just walking the eerie council estate parks and entering the piss-stained lifts that would hopefully shunt me to Grant's floor, before a sprint to his door. He was visiting me for song sessions now, reversing the trend of a lifetime.

In the middle of the year we went to the US again, this time touching down in the Midwest, playing to a few fans and *NME* readers in Columbus, Ohio, and Lincoln, Nebraska, then playing San Francisco and a bizarre gig in LA, supported by a buckskin-wearing singer-songwriter with two hippie maidens in tow. Given a broader view of the task, we realised that the US was going to be like France – a hard nut to crack, although we had a cultural fix on the country. In the US I really thought we had a chance; not only were many of our influences from there, we were writing strong, melodic rock songs that lyrically, while not pandering to the 'Girl, you set my world on fire' crowd, pertained to life. In LA we did make some converts, a great gang of people, friends of REM who hung around Texas Records and public radio station KCRW, and it was to become a town with a few influential supporters of our music.

*

At the end of the Aztec Camera tour, the band's manager, Bob Johnson, had told Clive and us to call him if we ever needed help. We now called, and went to the South Kensington mews office he ran with his wife Sharon in search of what most down-at-heel bands need – a record deal and money. Bob was very different to Clive. He was English, older, had been a mod, a hippie in India and Australia, and had worked in a record company selling Bert Jansch records. He got into management, discovering and guiding Frankie Goes to Hollywood to the cusp of stardom and taking Aztec Camera from Rough Trade to Warner, where they were high priority. Bob was a music business insider with a reputation for being able to handle difficult artists, not that he would have necessarily considered us as such on first meetings. We were well mannered, smart, a little hopeful ('good songs will win through') and self-assured. Lindy was in her mid-thirties, and Grant, as writer and singer of our recent singles, would have seemed to any reasonable eye the 'pop' focus of the group – important in London. And yet, in a warning of the complications involved in handling a group with two singer-songwriters, I was about to reassert myself.

Bob's first move was to get 500-pound advances from major record labels, for us to make demos to present in the hope of being signed. We started to do one- or two-day sessions budgeted to leave cash in our pockets. The songs we were recording had us excited, coming as they did over a summer as magical and warm, and for myself as secure, as the summer of '82. With melody and a take on rock classicism now back in play, the thought came to me that I hadn't written an A side since 'Man O'Sand', and before that 'I Need Two Heads'. Wasn't I once the pop kid? Fired as ever by the distant voice of Alan Horne ('Just write classics'), and the pointed intention of a recent hit song ('Gonna write a classic/ Gonna write it in an attic'), I wrote 'Spring Rain', 'Head Full Of Steam' and 'To Reach Me', all pop songs, in months that felt like weeks. 'Bow Down', a ballad done then too, completed the best set of songs I had ever written.

'Spring Rain' was my second song – there are now four – with the word 'rain' in the title, in homage to the Creedence Clearwater Revival hits 'Who'll Stop The Rain' and 'Have You Ever Seen The Rain?' And instead of labouring over lyrics, as had been my way, I wrote quickly, first thought best thought, taking Grant's example of delving into the past, to stop at eighteen: 'Driving my first car, my elbows in the breeze/ With all these people that I never never need.' Another inspiration that summer was Prince. Everybody had been taken with 'When Doves Cry' and his following albums and singles, including 'Raspberry Beret'. The longstanding division between mainstream and underground bands was being driven further apart by video and studio costs. (Video especially, with MTV as the new grail, pricing a hit out of the reach of non-major-label bands and artists.) Prince was a bridge, witty, playful and eclectic. He could have been on Rough Trade. By '85 he was in his Sex God phase, and his power over me was strong, not only the snap of his songs, but the man himself; he was provocative and funny, doing exactly what Grant and I would have done when becoming pop stars – making films. The latest, *Under the Cherry Moon*, had been shot in black and white on the Riviera.

*

Amidst the songwriting, rehearsal and record-company adventure came an offer to play WOMAD – our first big festival show. The band was to perform on sundown, and having been given the chance to escape London for the countryside, something we seldom saw, we pulled up at the site in the early afternoon. I had just stepped out of the backstage area when a young woman approached me with a large plate of biscuits.

'What are they?' I asked.

'Hash cakes,' she said cheerfully.

I held my surprise. 'Ah, how much do they cost?'

'A pound.'

I had a pound, and with the transaction made the cake seller turned, and in her turning a hash cake fell off her tray to the ground. I was presented with my first moral dilemma of the afternoon. Do I run after her and tell her she's dropped a cake, or do I keep it? I kept it. The second question was, Do I now take both? I took both. My rationale the light state of self I was feeling at a world music festival in the English countryside on a sunny afternoon, and the fact that our performance was still five hours away, and surely whatever effects the hash cakes brought on would be diminishing by then.

They came on in thudding waves, setting off great mental and physical disorientation. I stayed close to the backstage area, repeating with mantra regularity the reassurance that our gig was hours away, and surely whatever effects the cakes brought on would be diminishing by then. Time, though, was . . . well, what was time? And to avoid being found curled up in a ball under our van, I kept moving around, wandering at one point into a room where a group of musicians were playing snooker. It was The Pogues, and taking a position against a wall and hoping to god I was projecting an appearance of sobriety and confidence, I watched a member of the band bend down, line up a ball with his cue, and shoot it to the far end of the table. The ball was setting off vapour trails, but more disconcerting was its sound – imagine a cannonball rolling down a wooden hall in an empty Edwardian mansion. This was still manageable, though, compared to the ear-blocking explosion I heard when it finally connected to the targeted balls. I was in very deep trouble.

Years later I realised that the only time I have ever been in a room with Shane MacGowan I was more out of it than he was.

The show, in a large tent with the last rays of the sun lighting thousands of faces, wasn't a total disaster. One of the advantages of having two singer-songwriters was that when either Grant or I got sick, the other could take over. I wasn't of any help that day, and it was a truly horrible experience being onstage. My vibe – late-period Syd Barrett. There was an occasional strum from me, a noise, but the songs, one of which I'd written, were like Russian novels, complicated and impossible to unravel. Grant did most of the singing, the band dredging up songs of his we hadn't played in years.

Driving down to London that night I was back on earth, relieved but still withered from the journey. One other member of the band had bought a hash cake and wisely waited till after the show to eat it. Their hysterical laughter spluttered through the post-festival festivities in the van. I sat in the front seat staring at the road, knowing I would never do vision-inducing drugs before a performance again.

*

The person engineering our demos was Richard Preston, who like most people that worked with us had been scooped up from the water as the pirate vessel veered past. Our first encounter had been at Pathway Studios, a noted eight-track studio in North London where Elvis Costello had done *My Aim is True*, Dire Straits 'Sultans Of Swing', and where we'd gone to make demos for *Spring Hill Fair*. Richard was an in-house engineer there. He was easygoing, and competent in capturing sounds while eschewing the twacking and whacking of much contemporary studio trickery. Such a person was harder to find than you might think, and with our wish to regain control of the recording process after Miraval, he was exactly who we were looking for. He was also connected to talented London musicians, leading us to keyboardist Dean Speedwell and the cello-playing string arranger Audrey Riley.

The major labels and their boutique affiliates weren't captivated by what they heard, bypassing future singles 'Spring Rain' and 'Head Full Of Steam', and Grant's amazing new ballad 'The Wrong Road' on one demo. We were contemplating alternatives when an offer came in from far left field. *Elektra*. A one-word sentence in rock'n'roll. Home of The Doors, Love, Tim Buckley, Television, and a hundred other groovy groups and artists, predominantly connected to the late sixties/early seventies. It *was* Elektra UK, and we knew what London chapters of prestige US labels were like; this was brushed away in excitement as we breathed the name into the astonished faces of our friends. We mightn't have had hits but boy, had we been on some labels. The band was signed by Simon Potts, an acquaintance of Bob's, who took his job seriously, wanting to sell records. The Go-Betweens was the second band he'd signed. The first was Simply Red. In October we began recording our fourth album.

The spirit we took into the recording session was aligned to the mood we'd brought back to the country at the start of the year. If this was to be our last shot, it had to be done on our terms. The production credit for *Liberty Belle and the Black Diamond Express* (what a wonderfully pretentious title) was going to read, 'The Go-Betweens and Richard Preston'. There'd be no drum machines, no piecemeal recording, no acquiescence to a higher authority – we were experienced enough in the studio, and flying on the strength of our demoed songs and Richard's easy, collaborative ways. Our intention was to expand upon the crisp, woody sound of *Before Hollywood*, to include a grander, more exotic range of instrumentation – vibraphone, oboe, piano accordion, and, at Grant's suggestion and to my apprehension, a string section. But he was right; we were making music and living lives that demanded strings. And we had a crack rhythm section, with Robert's swinging melodic bass and Lindy's signature rolls and fills, inventive and sturdy under every song. We were recording well at Berry Street studios, a mid-priced London studio (another lesson from Miraval and 'Man O'Sand': indulgence leads to loss of control), when two weeks into the session, Elektra UK collapsed. It really did feel like we were cursed.

After a few fraught weeks we returned to the studio, Simon, in a generous gesture, privately financing the album's completion. We were now making a record for a label that no longer existed, to hopefully be released by a label that didn't yet know of the album's existence – a circumstance that could only befall The Go-Betweens. The unpredictable nature of the process, one more chapter in a band story becoming ever more comic and tragic, reflected the content of two of the record's finest songs – maybe the best, taken as a pair, that Grant and I ever wrote for the group. 'Twin Layers Of Lightning' was a portrait of the increasingly sparky relationship between Lindy and myself, played against the ache of our ambitions: 'It's written in big letters/ Graffiti all over town/ It reads TROUBLEMAKERS ON THE RUN/ And both our names are written down/ Oh, but infamy or fame/ Each came in a small dose/ I just wish the day would come/ When the last one would be so close' – 'infamy or fame' being Lindy's reply at twelve to what she wanted in life. The six verses of Grant's 'The Wrong Road' have him chronicling in images more consciously literate than mine, as was his way, the scars and frustration of dream-chasing in a foreign city: 'A room in a lighthouse near the park/ The ghosts in the next room hear you cough/ Time drags on Sundays spent in Mayfair/ With all your riches, why aren't you there?/ The wind acts like a magnet/ And pulls the leaf from the tree/ And the town's lost its breath/ I took the Wrong Road round.' The Go-Betweens had been in London a long time; *Liberty Belle* is where we let the city in.

Dean, who we took out on a UK tour for the album's release, added fantastic textures to our music, proficient as he was on anything involving a keyboard. On top of his playing, as a third layer of the cake, came Audrey's strings, swooping in like birds, to soar off again through the clouds. She would go on to work with Coldplay; her start was *Liberty Belle*. We also needed a voice from the town, and who better than Tracey Thorn. I'd met her and Ben Watt separately at Cherry Red, where they were signed as recording artists before starting Everything But The Girl. They were a showbusiness couple, like Lindy and me, but younger, and as they were signed by Geoff to Blanco y Negro through Warner, more successful. The four of us were friends, and they were feistier and funnier than their public image let on. They pointed out to me Morrissey's use of 'Eskimo blood in their veins' from 'Karen' on a recent Smiths B side, 'Stretch Out And Wait'. Tracey's singing lifted the chorus of 'Head Full Of Steam': unlike myself, she can hold and bend notes. On Grant's 'Apology Accepted', the last agony-of-commitment song he wrote for a few years, she stayed with him as he delivered an unusually impassioned performance.

Album done, Bob signed us to Beggars Banquet. There would be no more New York phone calls – most business was done in a pub across the road from the label's Wandsworth offices. To our delight the label had a gothy image, despite being financed by Gary Numan's success; Bauhaus had left their inky stamp. The company had money, but not too much, no rope for folly or indulgence, and they were interested in supporting groups album to album. Had we found a home?

'Spring Rain' came out and charted outside the charts at eighty or ninety, windblown oblivion, yet our highest entry to date; and we played our best London show leaning heavily on songs from the forthcoming album, the cover of which had us laughing on a couch in Bob's office. We had done it – believed in ourselves, taken control and made our best album. To round out the year we left for Australia, to avoid what were always sad Christmases away from home.

1986

Michael Crawley was typical of a type of Englishman who, seduced by the lifestyle and beauty of Sydney on a visit, returns with family to live and work in the city. Michael had been involved in the London music business, and having spotted a niche in Sydney had begun True Tone Records. Ed Kuepper and soul-singing wonder boy Peter Blakeley were signed, and former Riptides singer-songwriter Mark Callaghan, having found success on the label with his new group GANGgajang, had been recommending Michael to me since our last Australian tour. The goal of True Tone was noble and clear – to put quality records in the charts. We signed.

Also in Sydney and about to meet The Go-Betweens in early 1986 was Amanda Brown. She was a twenty-year-old violin-playing university student, whose then boyfriend,

Michael O'Connell, had been a guitarist and songwriter in The Apartments in the late seventies. Fresh into their romance they had started a musical duo playing Michael's songs and some covers, one of which was 'Draining The Pool For You'. Lindy and I were invited to a small cafe in Kings Cross to see them play; they were impressive and it was hard not to be taken by the musical ability and beauty of Amanda.

The Go-Betweens were in town preparing for an Australasian tour, and shooting a clip for 'Spring Rain'. The age of video had not been kind to us. Rough Trade hadn't commissioned anything for 'Cattle And Cane' or 'Man O'Sand'; the clip for 'Bachelor Kisses' was amateurish and clichéd – Grant sings 'diamond ring', camera zooms in on a diamond ring, that sort of thing. Five years back, when we were young and tender, miming to 'Your Turn, My Turn' in the burnt-wood, boho splendour of Grant's Dahrl Court apartment, an essence of the band had been caught. We needed that to happen again. And there did seem to be a more creative approach to music videos in Australia than in England, a greater awareness of their importance at least – I certainly ran into enough people in Kings Cross bars in the eighties who told me they were video directors, and Michael knew the best and could pay them.

There were three filming locations for 'Spring Rain', the last under fire-truck hoses on the hill in Ultimo, and as I danced and pranced around the group with an umbrella in my hand, indulging every lead-singer fantasy I ever had, there was a feeling, with Sydney gleaming below at night, Michael beaming at the edge of the falling water, that record company, band, single and video were in their best alignment to deliver that elusive hit record.

London was also calling. On the back of an enthusiastic response to the album by the English and European press, journalists were wanting to speak to the songwriters. Lindy was not happy with this development – the first time Grant and I had flown off to do band business alone – and in a piece of manoeuvring designed partly to remind us not to get too big for our boots, we returned to find that she'd asked Amanda to join the band as a guest musician on some upcoming shows.

Unrelated to this, and yet part of a shifting of things that can happen in a band's or a person's life, or two people's lives in a band, Lindy and I broke up. The *Liberty Belle* sessions had been cohesive for the group, but scrappy between us. There were no other people involved; it was exhaustion with each other, our ever-increasing fighting, and we needed it to stop. It was a true showbusiness split, a break-up in the morning, to face each other at soundcheck in the afternoon, and like so many of the exchanges between us, it had to be done under the eyes of the group, before whom, I always thought, we conducted ourselves with some dignity and restraint. Grant and Robert must have wondered what would happen next, as normally when couples separate they . . . separate. And none of us were to know that the band was about to get bigger.

Just as *Before Hollywood* had popped Grant out from bass to guitar, bringing in Robert, so *Liberty Belle* signalled the need for a keyboard player or violinist. The will within the band leant to a keyboardist, and Bob thought this too, although he was discovering we weren't the easiest band to manage, especially when far from his influence. But Amanda, meanwhile, had learnt Audrey's lines, and written her own to some of our back catalogue, the number of songs conducive to violin being surprisingly high, and at the shows she performed with us, primarily in Sydney, the response from the audience was very positive. The Go-Betweens weren't a consistent live band; we were too mercurial for that, 'plodding' and 'workman-like' not terms journalists had cause to turn to when reviewing us in concert. Onstage with Amanda we were more dynamic and cohesive, a power we felt, and even when we weren't playing well the band was now so charismatic people were happy just to stare at us.

At the Cosmopolitan Hotel on the Bondi waterfront, Nico and her Manchester band three floors above us, we asked Amanda if she wanted to join the group permanently. We were following our protocol; she had arrived not via advertisement, and at the moment of need. She was young and ambitious enough to say yes and walk away from a comfortable Sydney life. Amanda brought a number of things to the group, the first being an optimism tinged with naivety that was good for our worn selves. She played oboe and guitar, sang, had studied ballet and said she would learn keyboards – the perfect Go-Betweens résumé. She was also funny and easy company, slotting into the mood of those around her while retaining a strong sense of self. And she was knockout beautiful, something she accentuated with a lean to fifties fashion. Strolling down the street with her was like walking with Monroe, men bumping into walls at the edge of my vision, ladders crashing behind me. She trailed a scene of destruction behind her, another Go-Betweens virtue.

*

A second blonde came into my life at this time, if only briefly, and she walked in from the past. I was staying in a flophouse Kings Cross hotel on days off from our tour, when I got a message asking me to contact a woman I'd vaguely known in the early days of the Brisbane punk scene. Jane Johnson had been a tall, striking-looking womoan with white make-up and cropped hair at Baroona Hall; she was now working as an art director on films in Sydney, the latest of which was a Second World War drama starring Lee Remick. Was I interested in meeting the subject of my song?

Two days later Jane and I were walking through the strip-joint and junkie streets of the Cross to the old-world elegance of the Sebel Townhouse in nearby Elizabeth Bay. I was hitting an all-time nerve high as we ascended in the lift, flowers in one hand, a copy of 'Lee Remick' nobly donated by Michael O'Connell in the other, to a suite where the famous Hollywood actress was waiting for me. Events then moved like stage directions in a play. We knocked and entered. A solid, older man, introduced to me as Lee's husband Kip, was talking to a woman familiar to Jane who had worked on the film. From behind a partitioned wall, where she was having her hair styled for a television show that night, Lee called out greetings to Jane and me. The agony went on – I could hear Lee Remick but I couldn't see her. Until, hair done, she swept into the room, took my hand,

and looking me straight in the eye said, 'So we meet at last.'

I didn't have a comeback line for that.

She sat me down away from the others and we chatted about Hollywood, her career, anything that came to mind, really. There was a particular film of hers I liked amidst many, *The Hallelujah Trail* with Burt Lancaster, and we spoke about that. She was gracious, having carved out time and privacy for us – I was getting a lesson in showbusiness etiquette. And all the while I fought the temptation to stare at her eyes, a startling pale blue, like diamonds in the sun; it was easy to imagine a casting director picking her from a thousand girls for her breakthrough role in Elia Kazan's late-fifties feature *A Face in the Crowd*. An hour later Jane and I were on the street, back in life, debriefing. I walked to my hotel on air.

There was a strange denouement to the day. In my room that night, between the shouts of people in neighbouring rooms threatening to kill each other over drugs and money, I watched the opening credits of the nationally broadcasted *Mike Walsh Show* on a television beside my bed. Lee was to be the first guest, and the host, I had been told, was going to present her with a copy of the single (her second that day, and the third in her possession; fittingly the subject of the song ended up with the most copies), which had been purchased from a collector for a hundred and eighty dollars. The first verse of the song rang out as she walked onto the set. Walsh explained the context of the music and the name of the group who'd made the record. Then, with a raised eyebrow to the camera and a theatrical clearing of the throat, he read out the lyrics to the second verse. '"She was in *The Omen* with Gregory Peck/ She got killed but what the heck/ Her eyes are like gems/ She's an actress for Screen Gems."' I was being humiliated on national television. Lee smiled coolly; having met the song's author that day, she knew his sincerity.

*

The Servants, named after *The Servant* (1963), a film by Joseph Losey, who also directed *The Go-Between* (1971), were the support band for our UK tour after the Australasian dates. They were one of a number of bands that had come out of the Ambulance Station scene. Skinny young men in dark clothing, mop-top hair and translucent skin – the next generation of Velvet Underground and anything-evil-floating-out-of-mid-to-late-sixties-rock worshippers. The Servants, who had good songs and a foppish image, also dug Postcard, early Orange Juice in particular, who had just broken up – Edwyn now solo. Accompanying the young band on some of the dates were their cheeky and attractive girlfriends – Sandy a photographer, Sarah a dancer – and at the tour's end I asked Sarah if she would dance in the 'Head Full Of Steam' film clip. This was my second single off the album, on the back of 'Spring Rain', our best video, in which I'd stepped out as a lead performer. I don't know if this was perceived as a challenge by Grant, or whether he simply wished to immerse himself in the spirit of the new video – a take on Prince's recent 'Kiss' clip, with me in my red flares and a skimpy black midriff top – but he suddenly decided on set with a make-up artist that he wanted to be 'dragged-up' as Wendy, the woman on guitar Prince performs to in his clip. This was weird and gave the video an odd edge. I didn't know what Grant was thinking. A team of psychologists at a lakeside retreat outside of Vienna would have to work that one out. I was still in costume a week later, Grant thankfully not, when we made our UK television debut performing 'Head Full Of Steam' on *The Old Grey Whistle Test*. Four years in London, four albums out, you'd think our star would be waning – but we were still contenders.

It had been a year since WOMAD and once again we boarded a van for a rock festival in the country. This time it was Glastonbury. This time we were brilliant, playing in mid-afternoon sunshine with a set that was now a golden hour. This was when we realised we could perform to thousands of people, many of whom had never heard or seen us before, and win them over. To become a big rock band you need to be able to do that. What had changed? Besides the fact that I wasn't on drugs, Amanda's violin gave us more rhythmic crunch and her solo lines did the job of a lead guitar. Also, violinists were a rarity in good rock bands, as were female drummers; we were starting to be recognised for the trail we were blazing. We didn't need a prowling front man – we had something else that elicited the same response.

It was also around this time, another summer phenomenon, that Grant and Amanda came together. Before more is said, a characteristic associated with the band has to be clarified. There were *never* two couples in The Go-Betweens at the one time. We weren't ABBA or Fleetwood Mac. There was, however, an element of inevitability, if only through the confinement of constant touring, that may have helped foster Grant and Amanda's relationship. A genuine attraction did exist between them, sparks were seen; neither was rushing, though, the example of Lindy and me no doubt slowing progress. Amanda was Grant's first real girlfriend. 'I remember when I met you, how slow I was to act/ But I hadn't used my heart before, that's a fact,' he would sing of this moment six years later in 'The Dark Side Of Town'. For now, the change was registered on 'Right Here', his new song, his declaration of love. 'I'm keeping you right here,' and 'Whatever I have is yours and it's right here.' Amanda had been won and he was proud. It's also a song offering protection, and through the entirety of their relationship there was this aspect to them as a couple. He would smooth things for her, ensure there were as few nasty surprises as possible. And although she enjoyed the benefits of playing in a band far more successful than the arty inner-city groups she'd been with in Sydney, The Go-Betweens weren't on the rock star magic-carpet ride. We were each on fifty pounds a week, seven pounds and fifty pence of that immediately going out on a weekly Tube card. Amanda's home was a Hackney tower. Still, Grant made sure everything was as comfortable as it could be. In turn she lightened him; he could no longer play the mysterious brooding poet, and it seemed he was happy to abdicate that role.

Her commitment to him unfortunately came at a cost. She was now in the middle of Lindy and Grant, my old station in life. The tension between those two, and the intransigent positions they held, the crack in the band. Whoever was linked to both had, as part of their duties, the ferrying of information between them, and the cooling of what were admittedly rare heated exchanges. And like myself, Amanda had to take this on when young.

As Grant settled, I moved into my second adolescence. My first had been a relatively quiet affair and there was lost time and much foolishness to catch up on. I was twenty-nine, the physical peak of most people, and rock'n'roll rations had me thin, and swivel-hipped dangerous. The person inside was a younger man emerging from a six-year relationship and out of practice, if he ever was in practice, with reading the signs and signals of love. A woman had caught my eye. Sandy Fleming, the girlfriend of Servants bass player Phil King, didn't seem to be his girlfriend anymore, and that she was of a rock'n'roll persuasion – black hair, black clothes, kohl eyes, snow-white skin – says much of the person I was when courting her: more flamboyant and confident, with my own rock'n'roll attributes to match hers. We were an eye-catching couple as we weaved our way through the pubs and clubs and the scene around her band, The Hangman's Beautiful Daughters, in which she played guitar. Sandy was fun, and it was freeing to have my emotional life separated from the band, and part of my social life away from Australians. It did mean I was moving twice as fast – pleasing and partying in two worlds, leaving Highbury for Brixton on mad-to-get-to-her train rides, in my red flares or other bedraggled rock-star wear that had jaded London commuters shooting me glances. If the relatively sane person I was at St Charles Square could have seen the ragged, pale-faced puppet

I'd become, he would have been amused and a touch concerned. Perhaps leaning over to whisper, 'Slow down.'

*

Accompanying this was a problem that grew more acute as the decade progressed – our need for a break from music. Not once since we'd been together had I or another member of the band had the opportunity to sit on a beach somewhere for a few weeks, to relax and reflect on next moves. We never generated the money to buy time for regeneration, or time away from each other. Here we were on the doorstep to Europe and the only occasions we went there was to play shows. So, having done a 29-date tour of Australia in August/September, and three albums in the last five years, the band went straight into preparations for another album. Recording meant budgets, budgets meant wages, and with our career momentum on a high but coffers low, I was walking around with plastic bags in my Chelsea boots, unable to afford repairs or thirty quid for a second pair: the hit-single option had to be examined one more time. Certainly Beggars and Bob were up for it, and the magic-wand effect that even a minor hit would have on our lives was enough to quell my reservations about trying to achieve one. Also I thought I'd make an interesting pop star.

Trouble was, I didn't have any hit singles in the bag. Do these song titles sound like top-forty contenders: 'The House That Jack Kerouac Built', 'The Clarke Sisters', 'Spirit Of A Vampyre', 'When People Are Dead'? It wasn't that I deliberately shied away from pop songs; whatever melodic clues I got from the guitar I followed to what I thought were true conclusions. That's what you do as a songwriter. Maybe I was just too focused on a few perfumed strands of thought outside of music. Rowland Howard had given me Anne Rice's *Interview with the Vampire* with his recommendation back in 1983, and at the very least I wanted to put 'vampyre' into a song. I'd just gotten into the blowtorch poetry of Anne Sexton and Sylvia Plath, and this fed into visits to Sisterwrite, a feminist bookstore in Upper Street, Islington. Part of 'The Clarke Sisters' came from there. 'Jack Kerouac' was a romantic-adventures-around-London type of song: 'You and I together with nothing showing at all/ In a darkened cinema I'll give you pleasure in the stalls' – I was trying double entendre. Again, not top forty. And 'When People Are Dead' was a beautiful tune, one of my best, worked from painful words in a diary shown to me by an Irishwoman I met called Marion Stout.

And it wasn't as if Grant was doing overtime in the hit factory either. 'Someone Else's Wife' and 'Hope Then Strife' and other bits and pieces he showed me were just as wild as my menagerie of songs. He did have a riffy thing called 'Cut It Out' that we would jam on backstage; it had a choppy, mid-sixties R&B feel to it. Plus there was the three-chord bang of 'Right Here', which, like 'Bachelor Kisses', sounded as if it could be a chart contender. With these numbers between us, and the possibility of something popping up in the next weeks, we went in search of that most mythical and elusive of all creatures in the music business – the hit record producer.

London of course was full of them. Most of them bright

and bushy with mullet haircuts and balloon-like bomber jackets. Craig Leon and Cassell Webb were an older American couple working as a team. He'd recorded and produced the first Ramones album, and worked with Richard Hell and the Voidoids, and Suicide. She came out of the late-sixties/early-seventies Texas psychedelic scene and could namedrop The Thirteenth Floor Elevators, Red Crayola, and some of the songwriters in the outlaw country movement. Amazingly in the there-is-no-yesterday world of the London pop scene, these two people had recently produced a number-one hit record for Doctor and the Medics, with a re-recording of Norman Greenbaum's 'Spirit In The Sky'. We hired them, Grant and I visiting their home with guitars to put our songs to a four-track, having given over the choice of what was to be the next two Go-Betweens singles for the first time. Craig picked 'Right Here' and 'Cut It Out', both Grant's. I wasn't pleased, yet there was no pop classic in my back pocket that I could claim had been overlooked.

We were in an expensive studio, Good Earth in Soho, owned by Tony Visconti, the engineer and producer of T Rex and Bowie; in effect we were back in Miraval. Craig and Cassell had led us there seductively – the drum machine for drums, after a slow wearing-down process on Lindy which had a deceptiveness that also affected the rest of the group. We were playing day after day, getting tighter and tighter, believing that at least two of us would be playing together on the recordings at the same time. Why did we bother? We arrived on the first day of the session to find Craig behind a bank of keyboards filling the control room, programming the drums, bass and organ lines. With costs high and deposit paid, the best we could do was slink off to a backroom and rehearse the B sides, to be called out one by one over the next four days, like witnesses at a murder trial, and feed our parts into an unremarkable mechanical churn that were to be our singles. Sensing our despondency and disappointment, Cassell tried diplomacy – nice as she was, it was too little too late.

The horror of the experience would have been alleviated if the recordings had charted or lifted our commercial standing. They didn't. 'Cut It Out' is the worst song in The Go-Betweens catalogue, and the label, management and band instantly realised it could never be released as a single. 'Right Here' is better, but for a recording from a production team obsessed with rhythm and timing, the track has little swing.

Friends of ours would have hits; all of them came in the nineties, a kinder decade for music, and in ways other than the methods we had tried. Tracey and Ben had 'Missing' remixed with a dance beat. Edwyn Collins built his own studio, and with time to tinker made 'A Girl Like You'. Nick Cave and the Bad Seeds kept recording with sympathetic engineers and producers in good studios, with the belief that one day a hit song or a strong concept ('Where The Wild Roses Grow' with Kylie) would appear. That approach (but without a guest singer) was what I thought we should keep doing, and in the depths of my frustration and with the explosive drama of 'Jack Kerouac' and 'The Clarke Sisters' in my head, I went to Bob telling him I was considering leaving the group. He listened and talked me down, and given the way events unfolded, I'm glad he did. But the episode came with a sting. Foolishly, I confided in Lindy about my visit to Bob, and when next she was caught out in the practice room by Grant and Robert over some unnecessary outburst or manoeuvre, she pointed at me and blurted, 'He wants to leave the group.' It worked; angry eyes swung to me. In the middle of torrid weeks for everyone, I managed to diffuse the situation and we carried on.

Christmas came. We were out of the new-album, tour-Australia cycle, and the pain of being far from home hit hard. Certain feelings pushed aside by the day-to-day business of the band came flooding in. We'd been away for four and a half years and although many of the winters had been broken up with touring, we were now at the start of a long cold stretch and there was a chill in our bones. Christmas Day was grey and biting, with little cheer and celebratory food or fuss. I put a quick call through to my family and tried to sound up; my mother wasn't fooled. I could imagine The Gap as it was being described to me, and there were things I could add – the colour of the sun coming through the loungeroom curtains, the taste of breakfast on the back verandah in the precious hours before the heat of the day came on. Above all I could sense the ease of life, and that's what everyone in the group was starting to miss.

The Blake Carrington
Interlude

London can make you do strange things. Especially when there's no one you've invested with any moral authority to curb your behaviour, and you're living in a world where eccentricity and eye-grabbing antics are actively encouraged. In early 1987 I walked into a Soho hair salon and asked for my hair to be dyed grey. The hairdresser at the front counter went off to consult with a senior colleague, and it was the second hairdresser, arriving with a concerned look on her face, who explained the intricacies of the process – my chestnut-brown hair would have to be bleached white before it could be further coloured, with the prospect that the grey might not take to the exact shade I had in mind. I went with my chances, and the most gruelling day I ever spent in a hairdresser's got under way.

Unbeknown to those working in the salon, there was a

philosophical treatise bubbling under my hair. It went something like this: rock music and rock culture were ageing badly by refusing to age well. Prominent artists from the sixties and seventies were still grasping for centre stage, the black-hair-dye bottle part of their elixir kits. Like the old-school showbusiness artists they'd replaced, they were going to cling to fame by whatever means possible. Mainstream rock was now essentially vaudeville – pile on the greasepaint, keep smilin' and dancin', and never admit you're one minute older than you have to. To my thinking, if Jagger, McCartney, Springsteen, Fogerty, Bowie, and all the other old dudes weren't going to be bold enough to play with the concepts of ageing and time in an art form that was supposed to be liberating, then I would. I'd be the old man of rock at twenty-nine.

My hero was John Forsythe, the elegant, grey-haired actor playing Blake Carrington in the popular TV series *Dynasty*. 'I want to look like Blake Carrington,' I announced to the startled hairdressers. They were right, though, the colour didn't take, and I came out more Jean Harlow than John Forsythe. Still, it played to the increasingly extravagant side of my personality that was the stuff of my songs and public persona – and there weren't all that many dyed blondes, male ones particularly, floating around the London rock scene at the time.

*

We had the title of our fifth album before we hit the studio. Pierre had married Jessica, an American woman living in Melbourne, and on our last trip to Australia we met their first child, Tallulah. I loved the sound of the name and thought it instantly worked as a title. The name, in turn, bounced back; in the mid-nineties I started to hear of and meet young girls who'd been named after a Go-Betweens album their mum and dad liked.

My mind was perhaps too focused on rock theory and not enough on the practicalities of record making, because in January we were recording *Tallulah* in a substandard studio on the side of a set of crumbling practice rooms in Camden. The circumstances so downmarket that at one point Kirk Brandon from Spear of Destiny wandered into our studio thinking it was his rehearsal room. Expenditure on the Craig Leon session had knocked the budget and therefore the strategy for the album out of kilter, and for the next weeks we played the game of catch-up that comes when you begin recording an album in the wrong studio. Those dreaded words 'You can fix it in the mix' were used as balm; trouble was, by the time the bills came in for the mixing suite in Shepherds Bush, and the residential studio out in the country that the remix engineer wanted to use, it would have been cheaper to be in a decent studio from the start.

So we never quite got the groove or the unified sense of mission we had on *Liberty Belle*. Richard Preston was engineering again, but the state of the studio put a worried look on his face. Amanda had written some great pulsing violin lines; Lindy, despite being bashed by the demands of the producers, was nevertheless still interested in the possibilities of drum machines, but she wanted to work with them on songs that were not entirely suited to mechanical rhythms. The clinching of my doubts came when I looked out the window to see Andy Summers, guitarist for The Police, pull up – ultimate confirmation we were in the wrong place.

Tallulah can be seen as the album that got away. The strength of many of the songs, and the salvaging of some of the band's character in the recording, and the whip to the sound that came from Mark Wallis's remixes all help to make it a good record. But a dark masterpiece was in the offing, one that matched the charisma of the group lounging on its cover: Lindy as Virginia Woolf, Robert in a cowboy hat and tie, Grant mimicking Dylan's pose on *The Basement Tapes*, a young Amanda with teddy bear, and I'm a blonde in Chelsea boots wearing my first pair of glasses. *Please* let this group into Abbey Road for a week, to bust or blow. But it couldn't happen. It was the time I felt most estranged from the group, and that was manifest in my appearance and my songs. I wanted to push things to an extreme, to an album I could see, one that our circumstances and our commitment to the singles didn't allow, and one the group couldn't or didn't want to make anyway.

That album, though, was heard live as we undertook the longest tour we had done. Where, without the squeezed crackle of the studio, and the imposition of two tracks that sound like nothing else on the record, songs blew up to their true size. Grant's majestic 'Bye Bye Pride', with one of the best opening lines ever, 'A white moon appears like a hole in the sky/ The mangroves go quiet' – I think of that line every time I look up at a night sky – was a ten-foot wave driven by Lindy's snare, with

Amanda's piping oboe the froth on top. 'The House That Jack Kerouac Built' howled, 'Right Here' swung, and 'The Clarke Sisters', with another good opening ('They had problems with their father's law/ They sleep in the back of a feminist book-store'), would wind from a whisper to a scream. The concerts for the album's release remain for many the best we ever did.

Three incongruous events stand out from the subsequent tours. One was being told we were to be supported by Alex Chilton on some US dates, and us insisting the headlining spot be alternated night to night. We'd had no connections with older musicians, no patronage from an older star, and it was interesting to watch someone who'd had both pop fame, with The Box Tops, and cult acclaim, with Big Star, negotiate his way at this stage of his career. Not that we drew many lessons, caught as we were in our own bubble: being Alex Chilton, how-ever, obviously meant accepting odd gigs.

Then there was Dublin. The city that housed the boyhood homes of Joyce and Beckett had me walking the streets as if on holy stones. We played on a makeshift outdoor stage in a cor-ner of Trinity College. It had rained most of the morning, and the crowd were as amazed at the appearance of the sun as they were at the sight and sound of the group. Our final note bring-ing a downpour, and a rubbed-eye, did-that-really-happen? experience that was pure Go-Betweens. And the third event occurred on 28 May 1987, when leaving the Schwimmbad, a bunker-like venue in Heidelberg, after a soundcheck. We met two people outside – Karin and Erhard. They had seen us play in Glastonbury the previous year. We chatted. The band then walked off to a restaurant, and after having gone a short way I had to turn and look again at the young, beautiful woman we'd just met. I smiled. She smiled back.

In the middle of the tour, and the year, I reached my thirtieth birthday. Sandy bought me an Italian-leather, blank-paged notebook I had coveted at Liberty. Up to then I'd been writing my lyrics and other things (of little consequence) in exercise books or on loose sheets of paper. It was time to house the words in a more permanent and ornate place; my intention was to write in green ink. Another friend gave me a stack of recent singles I liked, including 'Ballad Of The Band' from Felt, and 'Velocity Girl' by Primal Scream – a new group formed by Jesus and Mary Chain drummer Bobby Gillespie. I didn't have the means to buy many albums, relying instead on night-time radio and seeing friends' bands live, like Microdisney, who practised next to us in Camden, The Weather Prophets, The Jasmine Minks, and Sandy's band. I was in the indie rock scene with all its poverty and flash. Someone else gave me a mixed tape and a song on it leapt out. 'Ashes By Now' by Rodney Crowell had a low, steady beat, no noise or weird, disorientating rock touches, and the well-written lyric told a clear story of lost love. The simplicity and freshness of the recording impressed me, and opened my thinking to another strand of music. Maybe there were more songs like this. By August I was sitting in the back of the tour bus as we zipped across the USA and listening to Gram Parsons and Emmylou Harris.

*

Returning to London it felt like we all turned simultaneously to each other to murmur, 'We don't have to live here anymore.' We'd spent almost a year on the road promoting our second album on Beggars; why stay here? That's what we'd come over to Europe for, wasn't it? To secure an international recording deal, tour the world and become famous? Now we could go home, the fear of being forgotten no longer there. If anything, our story was starting to get a little too predictable – it was time for another twist to the tale.

The reverberations came quickly. Robert Vickers didn't want to come to Australia, wishing instead to return to Janie and New York – we lost a great bass player and the most level-headed member of the band. The diplomat had left the embassy. I had to tell Sandy I was going, and our relationship wound down with some amicability. I informed The Corn Dollies, a London group for whom I'd produced a good single, 'Forever Steven', that I couldn't do their album. And at the request of Manchester friend Dave Haslam, I finished an article on my hair obsession called 'Hair Care' for his fanzine *Debris*. An obscure start to journalism. At the last minute, Cathal Coughlan, the lead singer of Microdisney, and one of the secret heroes of London, pressed a cassette into my hand. 'Take this,' he said. It was the first two Tim Hardin albums.

Looking back on my last year in London, I'm reminded of a sentence from primary school. We were being taught the deeds of the New World explorers, men with fantastic names like Vasco da Gama and Dirk Hartog, whose historic voyages down European and African coastlines we traced with red arrows on blue paper. At a certain point on each of these journeys, the teacher would say, 'And this is as far as they got.' The past year was as far as I ever got away from myself. There were times when, catching a quick look at my face in a mirror before dashing out, or in the curved windows of a Tube carriage while dangling one-handed on a strap, I'd think, Oh my god. That's you! I was ragged and running fast. A dandy underground rock star who'd pushed himself harder and harder through the decade, to the point where the ropes were pulling on the moorings. I'd gone there willingly, in step with my songs. How sane was Bowie when writing 'Life On Mars'? How normal a citizen the Dylan of 'Visions Of Johanna'? With my blond hair growing out, my gaunt face, a Sherlock Holmes-inspired wardrobe, parties and pubs, alcohol and drugs, in love with all extremities of art, my family far away for years and no angel on my shoulder, it felt like I was without a weight to the world. All extravagances of my behaviour very conveniently confirmed by the recent publication of Richard Ellmann's latest, and last, biography, of Oscar Wilde. My golden book. Wilde: someone who'd walked to the edge, thrown his arms triumphantly to the sky, and jumped off.

Beside me, bemused at my transformation and with never a call to pull back, was Grant, steady and understanding, encouraging of my eccentricities and excesses, which ran all the way back to my first songs. I'd just taken them further, to the point where I was starting to lose myself. It was in this year that Grant's and my public personas solidified, to remain with us to the end. I was the flamboyant, powdered showman, he buttoned-down and sincere. These were not true representations of ourselves at the time, our differences exaggerated through the built-in distortions of the media and the clear lines demanded by rock myth. In primary school those arrows would curl in a half-circle, and while not necessarily tracing the same tracks back, would head in the direction of home. Like all explorers who survived, I was to always know how far I'd got.

With a departure date set for mid-November, a greater affection, a nostalgia even, came to us for the city. Five and a half years we had devoted to it – the life of some bands our London phase. For Lindy and me the time had been sweetened by Highbury; we weren't so much abandoning a city as a neighbourhood. The warmest memories of the town, the ones that carry an ache in their recollection, are from here: Lindy and I carrying home bags of books from Islington Library to devour over long lazy days. The night walk I'd take from the Highbury & Islington Tube station, past the toilets at the edge of the fields that Joe Orton was said to frequent in the sixties, a little further to the Walter Sickert house with its blue plaque, and then the council tennis courts where Lindy, David McClymont, Robert McComb from The Triffids and I played doubles in summer, to reach the thin strip of shops in the Barn – the brothers at the fruit shop, and the surprise of a good delicatessen – and then first right down to our home, key in the door, the attic good to the end, with 'Love Is A Sign' and 'Dive For Your Memory' under way. Outside it's foggy – soft rain, yellow street lamps – and although I crave sunshine, a part of me will miss the gloom. Goodbye darkness my old friend.

Amanda, Grant and Lindy flew to Sydney to set up homes. I went to Brisbane, in need of family-tendered rest and to touch the ground before the onslaught of another demanding city. And to write songs I sensed were there. The pace never slackening. We were to start work on a new album early the following year.

Zap. Back at The Gap. Where I was more comfortable at thirty than at twenty. My brother had married and moved out, and with both my parents working I had the house to myself each day. I'd get up about nine, breakfast, and dress in blue jeans, a work shirt and my black schoolboy-style shoes. The Chelsea boots hung up. I'd make coffee, and with the stillness of suburbia around me, childhood associations everywhere, go to the stereo to fire up the two albums that were my fuel for those weeks. *Born in the USA* by Bruce Springsteen, and *Darklands* by The Jesus and Mary Chain. Some people think the 'real' Boss is the left-field artist of *Nebraska* or *The Ghost of Tom Joad*, and that his other albums are genuflections to the mainstream. At heart, Springsteen is a bar-room rocker, and *Born in the USA* is his best set of bar-room rock songs. I loved the melody and beat-up regret in 'Bobby Jean', 'I'm Goin' Down', 'Dancing In The Dark' and 'No Surrender', and while listening would pull back the curtains onto Glenmore Street, urging myself to get these qualities into my songs. As for *Darklands*, it's the best Jesus and Mary Chain album. The difference between the Mary Chain and the Boss is negligible – the Mary Chain could have made *Born in the USA*, and Springsteen could have done *Darklands*. The Mary Chain are slowed-down Boss. 'I'm going to the darklands/ To talk in rhyme with my chaotic soul' – I knew what that meant. I'd switch between these albums and when in want of a touch of acoustic guitar and sixties poetry, there was Tim Hardin.

I wrote in a frenzy. A spidery scrawl covering the pages, lines razored as I shot for a sparser, more emotive touch. I finished 'Love Is A Sign' and 'Dive For Your Memory', and then hit pay dirt with a new song, 'I'm All Right' – 'She knows that I'm not ready/ When my nerves are steady/ When my eyes are free of tears, someday/ . . . She doesn't want to hurt me it's OK/ I'm all right' – blurring myself with the hard-done-by guy in the Springsteen songs. 'You Can't Say No Forever' popped out before Christmas. A last song, the precious fifth, I thought I already had in 'Wait Until June'.

There didn't seem to be anyone or anything left in the city. Almost twenty years of Bjelke-Petersen had made sure of that, and those who'd stayed were heads-down in jobs and family. I went out to a gig and knew no one and no one knew me. My pleasure was walking down to the local shopping centre in the midafternoon, to maybe drift further on and see the children coming out of my old primary school. I'd try to get some of that sweet tender ache into my songs, too. Then home to dinner, TV and reading. Bob might call from London, telling me that with the success of Simply Red, Simon Potts had joined Capitol Records in Los Angeles and was thinking of signing us to a US deal. More money for our album. Grant and Lindy would phone too, happy and excited in Sydney. 'You've got to get here. It's beautiful.' I told them I'd be down in the new year.

16 Lovers Lane is
a Long Road

Sydney *was* beautiful. Sparkling. Shimmering. An eye-squinting paradise with a summer a good five degrees below Brisbane's. The city tilting above the water felt like a stage or a catwalk, and arriving with an album to be done gave our arrival, if only to ourselves, a sense of drama and destiny. The Go-Betweens were in town. For Amanda it was home, Lindy had a brother living in Potts Point, and to officially greet us was Roger Grierson, our new Australian manager – effusive, culturally savvy, and with a spare room in his Woolloomooloo house for me to move into.

I went to see Grant, who was living with Amanda in a set of red-brick flats at Bondi Junction. It was song-playing time. What did he have? More songs than me, and his usual trail of riffs and sketches. I could see, though, that his material, like mine, was compact and sharply themed; he even had a song

with 'love' in the title, a word that both of us, two songwriters
obsessed with relationship songs, had conspicuously avoided
on our previous five albums. He showed me 'Love Goes On'.
I played him 'Love Is A Sign'. And *16 Lovers Lane* can be
understood in their similarities and their differences. I'd under-
gone a bumpy couple of years with my affections, was working
through the break-up with Sandy, and was single – nuggets of
gold for a songwriter. Grant was buried in love, and when he
played me 'The Devil's Eye' I was hearing the first in a set of
songs he'd written for Amanda: 'I don't want to let you out of
my sight.' He was inspired, and shortly after he would write
his best, certainly his biggest, song for her – 'Quiet Heart'. We
played everything we had, card laid down after card, and saw
the fit.

John Brand had begotten Richard Preston, Richard begat
Mark Wallis. Mark had remixed some of the tracks on *Tallulah*
and we could hear, in the space he gave to the songs and the
lush swirl he put into the guitars, a way forward for our sound.
We'd had a drink with him before leaving London, talking over
the album. We wanted to record and mix it in one location,
and the commercial aspects of the record, hit singles and such,
were barely mentioned; our wish was to make a cohesive album
bearing Mark's sonic print. Our problem was that his career
in early '88 was in terrific shape. The two most recent albums
he'd worked on being U2's *The Joshua Tree* and Talking Heads'
Naked, and he'd just produced a single for The Primitives called
'Crash' that was sprinting up the UK charts.

Bob told us to at least consider the possibility of using

another producer, as Mark was expensive as well as popular. But the band wanted to work with him. So Grant and I went into Trackdown Studios in Bondi Junction and cut eight songs over two days on acoustic guitars. The tracks were 'Was There Anything I Could Do?', 'Wait Until June', 'The Devil's Eye', 'I'm All Right', 'You Won't Find It Again', 'Love Goes On', 'Love Is A Sign' and 'Dive For Your Memory'. We sent the tape to Wallis and we waited. Bob phoned to say Mark was coming to Sydney to make the album. 'He *loves* the demo.' Wallis's first words to Grant and I upon arriving were, 'It's the best demo I've ever heard.' That's what you want a producer to say.

I liked Mark, and not only because he rated our band and our songwriting. He was roughly the age of Grant and me, and had begun working in London studios in the mid-seventies. He was not a musician who'd drifted into recording, but someone obsessed with sound, who had learnt the art of microphone placement and of putting instrumentation to tape from experienced engineers. By the eighties he was the chief engineer for slick hit-making producer Steve Lillywhite, although he looked like he'd just stepped away from making *Exile on Main Street* – a big man with a full head of shaggy brown hair to the shoulders. Mark was how you imagined all those late-sixties and early-seventies rock band producers like Andy Johns or Jimmy Miller to be. And yet none of this was a problem, and it was down to his personality; he was quiet, with no arm waving or ego imposition. In the practice room with us in March he'd be taking notes as we played and at the end of a song he'd say in a dreamy voice, 'Could you play that again, please.' The whole sonic pattern of the album was being put together in his head.

Thinking I was a strong song short, and usually hopeless under pressure, I'd written 'Clouds'. A song willing myself to be a more clear-minded person after London: 'I said to these clouds/ "No more am I blind / I have to see straight/ And that will make me unkind".' Grant had 'Quiet Heart' and a new song I could hear him strumming in the practice room, which he wouldn't, or wasn't yet ready to, play when we met. Strange. Amanda would sometimes sing along with him on the chorus, just at the edge of my earshot. 'Round and round, up and down, through the streets of your town.' I could hear it was very poppy.

We'd handed the decision of which tracks went on the album to Mark, and as I'd lost out with Craig Leon, and as Grant possessed, to any producer's ear, the more conventionally sounding pop voice, with lyrics and melodies to match, I awaited the decision with trepidation. We sat in a circle after practice one afternoon in a park opposite the rehearsal room in Ultimo, Mark standing before us holding a scrap of paper. It was like being at a sports carnival and hearing who'd been chosen for the rep team. He started reading and had come to eight songs, four by each, when he stopped.

'There's one song we haven't rehearsed that I think is tremendous. Grant and Amanda have played it to me and it's called "Streets Of Your Town". We have to do it.'

I glanced at Lindy. She hadn't heard it either.

And then it was down to the last song. I was sure it was going to be one of Grant's, and tensed my body in preparation.

'"You Can't Say No Forever". . .' Long pause. 'Is a challenging track, and I think we should do that too. And that's the ten.'

I never knew how aware Mark was of the discomfort between Grant and me over the song selection. Maybe he'd been briefed by Bob, who'd also told him to go out and make a 'rock' record, which didn't happen. I was mad at Grant and he knew it. The wind blew bitter for a week. Typically for us, I didn't press him as to why he'd shown 'Streets' to Mark before me. I didn't because we weren't two hot-headed guys, or one hot-headed guy and one of reason, the way it is in many partnerships. We were both taciturn, avoiders of high emotional interactions such as anger; the downside of this was that certain things between him and me didn't get discussed, and festered a little, only a little. The upside was that it didn't tear us apart. It remains an odd fact – the one Go-Betweens song Grant and I never played together before recording was 'Streets Of Your Town'.

Also on the grass listening to Mark, probably with a lop-sided grin on his face and a gin and tonic in his hand, was our new bass player John Willsteed. He had been a staunch supporter of Brisbane, believing, perhaps, that a career could be built from the town, but he'd been worn down and moved south. He wasn't a conventional, low-end-of-the-bass style of player, or person – he was quirky and inventive. In an unlikely twist, the Zero rhythm section was now driving The Go-Betweens and that brought its own dynamic. Lindy's mood had ruled the practice room; it was her domain, and it meant that the discussion of rhythms or suggestions for a song had to be proffered tentatively. Willsteed wasn't intimidated by her,

GRANT & I

he hadn't been in the late seventies and he wouldn't be now. His place in the band, however, wasn't secured by his ability to go measure for measure in counting time signatures with Lindy; he was a good musician, and some of the best guitar parts on the album, including the incredible flamenco solo on 'Streets', were played by him.

Lovers Lane took eight weeks to record and mix, and was done at 301 Studios in Castlereagh Street, in the city. The studio was on the seventh floor of an office building: get out of the lift and bam, it was rock'n'roll – high-end rock'n'roll with a large SSL desk and plenty of studio and recreational space. The session went smoothly; the first hurdle, the question of a drum machine or live playing, was settled with Mark's diplomacy and Lindy's pragmatism. The songs required less percussive drive than any record we'd made – Grant's and my songwriting was quietening down. Mark was calm and in control, clearly intoxicated with the album he was recording, and the mood in the band was good, aided by being perched above a city that seemed in step with our music – shimmering and sunlit. Mark's ability to record and manipulate instrumentation into a rich and dynamic weave suited our material, and as the weeks went by and we reached the mixing stage, the sound coming out of the speakers was at times almost overwhelming in its size, beauty and sparkle.

Too sparkling?

I had trouble with *16 Lovers Lane* for a long time. It wasn't until the late nineties that I recognised the album for what it was – a pop record, a far but true side of what we were as a band. With its spiralling guitars and narcotic groove it became an influential album in noughties pop. On its release my fear was that the production obscured the grit in the songwriting, the added heart Grant and I had put into our lyrics. I also knew that the luxurious sound, our biggest sonic jump since *Before Hollywood*, would split the fan base, and in hindsight I was too defensive about that. (A few reviews in Europe compared us to Prefab Sprout – enough to send me off on a three-day depression.) Most critics adored the record, *NME* the exception, lashing it with a six out of ten rating. Five years later, sitting between *Clear Spot* by Captain Beefheart and *Pink Flag* by Wire, it was at number seventy-six on their Hundred Greatest Albums of All Time list. *Rubber Soul*, another good pop record, was at ninety-six.

*

You can forget you're anywhere near a beach when strolling in the fumes of Woolloomooloo and Darlinghurst. My exposure thus far to the eastern-suburb beaches was Bondi – the end station of the inner-city. The pleasures to be had in the town's delightful sea and salt lifestyle began when I moved into an apartment on the northern hill of Coogee Beach belonging to my new girlfriend, Kathleen Phillips. She was part of a group of friends we knew in the city, while retaining a distance from the scene with her home and her dedication to a good nine-to-five job. My life sweetened and further normalised in her presence, and yet a built-in incongruity existed between us. One day she asked me to write a song about her, and putting myself in her

GRANT & I

shoes, looking back at me, I wrote 'Rock'n'Roll Friend': 'You're home late and you smell/ Of the music that you make/ All my patience, all my love/ That's now all at stake/ And it amounts to a lot, and it seems like I'm trying and you're not/ So do something about me, my rock'n'roll friend.' The swift truth of a song. She introduced me to a number of things: the music of Lucinda Williams, Ella Baché beauty products, and, through her circle of sharp, femocrat (their term) friends, the novels of Jane Austen. Suddenly it was 1816, and Austen seemed to get Sydney better than any other writer I knew: plenty of Elizabeth Bennets around, lots of two-timing Wickhams, particularly in the rock scene, and far too few Mr Darcys. In fact, most of the best looking men in town seemed to spend their time in bars together.

*

'Streets Of Your Town' just had to be a hit. Everybody told us so. We'd signed to Mushroom Records, the country's biggest independent, Kylie Minogue another recent signing. We made not one, but two videos; the first, the 'artier', was the better one, capturing the character of the song and group. It was done by Kriv Stenders, who later made the feature film *Red Dog*. The second was a big-budget, MTV performance clip for Capitol. All the carriages seemed to be in line *again*. And whereas 'Spring Rain' may have sounded a trifle indie, and 'Right Here' too contrived and thumpy, 'Streets' was foolproof to all ears – a ridiculously catchy tune enshrined in an enormously appealing, crystal-canyoned production from Wallis. And for a few weeks we felt a delightful puff of wind under our wings (imagine the gust a hit would bring) as radio stations that had never played us played us, and both videos appeared on Saturday-morning pop shows watched by record-buying teenagers and drunken, amphetamine-driven musicians still up from the night before. But it was not to be – the song stalling at the bottom end of the top forty, veteran record company people genuinely surprised.

It didn't destroy us; there was the roar of the album reviews, an Australian tour, and the usual bustle of a band with an album out. It did deny us success, and that was something we needed, if only because it would have presented the band with a new set of experiences. Forget the money, it was the fresh streets of stardom that would have rejuvenated the group. One advantage we had was that, unlike most local groups, all eggs weren't in the Australian basket; the London years had given us a UK and European audience, and there was the citadel of the US to be approached seriously for the first time.

We went to Europe to promote the album and I saw Karin again at a few of the German shows. Since I'd met her eighteen months before she had grown more beautiful and further into her own style – long vintage dresses and boots, a scarf in her hair. We had talked in Heidelberg after the show, and now, in grabbed moments backstage amidst the chaos of a rock tour, with her friends and The Go-Betweens always in attendance, we got to know each other a little more. My mind having to be continually refocused as I drank in her looks – a sixties, Jane Birkin quality she had, thrillingly tall too – while pondering the fact, the miracle, that she seemed to be interested in me. She was studying psychology at Regensburg University and had a gravity and seriousness, a German-ness if you like, that I found appealing. To add to this, she not only knew her Dylan, she had his bootlegs too. We connected while people walked over and around us; were sympathetic to and lost in each other from the start. Nothing was pushed, though: with the next Go-Betweens album and European tour probably years off, if we did meet again, how many changes would there have been in our lives by then?

The band also pulled into Manchester, where Dave Haslam was DJ-ing at the Hacienda and invited us down to the club. It was a crazy scene. The acid house movement was getting into gear and this was its epicentre. There were people dancing on podiums and the room had the feel of being at the edge of going out of control. The signifiers of the broader experience – the baggy clothes, beads and ecstasy-taking – didn't get to me, acid house being the first UK musical movement since glam that I wasn't curious or enthusiastic about. The one band I liked was The Stone Roses, who had supported us in Stockholm a few years back, and had obviously listened to The Monkees – 'Last Train To Clarksville' and 'Pleasant Valley Sunday' in particular. The English music press went nuts for the movement, and a process began where reporting on favoured groups went over to tabloid-like hype and never returned.

From London, Lindy and John went back to Australia while Grant, Amanda and I travelled to New York to make first contact with our US label and play a few showcase acoustic shows. I thought we were a strong three-piece. How many other trios in the world consisted of two singer-songwriters and a violin and oboe player who sang? And the songs of *16 Lovers Lane* suited this approach. Grant and I fulfilled a dream of playing a Greenwich Village folk club, and it was there that we met Steve Kilbey from The Church. They were riding high in the US top forty with 'Under The Milky Way', they'd got their hit, and Steve told us the only album his band could all agree on being played in their tour bus was *16 Lovers Lane – that* was a compliment.

Capitol Records was headquartered in LA, most of the operation housed in a six-storey, saucer-shaped building straight out of *The Jetsons*. We looked out over the city from the rooftop, a stop on the in-house tour that included the studios where two of the label's biggest acts, Sinatra and The Beach Boys, had recorded. We also met various marketing and label managers and I got to talk to someone in accounts in touch with the reclusive singer-songwriter genius Bobbie Gentry. It was a blissful morning from a fan's perspective; other business commitments, however, had kept Simon and Bob out of town, and we were wandering around alone, a rare thing for a band when meeting a major label record company for the first time. Having someone with us might have saved us from what happened next.

In the afternoon we were told to go down to a small basement studio and do radio and video IDs – identity spots for promotion. And for the next three hours, hidden from the rest of the company (the torture chamber not in view), we were coached, cajoled and bullied by a pig of a man to read out grovelling messages begging people to play our record at every radio and TV station from Alaska to the southern tip of Florida.

'Hello Barry at KMPW Salt Lake City, we're The GO-BETWEENS! And we know you're a big FAN! And we've got a new single out called —'

'Guys, guys,' the Pig interrupted. 'Could you do it with bigger grins. And maybe do something wacky when you say Barry's name.'

We knew that in return for the company's support there would be promotional duties requiring an adjustment in our attitudes, but this was brutal and left us feeling humiliated. Amanda was close to tears. Grant very angry. As good as it was to be on a label with such a fantastic history, we could tell we were in a culture where there was little to no comprehension of ourselves or our music. It was as if IBM or the CIA were putting out our record. The groovy indie guys and girls that came with alternate rock weren't yet in major label offices. We were trailblazers and in late '88 the puffed-haired spirit of Toto and Kansas still held fast, with Guns N' Roses the fresh-faced new boys on the block. The town's A&R men, taking the hint, were down at the Rainbow Room on Sunset Boulevard looking for the future of rock'n'roll. It was in stacked heels and spandex pants, and none of the bands had a song.

What saved the situation was playing our showcase shows and meeting friends who'd supported us in the past. Deirdre O'Donoghue was a radio announcer and a passionate believer in new music at KCRW. We'd done a live session with her before and now we played a magic four-song set, including a version of 'Quiet Heart' that has to be one of the best recordings we ever did. Grant is singing for his life. Amanda's violin is extraordinary, and I'm along for the ride on harmonica. Deirdre's on-air response: 'You know, every time I think that it's been completely done, and I feel as though I'm absolutely, totally, permanently jaded, The Go-Betweens come along with a new record and take me apart cell by cell.'

We also performed at McCabe's Guitar Shop in Santa Monica. Another advantage of playing acoustic – it got us, if only for a second, out of the rock clubs. The back room at McCabe's was rows of folding chairs with a low wooden stage, guitars hanging from the walls like icons in a church. If you had songs you could stun two hundred people there. We were backstage before going on, when a tall, broad-shouldered man in his mid-forties ambled in. It was Guy Clark, down to check out who was playing the night before he and Townes Van Zandt were to appear. We shone, and when we returned the next day and peered into the dressing room, Guy said, 'Hey it's The Go-Betweens.'

I took a seat in the second row for their show, my acquaintance with the work of both singer-songwriters sketchy. I knew that Guy, who was to play first, had put out a classic album in 1975 called *Old No. 1*. *ZigZag* magazine, in the months before punk, had raved about it, and 4ZZZ had played a couple of songs – 'Desperados Waiting For A Train' and 'LA Freeway'. That was a long time ago, when slow ballads about old men and trains were not what an eighteen-year-old wanted to hear. I was ready now, and two songs in I knew I was in the presence of a master singer-songwriter, the best I'd seen up close. His guitar-playing was good, but not flashy – no barre chords, instead open-handed folk/country shapes with melody runs between changes. The songs were of that persuasion, but taken out to the edge with heavy poetic intent. No sugary philosophy or grinning showbusiness in the delivery either. Just bang, bang, bang, one outstanding number after another. The songs the work of someone who'd lived, taken down the details, and then, with a stack of tunes that, like everything he did, averted the cliché yet acknowledged the formula: Guy put lyric to melody with a talent equal to Lou Reed, Dylan, or anyone else you'd care to mention. At the break I went out on the street: a warm Santa Monica night. My mind too blown to go back in and catch Townes.

*

The day I got back to Sydney my parents called. 'You're going on tour with Rem.'

'Pardon?'

'It says in the paper you're going on tour with Rem.'

I had to untangle this.

'Mum, they're called R-E-M.'

I had a fantasy that my parents were right. That the band, when they were in the practice room alone, always referred to themselves as Rem, and were mystified why people called them anything else.

Early in the new year, before going on the tour, I went into Judy Morgan's clothes shop in Surry Hills to talk to her about making me a dress. For the past year or so, at occasional shows,

I'd come on for the final encore wearing one. Why? I don't really know. They felt comfortable and lithe, for a start, and like the red flares and capes I favoured, were part of a set of feelings I had concerning the group's image – never be bland – the content of my songs, and what I wanted to do as a performer. There was no drag aspect to it, no make-up; I just stood onstage playing my guitar – singing 'Draining The Pool For You', usually – and then walked off. A difficulty was buying the dresses, which I did in op shops, pretending I was getting something for my girlfriend who just happened to be the exact same weight and height as me. Judy sent me off to a fabric shop and I bought some meshy black and white material that she then tailored into the style I wanted: in my mind I saw a lounging-around-the-house, ankle-length hippie dress. Check out Emmylou Harris on the back cover of *Pieces of the Sky* – something like that.

The dress was packed when we rolled into Perth for the first show. I intended wearing it through the entire performance, and had the support of the ultra-competitive Go-Betweens, who wanted to throw a challenge out to the headliners. As I walked onstage the crowd cheered, as they always did when the dress came out, and we played a blistering set; REM, with command, rose to the occasion. After the show Michael Stipe came up to me and said, 'I wear dresses too.' It can take time for bands to be become friends when touring, if friends is what they will be. By the next date, Adelaide, both groups were getting on well, and by Sydney REM, who were on Warner, forswore the rock-star harbour yacht cruise to crash a small party some friends of ours were having in a park in Elizabeth Bay. REM were lovely people. We went to another party together, at the Melbourne home of Michael Gudinski, owner of Mushroom Records and the booker of the tour. Many revellers were there enjoying themselves in the afternoon on a large verandah when Peter Buck, who usually drank little but on this day was drinking a lot, tipped and crashed heavily off a high stool to the ground. The party froze in horror. The first movement came from Michael Stipe sliding at speed through guests to bend down, pick up Buck, put him on his stool and check he was okay. It was a very impressive act, and it made me wonder who would do that for me in my group – it wouldn't have been everyone.

This touches on something else we were being exposed to. If Orange Juice were the first great group Grant and I saw up close, then REM were the first great group who were going to be stars that we saw up close: touring and hanging out with them, we got to see it all at point-blank range. What it takes to be a successful rock band. They were promoting *Green*, the forerunner to *Out of Time* with its breakthrough single 'Losing My Religion'. The first thing to note was that the band had a classic shape: Stipe up front and free to toy with the media; Mills, Buck and Berry happy in the shadows, pumping out the great music. In The Go-Betweens everyone wanted to be the centre of attention. No one wanted to be Bill and Charlie, or the rhythm section of U2. And yes, that was a reason people loved us. However, two and a half years after Glastonbury, and with the band still on the same career level, something had to change if we were to scale the last Everest steps to stardom: a greater focus on the singer-songwriters? But that wasn't going to happen. It hadn't been woven into the fabric of the band, and we weren't united or flexible enough to change. Personalities were too strong, and things trundled on as they were. And while it certainly made us an interesting and volatile group, my dress a part of the spectacle, volatility was not what was wanted. The evidence was seen in calm REM.

New Zealand was next, and then on to our first proper tour of the US: six weeks long, a four-man Australian crew, playing to four hundred to six hundred people a night in the big cities – in the smaller towns, many of which we'd never visited before, significantly fewer. Confirming that the US required regular, punishing visits to build a band's profile. As on the acoustic run of dates, the tour hung on LA, where other duties kept Simon and Bob from being there to grease the wheels. It must have been another bruising day with the record company, because when I returned to my hotel room from soundcheck I had Grant on the line.

'Are you going to wear the dress tonight?' he asked.

'I was thinking of it,' I said.

'Good, I think you should.'

The dress had made one appearance after Perth, in Sydney. There Michael Gudinski took Grant aside after the show. 'You run the group, right?' 'Yeah,' said Grant. 'Get rid of the guy in the dress.' The guy and the dress were about to come out in LA.

Wearing it onstage that night was in part an act of provocation. But if I was going to wear it in the US, where better than glitzy LA? The difficulty for the record company was that the dress had no cultural context. When Kurt Cobain, and Evan

Dando from The Lemonheads wore dresses onstage a few years later, it was instantly accepted, a dress becoming a grunge-era accessory for the handsome young rock star. But in early 1989 the reaction from the Capitol staff dotted through the show – and this *was* the first time they were seeing the full band – was one of shock and displeasure. Besides being affronted themselves, there was a question: How to sell this to Idaho?

Bob, bewildered and a little angry, was on the phone the next morning. I told him of our day with the label and Grant's call, knowing that he regarded Grant, as did most people in contact with the group, as more reasonable and level-headed than I. It might have been on this call, having been informed that our career was 'in ruins', that the offer to support REM on a string of shows through Europe was raised. Did we want to do it? The band said yes.

*

Unless you're playing to five hundred people a night, a band going on tour in a foreign country with any crew beside an amphetamine-riddled van driver, who, if he's mad, which most are, will also agree to mix the sound, do merchandise, carry the gear, tour-manage, and oh yeah party, is going to be losing money. A way around this is when the record company, believing a band to be advancing their career and in need of as much exposure to audiences as possible, will offer to pick up the shortfall between gig wages and actual gig costs. This is called 'tour support'. It looks good, almost like free money, when in fact it's an advance on your future record royalties. So far we had paid our own way. The stakes, though, were rising, and with the potential of *16 Lovers Lane* still not felt to be fully realised, we accepted tour support. From Capitol and from Beggars. Two months zigzagging across Europe with four crew, transport, hotels and wages ran to forty thousand pounds. You have to sell a lot of records to earn that back.

And for a few magic weeks in London in May, it looked like the gamble would pay off in spectacular fashion.

Beggars, in one last push, had re-released 'Streets Of Your Town' and to everyone's amazement and joy it was A-listed by BBC Radio 1. Guaranteeing thirteen precious plays a week and stamping it as a hit. Walking through Soho in spring sun I'd hear our song coming out of the radio in one shop, to quickly walk into another and hear it again. See how I got my kicks? Long-time industry friends of Bob's phoned to declare, 'Your band's got a hit.' For three weeks we were A-listed, the time it takes Warner or Sony to swing the machine behind a record, and lodge it high in the top forty. First week in at twenty, that type of thing. Beggars didn't have the muscle. We didn't even crack the top seventy-five. The domino effect a UK hit would have had on our career gone in a movie-sound-effect *whoooossh*. The failure of our record companies worldwide to get a song as ridiculously catchy and luxuriously produced as 'Streets' away meant we had to at least question why we should continue to make big-budgeted pop records and hope they would chart.

And the forty thousand pounds? For the next twenty-six years we received no record royalties outside Australia for

Liberty Belle, *Tallulah* or *16 Lovers Lane* – until Beggars wiped the remaining twelve thousand pounds of debt in 2015.

*

The European dates with REM were a mixed blessing. We got to play in bigger venues in countries where we weren't so popular – so one and a half thousand people saw us at both the Grand Rex in Paris and the Palasport in Bologna – yet when we were performing in Bielefeld to the same-sized crowd as we'd played to as headliners the previous year but earning a fraction of the fee, it seemed to make less sense. Our German fans felt comfortable enough to tell us as much. 'REM should be supporting *you!*' And among those at the first German show, at Düsseldorf, was Karin.

She and I were coming up to our third time around. Our 'relationship' moving at the pace of a romance in a Victorian novel – including the exchange of infrequent letters, and months of no contact but fervent contemplation of the other. It was now to be put to the test once again amidst the madness of a rock tour. And for this, being the support band helped.

In Munich, the date after Düsseldorf, Bill Berry, REM's drummer, came down sick and the night's show was cancelled an hour before the doors were due to open. Karin and her friends were among the hundreds of people waiting outside, and after linking up with them, the band decided we'd all return to the bar of our hotel. The awkwardness between Karin and me stood in contrast to the band and the other Germans, who got down to some serious drinking, till Karin whispered to me she'd like to see my dress. We went to my room and it could be said our relationship began then. (If you are reading this, thank you, Bill.)

Not to make light of his bad health or audience disappointment, there was more good news. The next three shows with REM were also cancelled and suddenly an unimagined thing appeared in a tour itinerary – a four-day break. This the day after I'd finally made real contact with a woman I'd been attracted to for two years. Madly calculating with our tour manager and Bob by phone, it seemed I could temporarily leave the tour – the money I'd save on four nights' hotels more than compensating for a flight to our next show, as headliners in Glasgow. I was actually saving the band money! Karin came to the hotel the next morning, and after waving the band bus goodbye – a strange experience indeed – she and I drove off in her white Golf diesel for a farmhouse an hour away. The two of us moving out of the city, onto the Autobahn, then a thinner road, to thinner roads. I was seeing livestock and villages, passing May fields filled with yellow flowers ('Raps,' Karin said), then a ridge, a street, a corner, a turn, and then a farmhouse in tiny Alteglofsheim that she shared with Erhard and another psychology student named Kerstin. In a blink I'd left the Holiday Inns, the tour van, the dark chill of rock clubs, for a student household in the Bavarian countryside. The merry-go-round had stopped, and I'd been thrown a long way.

When the tour recommenced in Scotland, followed by England, Portugal and Spain, each day, each show, brought closer the moment of reckoning. What was I to do? I'd never had two women in my life at the one time before, and in defence of my behaviour I pleaded to myself the extraordinary circumstances of the situation. From Bologna I wrote to Kathleen, ending our relationship. Cowardly on the one hand; on the other I was following what I knew to be the true course of my heart. Karin Bäumler was the woman I'd been searching for.

The last performance of the tour rewound everything to the start: Munich, the cancelled show rescheduled. It was also my thirty-second birthday, and for the second time in two months I drove off with Karin. On this occasion not just for four days, but for time unknown.

Bliss and a Bang

Days after the rest of the band got back to Sydney, Grant had to tell John Willsteed that he was out of the group. Most of us had been drinking rather heavily on the road, myself as much as anyone; John, though, had taken it a step further and it didn't seem like he wanted to wind it down anytime soon.

We were a four-piece again, with songs to be written, producers and engineers to be considered – the whole business of constructing a new album starting up straight away. If we followed our plan to record early the following year, we would be making our seventh album in nine years. No wonder we were starting to get a bit wobbly. My consolation was not having to face this from Sydney – finally there was distance on things – but from a room with a view of a pig farm across the street. Down the hall my bath was heated from a stack of wood I had to hack, bought from the farmer next door. Around me people spoke not only another language, but a regional version of it called Bayerisch. The only sound breaking hours of silence during warm summer days were tractors returning from the fields. After a few weeks I was getting nods from the cloth-capped drivers as they passed.

If my surroundings were foreign, the house and those attached to it were familiar. Karin played violin and sang with Baby You Know, a raucous folk-rock band with fine songs whose members – Erhard as lead singer, Robert and Mickey on bass and guitar – had been part of a gang of friends coming to Go-Betweens shows. Alteglofsheim was the band house, with curious neighbours clocking the comings and goings of a wide variety of people who now included an Australian. There were band songwriting sessions in the kitchen, and upstairs a record player with floor-to-ceiling shelves of quality records gathered by Erhard, who worked at a record shop in Regensburg, half an hour away. In a beautiful coincidence, Guy Clark and Townes Van Zandt were followed here too, and, in true German style, were followed in depth: a bootleg video of the seventies Texan-outlaw, country-scene documentary *Hardworn Highways*, with eye-popping footage of Guy and Townes and a sixteen-year-old Steve Earle, was a key inspiration. From my upstairs room I began songwriting, and with Karin and Kerstin at university and Erhard at work, the reality of my recent decision hit hardest and sweetest as I sat in a creaking farmhouse, no car at the door, to write my next chapter of songs.

It was a golden summer. A season so long and hot rolled around only once every ten years. In the afternoons Karin and I would walk through the surrounding fields, talking, shyly trying to hatch a future, the world always at bay with us. Some days we'd drive down back-country roads to swim in forest-shrouded lakes, and when in need of cafes and seventeenth-century streets there was Regensburg, a breathtakingly beautiful Imperial city on a turn of the Danube, where we'd meet up with Baby You Know and other friends. It was a heavenly state of affairs and I felt comfortable and welcomed, living on a fraction of the money it would have cost me in Sydney. While always knowing I'd have to leave the love story and return to the business and bustle of constructing yet another fucking (sorry) Go-Betweens record. The shadows fell in early October and I left thinking I'd see Karin in six months.

Grant and Amanda had vacated their flat, which I took, and they relocated to a small house nearby. I was desperately hoping the slap in the face that work and Sydney provided would be enough to keep my mind on the tasks at hand, and not have me at every free moment longing for Karin and the Bavarian idyll. Grant came over and this time I could match him number for number. We brought Tony Cohen up from Melbourne with his four-track, and over two days in my bare flat we recorded twenty-one songs. I had four that I thought were keepers, good enough for an album – 'Is This What You Call Change', 'I've Been Looking For Somebody', 'Dear Black Dream' and 'Danger In The Past'. The latter the jewel in my crown. A six-verse folk ballad that whacked the Guy Clark/Anne Sexton synthesis (folk tune/neurotic lyric) together with real finesse: 'So I went and I saw you/ We walked through the hospital grounds/ I took your hand and I told you/ Never show your problems in a country town.' The next album was going to be different just by having

213

this song. Grant's best, from a bunch of surprisingly downbeat material, was the pop of 'Easy Come Easy Go', plus 'The Day My Eyes Came Back,' 'Haunted House', 'Broadway Bride', and, my favourite, an epic rolling ballad that we loved playing called 'Dream About Tomorrow'.

We were close to having an album's worth of material when our minds turned to who was going to engineer or produce the record. There was broad agreement that we didn't want to work with Mark again: we wanted another sound. The alternatives showed the struggle we were going through in trying to dis-cover what kind of album and group we wanted to make and be. Grant had suggested Hal Willner, whom I'd visited in New York in August, to find that his speciality as a producer was esoteric solo artists like Marianne Faithfull and Gavin Friday. I didn't have anyone in mind, only a few diary pages of riffing with the mad idea of getting Sydney painter Brett Whiteley involved. Had anyone in the world made an album produced by a famous artist since Warhol did the first Velvet Underground LP? Tony Cohen was probably the most likely candidate, and at a cafe in Oxford Street we met a young engineer from one of the big studios, put forward by Lindy and Amanda – his latest project was *Tin Machine II*. I adored Bowie; Pixies-style rock, though, was not the direction our songs were taking us.

The demo was the problem. A listen showed two songwriters in their early thirties moving away from the angular rock and pop that had once inspired them to their own twist on clas-sic singer-songwriter territory. Three of my four songs could be done without drums – many of Grant's too. This was echoed in the practice room, where we had trouble putting rhythms to songs, more time being spent playing the second-tier material than the numbers intended for the record. With us was our new bassist, Michael Armiger, a friend of Roger Grierson's, a good player and an easygoing guy, and the first musician since Tim Mustafa to join the band whom we hadn't known before. He listened a little perplexed as ideas flew about; Lindy and Amanda, who had spoken in interviews of one day forming their own band, were drawn to a more electronic pop approach – drum machines and violin-triggered keyboards – believing perhaps that hits were still to be had.

For all this activity, the mood in the band during the first weeks of my return was languid and unfocused. Certainly there wasn't the gritted 'here we go' feeling that had propelled us into our previous albums. Maybe it was still to come. I suggested we do a few small gigs to help offset wages and road-test new material, hoping to knock some of the knots out of the problem songs. With this in place and a few weeks to spare, I flew off at short notice to Germany. It was a colder month there, my feelings for Karin and the cosy wooden world in the farmhouse just as strong. My songwriting recommenced; I'd written a melody and was in need of a lyric when a friend of Karin's visited with boyfriend problems, there being two of them. Subject matter found, I placed myself as the aggrieved partner addressing his girlfriend: 'You say there's nothing wrong with us/ That what we have here is good/ But you have more needs/ And the fire cannot burn on the same old wood.' I called the song 'Baby Stones', and a late chorus celebrated walking free: 'I missed the turning back, I walked on by/ Old situations can make you just want to lie down and die.' Prophetic words.

*

In Sydney a few weeks later, we were rehearsing in a large room near Town Hall; without Willsteed or the presence of a producer, the practice room had the rough and tumble of late London rehearsals, one or two of which I had walked out of. Things boiled to a moment when Lindy turned on Michael over a difficult beat and snarled, 'Just play this, ah . . . whatever your name is.' He was silenced, and it was the shock of seeing someone unprepared for this kind of command that was so affecting. He was being blooded to join our group. In reflex I looked over at Grant, to find his eyes already on mine, a very flat expression on his face, and for once his gaze didn't shift. 'I'd like to see you after practice,' he said to me quietly at the next break.

An hour later we were at a bar around the corner, alone. 'I want to leave the band,' he said, and before I could add anything, 'you can keep the name if you want. I don't care.' He really had had enough. His courage in saying so greater than mine. I now knew my own feelings, having heard his expressed. 'I want to leave too.' We both wanted to leave our own group. Ha!

A weight lifted. Our rock band in debt and limping to its seventh album, ourselves drunk on relief and the drinks we're throwing down, we immediately start tossing around ideas for the album we really want to make, and as at the beginning, we find ourselves in step. Damian Nelson could have walked in. An hour after splitting the old group, we already know how the new one will be. An acoustic duo with a splash of bass and organ, cherry-picking the numbers from the demo that suit this approach to make an album bold as brass, with the opposite dimensions of *16 Lovers Lane*. We bubble with excitement while toasting ourselves. We sniff freedom, misjudging all danger.

The secret is held tight although it feels hot. Band meetings, with Lindy ramming through agendas – I'd returned from Germany to be told my wages had gone on a new drum kit, Roger palms-up: *What could I do?* – are at times no less fractious than rehearsals. Not an option for airing concerns or declaring plans. And really, there's nothing to talk about, the scene in the practice room not the game-changer, but the last sprinkle of sand tipping the scales from wanting to go on to wanting to walk away.

*

I went to The Gap for Christmas with Grant's instructions in my head: 'See how our decision looks from Brisbane and ring me.' Brisbane, the spiritual home of the group and a vantage point over Sydney. After a week, I phoned him to say we were doing the right thing.

'Good. I think so too. Let's do it.' We also agreed on the method. I would tell Lindy at the moment he was telling Amanda.

I got to Sydney after Christmas and went to Lindy's the next day.

Her bitter laugh almost held a touch of admiration. How had two guys she'd always regarded as being weak-kneed suddenly found the balls to do something like this? Of course in the flutter of explanation I'd told her everything – not only were Grant and I breaking up the group, we were going to continue working together. She wanted to know if Amanda knew, and I told her that she was being told now.

Lindy walked to the phone. She looked back at me after dialling and then turned in profile to talk. Her first words: 'Leave him.'

She was either issuing instructions or confirming Amanda's reaction on being told. And it was by watching the connection between Lindy and Amanda that I could suddenly picture Grant, distraught and begging, looking at Amanda on the phone to Lindy, no friend of his, realising the ugly twists still to come. Our news, cupped in our hands like a bird, had flashed into a fire-breathing eagle with talons of steel. Our naivety and belief in the worth of our project, our strength in the past, was now our weakness, blinding us to all consequences. Of course Lindy and Amanda would feel betrayed and angry after the years of work and emotional energy they had put into the band, to rebound with a punch as great as the one we had just given them. Amanda, shocked and upset, wanting to leave Grant.

I looked on in horror, while a note an octave down I couldn't ignore still sang relief. It was over. I'd seen the flashing of knives, the brutal last scene that finishes every tragedy, which is what The Go-Betweens had become. Grant was on the ground, the one of us without a survival technique. I could walk away – from this room, from Sydney, from whatever remained.

My only concern Grant.

The Intimacy of Grief

I visited him the day after Amanda left. She had held to her first impulse and was packed and gone by the following afternoon. From the delivery of his news to her closing of the front door, it must have been one hell of a 24-hour stretch in the house.

'She's so innocent,' he pleaded to me through tears. He was sitting on the loungeroom couch with his face in his hands, rocking back and forth. I bit my tongue. I wanted to say, *You're* the innocent one. *You're* the one left in the house crying. Amanda was young, but not as guileless as he wanted to believe. She'd had boyfriends, and so when the crisis in their relationship came, further proof of *his* innocence, she knew what to do.

I didn't think of it immediately – the question came later. Why didn't Grant and I include Amanda in our plans? After all, the three of us had played successful shows together, and her violin and vocals would have fitted the new material. As strange as it sounds, Grant never thought to bring her in and nor did I. I did ask him how he thought she would react to our announcement and he didn't seem concerned. 'It will be all right,' he said. A massive miscalculation, since he'd been with her for three and a half years, but then I didn't reckon things any better. No storm warnings from me. We knew Lindy and Amanda were very close, and there was no guarantee, given the opportunity to play with Grant and me, that Amanda would have chosen to join us. She also had a suspicion of natural recording, and our next album, working title 'Freakchild', was being referred to within the group as 'Robert's album'. So we didn't consider bringing Amanda in: artistically perhaps the right decision, but as a reading of an emotional situation, a disaster.

One other thought occurred long after the lightning days that tore the group apart: after the European tour, Amanda and Grant may not have been as harmonious as they once were. Grant's songs support that story, the swoon and boast of *16 Lovers Lane* gone, replaced by 'Haunted House' and 'Broadway Bride': 'Got himself a Broadway bride/ Now the misery is his'. So when he uttered the unexpected news, the bond between them might not have been strong enough to weather it or seek solutions, making the leaving of him a little easier for her. But if they were unstable, why had he thrust things into crisis?

I walked down to his house every day, and each time Grant was a mess. Whatever control he'd stored up to get him through the night would have collapsed, leaving him bewailing his predicament. The force of his grief transforming him into a person who bore surprisingly little resemblance to the friend I'd known for almost half my life. And in his transformation was mine. I was now the rational one, the voice of reason talking him back from the edge. It happened during these days – a switch in the roles of our friendship that would play out over the remaining years.

It was a twilight world we were in. End of the decade, end of December, end of the band, the de Chirico-like emptiness that befalls city streets between Christmas and New Year. It felt as if there were five people living in Sydney. Actually, the closing of the year and the eighties had given momentum and meaning to our decision. The Go-Betweens weren't going to splutter out; the last days of a six-albums-in-a-decade career was a dramatic place to pull up stumps. Theorising aside, everything had the feeling of having stopped, and my duty was to visit Grant, listen, chip in with clearer thoughts, listen some more, and help get him through another day. Few knew what had happened, enforcing the sense of it all as a private drama. For almost a week he saw no one but me.

To add to the atmosphere, storm clouds came in over the city at the end of each afternoon, their march seen from the hills of Bondi Junction as they swung low and slunk past, or dumped an hour of violent rain. Two hours later the air would be cool. Sydney, never the most comforting of cities for Grant or me, was not the ideal place to dissolve the group. It was a town and a time of year when you wanted to be at the beach laughing and living, not walking back and forth between two houses trying to cope with the unintended consequences of breaking up a rock band. Some days I went to Grant's in dread. He'd hinted at suicide. I didn't take it too seriously, but there were times I'd knock on the front door in the early afternoon and wait, knowing he was inside but not coming; I'd then peer through windows, looking for a moving figure, and it was with some relief that I'd see him limp to the front door and let me in.

He didn't get better, but the shock and despair, the wreckage in his eyes left, and after a week he began trying to string some quasi-positive thoughts together. The first wave of stunned crisis was over.

I was keeping Karin up on events, throwing coins into public telephones and hoping she'd be at home. And when she was, pouring Sydney madness and my love, often in equal doses, down the line. I had her, and the reassurance of that, and knowing that Grant and I had made the right call for our music, no matter how bloody the ramifications, allowed me to focus on him. To my shame my eye was also on the calendar. Even though Karin and I had parted at Vienna airport in November not expecting to see each other for months, I still wanted to get back to her as soon as I could. My sense of guilt about leaving Grant lessened when he made contact with more people; Bob and Roger were phoning him, a few Sydney friends crept into the house, and he was leaning heavily on Golding Street friends Andrew Wilson and Karen Byatt, who had recently moved down from Brisbane. Also, we would be making an album in February or March, probably in Europe, but maybe, with a new start in mind, the US. The fabled New York album?

In any case, I'd be seeing him soon.

There were two goodbyes.

My mother combined a visit to Sydney relatives with seeing me off. At thirty-two I was leaving Australia yet again, this time for a German woman she and Dad had seen in photos standing before a farmhouse in the snow. What were they to make of their eldest son and the ever-twisting tale of his rock band? I must have still been a worry to them, and I was coming to hate that.

As for Grant, this was the only time he came to visit me, at his and Amanda's old home, in the weeks after the break-up. There must have been effort in that. It was 17 January 1990, the day I was flying out. He watched me throw my clothes into a suitcase – I could still pack my life in an hour. An acoustic guitar waited at the door like a sentinel, my constant companion in bedrooms, hotels and airports around the world. Closing windows, emptying the fridge, carrying a last bag of rubbish down to the bins. It was a weird farewell when it came. We were brought face to face with the consequences of our actions, and although we'd be seeing each other soon, there was a sense that this was our first real parting.

We hugged, something we rarely did.

'You're my best friend,' I said to him, and I'd never said that before. What did I know? That brought his eyes up to mine. He smiled and nodded and then walked off down the stairs. Something was going on between us. Two moons passing is what it felt like. A ritual crossing: me on the up, maybe, him on the down. Would our lives ever be in synch?

REEL II

First Steps

'Have you heard the news?' asked Bob.

I'd been back in Alteglofsheim a couple of weeks. Days after arriving I'd phoned Grant and the call was much like visiting him – he held up for a few minutes and then crumbled. At the end of the conversation he promised he'd phone me, and I'd been expecting to hear from him for a few days.

'I've heard nothing. What do you mean?'

'Well . . . I've just had a call from Beggars. Grant's contacted them and told them he wants to make a solo album.'

A slow, disbelieving 'No' falling from my mouth. I was stunned. After the call I went to Karin. 'He's stabbed me in the back.' My hurt and wrath were undercut only a fraction by immediately knowing why he'd done it – to get Amanda back. To have a reason for establishing contact. 'Do you want to play on my solo album?' He'd withdrawn music from her and she'd left him; now he had to re-offer it and hope she'd return.

Two weeks later he called with an apology, and in his defence quoted advice he'd got from friends, which he was intent on following. 'I have to concentrate totally on getting the one thing that I want.' I thought it was hopeless. Amanda wasn't coming back. She'd been humiliated; she was gone in a day, and somewhere in the city she was already building a new life. Grant, though, was determined, and it was to cause him a lot of pain. It also chained him to Sydney; his reasoning seemed to be that if he left town she'd be lost to him forever. His fear big enough to stop him coming to Regensburg, to join my rejoicing parents and brother at Karin's and my wedding in May as best man.

With the bucket of cold water over my head that Grant's turnaround was, I felt a need for action. I enrolled at a German language school in Regensburg and went there four mornings a week, sitting beside Polish au pairs and gruff Russians who'd piled into the country in the months after the fall of the Berlin Wall – like me, they were looking for a new start. In the farmhouse kitchen was a piano, an instrument I'd always wanted to learn, and with the help of a teacher I banged away on that. And I approached a big reading project: Proust. I had the three-volume Terence Kilmartin translation of *Remembrance of Things Past* in paperback – stacked side by side, a daunting amount of fine-paged, long-paragraphed reading. An early glance located the first sustained dialogue on page 25, and I liked dialogue. All roads led to Marcel, though, his book namechecked whenever my reading took me to literature's most delicate rooms. I now had time.

I'd also begun putting things in place to record a solo album of my own. I was still under contract to Beggars, and the challenge of writing the remaining songs for the record, not stopping at five, was enticing, as was the prospect of them shaping the album's mood. For as satisfying as it had been making the Go-Betweens LPs, it can't be denied that the opportunity to write *all* the songs and tell the *whole* story, even if it potentially meant selling fewer records, was attractive. Grant's decision, and the betrayal I caught in its tail, gave us both something precious – our freedom from each other, and the chance to each make an album exactly to our own specifications.

*

When The Go-Betweens had arrived in West Berlin on tour in May '87, I phoned Hansa Tonstudios asking if I could come down to see their recording facilities. The next morning, hungover, and with no one from the group wishing to accompany me, I caught a cab to a part of town I'd never been before, a corner of the city where a row of five- to six-storey buildings faced the Wall across open land. Bowie and Iggy Pop had recorded vital albums here, and I'd never visited a famous studio in cities we had toured. Hansa drew me in. And as I stood in the ballroom-sized recording room of Studio Two, all fairytale dark wood and high-panelled windows, I said to myself, so it would come true, I'll come back here one day and make an album. At the time I was thinking of The Go-Betweens, but it was where I would make *Danger in the Past*.

Galvanised by the opportunity, and with classic singer-songwriter debut albums streaming through my head, I wrote 'Heart Out To Tender' and 'Leave Here Satisfied' back to back in February and March. 'Heart' was an image-flecked chronicle of Karin's and my courtship: 'Put yourself in my shoes/ Look on down my line/ She gets bigger in the mirror/ I have to be with her this time.' 'Leave Here Satisfied' was the first song I'd ever written about Grant:

> Found myself in an empty house calling out is anyone there
> Thinking someone must be here somewhere.
> No one stepped up at all, no one I could see
> No one tapped me on the shoulder and said, 'It's me.'
> And I just wanted to run and hide
> Felt a drop of water deep down inside
> I could go, but I wouldn't Leave Here Satisfied.

On the first day of recording we recorded nothing, and even that was liberating. Bad Seed Mick Harvey had been my first and only choice as producer, and he stood in the Hansa control room assessing what we needed to record and mix an album in the twelve days our budget permitted. With his waistcoat and noble profile, he looked like an eighteenth-century sea captain planning an adventure – I was willing to follow him anywhere. Beside him sat Victor Van Vugt, a handsome young Dutch-born Melbourne engineer I'd met in St Kilda, when his main gig was doing live sound for The Moodists. Our drummer, another Bad Seed, Thomas Wydler, was holidaying somewhere on the Mediterranean. 'Hopefully he'll be here tomorrow,' said Mick. We thought we might need a lead guitarist on some of the tracks, but neither of us knew who that could be. I walked over to a cupboard and pulled out a dusty old Guild twelve-string guitar with no strings. 'We'll use that,' said Mick. So ended our first day's work.

That night I went to a bar of the typical Berlin style: no furniture, bare concrete walls and floor, and cigarette smoke so thick the bartender looked like a nightwatchman in fog. Behind me queuing for a drink was Hugo Race. I'd known him in St Kilda too, when he'd led an art-rock group called Plays with Marionettes. He was in town hoping to start a new band. 'What kind of music are you wanting to make?' I asked. He smiled. 'I'm going for a *Highway 61 Revisited* kind of sound.' The next morning at the studio I suggested Hugo as our lead guitar player. Mick, who knew him through his short stint in The Bad Seeds, pursed his lips. 'He'll do.'

Meanwhile Thomas had arrived and we started running down the songs. Our work method was simple. Thomas would listen to a demo; Mick, on bass, would talk him through the arrangement; we'd go into the recording room, play the song no more than four times, do a take, and then go on to the next number. In this manner we were doing three or four songs a day. I was skipping between the recording and control rooms exalted: this was exactly how I'd always wanted to cut an album. In a big room, not a box, with dynamics in the playing, and quality recording gear to catch it all. And if the tempos sped up or slowed down a touch, we took that as excitement, not a crime. Hugo came in to spray some great Mike Bloomfield riff-age over four songs, Mick overdubbed keyboards and sang, and with the album nearing completion the last piece of the puzzle was Karin joining me to sing three words on the title track: 'Danger. Danger. Danger.' It was in the past, and she'd helped put it there.

For the cover I'd found a photo of James Joyce in a biography at Regensburg University library. He was sitting cross-legged on a chair and holding a Spanish guitar. With his round wire glasses, moustache, and swept-back hair, he'd always reminded me of my father's father. Joyce could have been a Forster, comfortable at Cranbrook. I was photographed in a similar pose.

Recording an album at thirty-three was easy compared to launching a solo career at that age. Morrissey was twenty-seven when he went it alone. Neil Finn was twenty-six. Dave Grohl twenty-five. Few have succeeded when starting much later than that. No second acts in rock'n'roll, F. Scott Fitzgerald could have said. My time for a clear solo lift-off was really back in early '87. In London, with music journalists on my trail, when I was rock-star-wrecked handsome with a handful of perfumed songs, and the inevitable stint in rehab still a few years off. As it was, having made a solo album equal to the best of The Go-Betweens', I didn't even want to tour, happy as I was to let the record go out into the world to seek those it would find. It was a romantic and somewhat sabotaging view, to stay at home and not chase an album down with six months on the road, but I was exhausted from the past decade, and not at all willing to part from Karin months after marriage. I lived off the reviews (some adroitly picking through the songs to find the album's story – upheaval and separation, to end in the calm of 'Justice': 'I'm a lucky man'), and a card from Edwyn praising the record and asking if I wanted to support him on a UK tour. That would have been a start. I considered it, walking the stone roads with Karin, but knowing Edwyn liked the album was enough.

*

I sent a copy to Grant in Sydney, to the Bondi Junction flat he shared with two female friends, and waited for his response. Then waited more. When I finally called he said he hadn't received it. Weeks later, he literally tripped over the record, weather-beaten and stomped on under the doormat, where it had presumably been left out of the rain. Any postman's note of its whereabouts long gone. 'It's warped,' he said to me on the phone, which held more metaphors than I wished to contemplate. I could only gaze up at the Alteglofsheim kitchen ceiling and take a breath, knowing that things between him and me in this new world order (the album betrayal still in my head) were occasionally going to be like this. Crosswired. A chance to see him came when Karin and I visited Sydney after spending Christmas in Brisbane in 1990.

Without the schedule of the band and the company of Amanda he was looser – dressed-down, drinking more, a free man although not necessarily a happier one. The fever of wanting Amanda back was still on him. She had played on his recently recorded solo album, yet to be released, and with Sydney rock gossip swirling over the break-up of the band and their relationship, he was riding highs and lows. A high, for both of us, was the solo gig he'd generously booked for me at the Three Weeds Hotel in Balmain. My one-show *Danger in the Past* Australian tour. I was apprehensive about playing alone, he was insistent and supportive. The curtains parted on a packed room, and with growing confidence I managed to front the audience, playing a mix of *Danger* and Go-Betweens songs. Towards the end of the show Grant joined me onstage, and the room exploded. Here we were, old friends, our connection known, the story of the last year not. Backstage there was a milling of people between him and me, and in the celebration I caught his eye. He flashed a big smile. And with a theatrical raising of the hands a *See? It all worked out* gesture.

'All of this could be yours'

'Here's a thing.'

I've heard this through the ages. It's Bob with a step to his voice, and it means an offer or a piece of news has come into his office, important enough to warrant an immediate call. Anything can follow. A movie company sniffing around one of our songs. Someone wanting to paint my portrait for an art prize. Maybe 'Streets Of Your Town' is number one in Montenegro this week. I pull up a chair and listen.

Lloyd Cole has asked if Grant and I would be interested in supporting him on a leg of his upcoming European tour, and on a string of US coast-to-coast shows. We'll be paid well, with transport and hotels provided, and all we have to do is forty minutes a night. Bob also tells me that Robert Vickers is in Lloyd's band, and that Lloyd is a fan of The Go-Betweens.

I already know this, as he's been graciously namechecking us in interviews since moving to New York, where he started a solo career after the break-up of The Commotions.

All of this is of interest, but Bob and I know there's another click to the story. The Go-Betweens are still signed to Capitol; the label has indicated through Simon Potts that they're willing to bankroll another album. Grant and I could pick it up. We could be The Go-Betweens on a major label in America. Bob's final words are, 'Why don't you go out on the road with Grant? Meet Simon in LA and make a decision on what you want to do.'

Nineteen ninety-one had been a quiet year for me so far. I'd done a few German and Austrian dates, and a London show with a great four-piece country-pop band from Hamburg, belatedly promoting my album. While on the road we recorded a version of 'Tower Of Song' for *I'm Your Fan*, a Leonard Cohen tribute album sponsored by the French rock and culture magazine *Les Inrockuptibles*. I was preparing to produce the second Baby You Know album, *Clearwater*, and besides that, after almost two years at the farmhouse, I'd been reading, writing songs, putting on weight, and by midyear starting to feel a little restless. So this offer, as unusual as supporting another song-writer was for me, was worth considering. Maybe it was time for me to go out and see the world again, hang out with Grant while filling my suitcase with the latest books, records and magazines, to bring back home and consume in my room. Well-stocked seclusion – my favourite position in life.

*

The tour began in the Netherlands. Grant and I rehearsed in our hotel for a day, the first shows were good, and a week into our dates we had our forty minutes down. We were a strong two-piece, able to capitalise on our working methods as song-writers – our interlocking guitar parts, the blend of our voices, the varied viewpoints of our songs – and with a little stage patter we were a convincing and entertaining duo. Also evident was Grant's love of touring, his all-access tour pass bouncing on his chest when he greeted me – the road is a place where music can be the only thing in your life. And for a couple of months I enjoyed it too.

Lloyd, whom Grant and I had never met before, was a dark-featured, good-looking guy who, having had hits in the eighties with his group, was carving out a new career. His latest album, *Don't Get Weird on Me, Babe*, was good. He was intelligent and literate, with a non-filter Lucky Strike at his fingertips as a prop for stabbing out a line of nervy, witty patter. I admired people brave enough to take on tough, 1950s-style cigarettes. Ben Watt had smoked Senior Service for a time, and another friend, Sydney rock journalist Toby Creswell, drew constantly on Camel non-filters, and had made the scrunching of empty packets and the patted search for a fresh one in his jacket pockets his trademark.

Lloyd was also a keen golfer, having grown up like myself with golfing parents near a course. He was a fan of the great Spanish player Seve Ballesteros, and had kept his game in far better shape than mine, playing off a handicap of around ten. In Lisbon we decided to have a game together, and it was with trepidation that his tour manager watched us climb into a cab and head off for a links an hour up the coast. We were the only ones out, and on some holes we'd see or hear the Atlantic Ocean pounding on rocks far below. I'd watch Lloyd take a drag of his Lucky Strike, throw it smouldering onto the grass, line up and hit his shot, and then, satisfied with the result, pick up the cigarette and walk puffing to the green. That was the European tour.

For the US dates we had a big overnight bus. I'd never toured like this and it wasn't my preferred option. We'd leave straight after the show, band members and crew sleeping in bunks, to arrive at the next city in early daylight and stumble into a hotel where a day room had been booked for everyone to shower, and then move on to the gig. It was practical because all the travelling was done at night, but it turned rock'n'roll into a freight business. I liked looking at the scenery during the day, knowing I was dedicating my night to the city I was playing in, even if after the gig I just went back to the hotel to watch seda-tive TV.

I wasn't the headliner, though.

Grant and I were the last ones to wake in the car park of the Hyatt on Sunset. Having fallen asleep somewhere south of San Francisco, to wake with LA sunshine streaming through the curtain cracks and the bunk above inches from my nose, my disorientation was heavy. I stumbled into hotel reception and got my room key. We were overnighting in the City of Angels – *please* let me write that – and in conjunction with the following night's show there was business to be taken care of.

The day before, Bob had asked if we had any suggestions for a producer for a possible album with Capitol, and this time I had a name – Pete Anderson. He'd done a couple of Dwight Yoakam albums, Michelle Shocked's *Short Sharp Shocked*, and most recently *The American in Me* by seventies singer-songwriter Steve Forbert; all of them were strong. Anderson was also a guitarist, playing twangy Telecaster riffs in the style of James Burton. I thought he'd be perfect for us, his sound authentic but commercial – a match for our songs and the record we needed to make. The power of the record company was on display when Bob phoned an hour later to say that Anderson would be in the hotel bar to meet us the following afternoon.

I recognised the broad shoulders and the bearded face from the back cover of *Short Sharp Shocked*. He admitted he'd never heard of The Go-Betweens, and I had expected that. The conversation went well. I took the chance to quiz him on the Forbert record, and he outlined his approach to recording: good musicians, live takes, some overdubs. He was impressive, quiet and reassuring, like Wallis, and we left the meeting thinking that here was someone we could work with.

That night we were collected at our hotel and driven up the winding roads of the Hollywood Hills to Simon's place. I don't know if he was renting or owned the house, but it sat on a ridge offering a glittering view of the city that I recognised from a hundred movies. He gave us the house tour, which included locations where *Playboy* magazine had done a photo shoot the previous day. One of the models had left a naked polaroid of herself on the fridge with a phone number. People desperately wanted to get into this house. We moved to the loungeroom, where Simon asked about Pete Anderson in a gambit to gauge our commitment to the project. Grant and I were being cagey: we didn't know ourselves yet if we wanted to do it, and we were aware that if we tipped our hand too much to a yes, the wheels would immediately be put in motion and we'd be trapped. Simon didn't push; answers, though, were expected soon.

New York was the last date. I'd been sober for a week, preparing to see Karin again, only to reacquaint myself with the bottle backstage and stagger through the streets with Grant in search of the perfect bar. Manhattan always overexcited us, but I knew our drinking would not stop here if we decided to make an album together. That, though, was not my reason for saying no to re-forming The Go-Betweens, and nor was it Grant's. The tour had done what it was supposed to do – lead us up to the edge of the cliff to look over. We were happy being solo artists, and with the freedom that afforded us. Going back to the band seemed like a massive retreat, and the thought of sitting in an LA recording studio while Karin worked alone in Alteglofsheim, studying for her final exams, sent a shudder through me. We said no.

For Bob it was exasperating. He'd got close once before to his wish of Grant and me re-forming as The Go-Betweens, before Grant torpedoed it. Now it had slipped away again. To see it from his side, it was much harder, and there was less money involved, managing two solo careers than one successful band, especially one with just two members.

The New York decision, and the understanding between Grant and me on parting, gave us something Sydney hadn't two years before. We let the ribbon of the band go out of our hands. We were now on our own.

Born Again Eyes

I realised Brisbane had changed as I watched Glenn Thompson make pesto and pasta. He was my new drummer, playing in Cow – a four-piece band performing a skewed take on 'country or western' music. Glenn and his girlfriend Jane had invited Karin and me to their rented West End deco apartment for dinner. He had made the pesto in a mortar and pestle, and having kneaded a big ball of dough was now threading it through a hand-operated pasta machine. This was the new Brisbane, and I was equally sure that there were few guys in their early twenties anywhere else in the world preparing a meal in such a way.

The rest of Queensland had gone through the wringer too. The Bjelke-Petersen reign was over, having ended in 1989 in the only way it could, in farce and ignominy. Like most politicians who preach God, Joh had tolerated shonky business deals, had no regard for the environment, and naturally no interest in the arts. And now, as in Romania after Ceausescu, or East Germany after Honecker, the populace were emerging pink-eyed and disbelieving out of the darkness, wanting to rejoin civilisation. Brisbane was in a rush and already blossoming when Karin and I moved there in July '92, soon after she gained her psychology degree. She was tentatively assessing the city from our rented inner-city Paddington worker's cottage, while loving the weather. I had come with songs and a plan – to find a young band and record in Brisbane.

Warwick Vere, the owner of Rocking Horse Records and one of the few people from the late seventies still on the scene, had led me to Cow; the studio I found myself. Remarkably, Sunshine Studios, where the first two Go-Betweens singles were done, remained the pick of the recording locations in town. I was going back in time. In my fevered mind it was like Elvis returning to Sun Studios, right down to the loungeroom-sized recording room and the pockmarked white walls. This chimed with the feeling that Brisbane was a kinda Memphis, a muddy, sweaty, rock'n'roll town with weatherboard houses, floods, a heavy cop presence, and people with eight tonnes of junk in their yard.

Back in time, too, was the light-handed touch of my band, led by gifted guitarist David McCormack. He was also the lead singer and songwriter of Custard, a young rock'n'roll group going places. They practised with Cow and me in a shed at the back of his parents' house in Spring Hill, a hundred metres down the hill from my old school. I couldn't help but notice, as the musicians and their friends clustered around the practice room raving about Jonathan Richman and Talking Heads, or cracked jokes and played cricket in the yard, that I had gone through something like this before. I phoned Grant. 'You won't believe it. It's 1979 up here.'

I produced my second album, *Calling from a Country Phone*. The title a tilt at where the songs and I had been over the past years. There was pedal steel on some material, but the mad, beautiful piano and violin of guest player John Bone, and David's crunchy licks, took the sound miles away from any form of country music. The band was adaptable and the material, after the catharsis of *Danger*, was smaller, and more content in tone. '121' combined two loves, Karin and Regensburg: 'And it's tombstones, cobblestones/ All those old bones/ That lie beneath this city/ But I want to see her one to one.' Another song, 'The Circle' – 'She's in a circle and they've all been with each other' – traced a single woman tired of the rotation of partners available in a group of friends. 'You got to live it breathe it seize it/ Outside the circle.' I was twisting perspectives – it was my story. The album, mixed by Tony Cohen, caught the boxy, innocent sound I associated with my hometown, but it wasn't going to reposition my career. Moving to a bigger city and plugging into a current style – grungey rock ruled – might have helped with that. I could only follow the songs, pulling in more tightly a diminishing yet devoted set of music lovers attuned to my material.

I had expected when arriving in town to add to the songs I'd written in Germany. None had come, only a strong guitar riff I wrote in the recording studio that became 'Cryin' Love'. Its lyric inspiration was from my latest golden book, John Richardson's *A Life of Picasso Volume I: 1881–1906*. Here was a spellbinding examination of early-twentieth-century Parisian bohemia, amidst which, in ramshackle rooms that housed his blue- and rose-period masterpieces, Picasso painted self-portraits. 'Cryin' Love' was a self-portrait in song.

My next new number didn't arrive until January '95. In the two and a half years between I panicked, realising it was 1980–81 again and I needed a 'By Chance' to break the drought. I tried all my tricks, writing first thing in the morning when dreams still pervade the mind, or in the last hours of night, loose on wine and cigarettes. I tinkered on piano and listened to lots of music. None of it worked. I had some promising song titles – 'Born Again Eyes', 'Carbon Monoxide', 'All The Love You Can Bring' – and sometimes they got finished. But they all sounded like B sides to me. I had begun to seriously consider that my music career might be over, that I'd written myself out.

A sideways solution was recording an album of cover versions in Melbourne in early '94 – the one mistake of my recording career. I had a last-minute chance to back out when Tony Cohen withdrew the night before recording was to begin. The studio, though, was booked, and the musicians, including Mick Harvey, Clare Moore, Conway Savage, 'Evil' Graham Lee and Warren Ellis, were all expecting to start the next day. The players proved to be heroic and enthusiastic, the fault of the session my overconfidence and lack of preparation. A fatal fault, considering I was the producer. I learnt some lessons – enough to be listed. My voice was too idiosyncratic to carry a whole record of other people's songs. (That was why Lou Reed and Leonard Cohen had never done one.) My strength was working with a few musicians, not a studio full. The material recorded was primarily sourced from what I'd been listening to in the late eighties – it was time to move on. I didn't want to produce my next album. If my career was to continue, it could only do so if I wrote my own songs. To find them, something had to change.

I went on a European tour, taking Glenn to join Robert and Mickey from Baby You Know on bass and guitar. For the first few shows, the Scandinavian dates, Mickey was unavailable; Oslo was the breakthrough. We started to concentrate on what we were doing as a three-piece, and not compensate for the fact that we didn't have another guitarist. Guitar, bass and drums – my god, it was as if I'd forgotten a band could be like that. We rode the bones of the songs in a minimal rhythmic manner that threw the material out on a journey, not having a fourth person allowing me to swing the band any way I wanted with the strum of my guitar. The audience picked up on it, clapping as songs broke down, and grooved on. I had a sound.

*

Jeff Erlbacher lived in a renovated corner shop in Sandgate, at the edge of bayside Brisbane. By the mid-nineties the hilltop end of the suburb was starting to get gentrified. Jeff, a quiet and dryly opinionated person, had done the live sound for Cow, Custard and myself, and worked at the hipper end of the town's folk and jazz scenes. I phoned him up.

'I'm looking for a bass player.'

Silence.

'I'm looking for a woman who can play upright as well as electric bass. And she has to be a nice person.'

'Umm . . . you've got two choices.'

They were Adele Pickvance and a name player on the roots scene. My gut feeling was to start with Adele. She arrived in a Kombi, hauled out her bass, and from her first note we didn't look back.

New beginnings. It was perhaps no coincidence that Karin and I were in a new house. After two and a half years in the antique-store bohemianism of Paddington, we'd moved across the river to the funkier precinct of Highgate Hill. The houses were tight together, with a much broader ethnic mix of people living side by side, and a tropical aspect to the vegetable gardens and fruit trees, which, miraculously enough, were walking distance to the city. This was a deeper step into the town for us, coinciding with Karin working at a women's health centre and a soundtrack to go with the bare-boarded house, including Roberta Flack's *First Take* – seven songs, lots of silky drums and upright bass – and Herbie Mann's *Memphis Underground* flute grooves. These produced the hey-presto moment that I'd thought would happen the moment I returned to Brisbane, and I wrote my largest and quickest collection of quality material since the late seventies. Starting with the three-chord round-and-round of 'I Can Do': 'This is something that I can do/ Pick up the rhythm I get from you.' Then the neighbourhood sounds of 'Warm Nights': 'Hear the bugs biting down to the seed/ Hear the dopers tripping on their weed.' This was what Adele and Glenn had walked into.

We rehearsed in the house, and under the moniker of Robert Forster and Warm Nights began playing local shows, the quirkier the better, our set including up to half an hour of unrecorded music. I switched from acoustic to electric guitar, Glenn from sticks to brushes, Adele from acoustic to electric bass, and the two of them sang harmonies – Glenn had a whistling solo. There were a lot of variations to be found in a few elements, the sound moving in waves. Tight rhythms, or 'crazy rhythms', as The Feelies used to call them. By the middle of the year an album's worth of material was in place. Leaving me enough time to start thinking of another long-held dream locked in my hometown.

G. W.

Contact with Grant had been intermittent but steady since New York. He'd visited Alteglofsheim for a few days while on a promotional tour, where he'd worked on a powerful new song called 'Riddle In The Rain': 'From my German window things move pretty slow.' It reminded me of Leonard Cohen, someone I'd never connected to Grant before, with its waltz-time minor chords, European imagery and multiple verses. The number appeared on *Fireboy*, Grant's second solo album, and was the dam-buster – a fiery rebuke after three years of songs filled with pleading, longing and regret.

By staying in Sydney, and being regarded as the more pop-orientated of the two songwriters in The Go-Betweens, Grant was signed after the band's break-up to the White Label, a boutique branch of Mushroom Records. He now had the platform to make hits, and could count on the confidence of Michael Gudinski. I was out of the way, as was a band name six albums old, and to this Grant added touches of reinvention, billing himself as G. W. McLennan and sporting American-style baseball caps, partly to hide encroaching baldness. He had been more of a chart-watcher than I ('with all your riches, why aren't you there?'), and with the playing field as level as it ever was going to be, and with his gifts and some luck, I thought he could have cut a career to the shape of Paul Kelly's. I would have been very happy for him.

His first two solo albums, *Watershed* (1991) and *Fireboy* (1993), were a pair. Both had been produced by hit-making New Zealand singer-songwriter Dave Dobbyn, and both pulled at the central dilemma of Grant as a solo recording artist. He was a confessional singer-songwriter who also had the ability to write stunning pop songs. In The Go-Betweens this had been checked by his ration of five songs per album, and by having to bounce his material off mine; alone, he could have created quality pop albums. The trouble was, at the very moment he had his chance at pop success, he was heartbroken, which the artist in him couldn't help but pour into songs. The albums he *could* have made were gorgeous song cycles of despair, records to make Scott Walker sound chipper. *Scott 4* could have been *Grant 5*. The melodic, up-tempo side of his songwriting hadn't died, and nor had the terrific ambition that envelops anyone making solo albums after a group career. A resolution between his competing sides was not aided by Dobbyn's production, especially on *Watershed*, where the crashing, programmed drums and slick keyboard washes that attempted to fire the rock songs leaked over to smother the ballads. The top-forty hit that would have justified this approach not forthcoming on either album. Success the one thing that might have blasted Grant out of his agony – 'I'm trapped inside forever/ loneliness is mean/ I want you to set me free.'

Most of the songs on the two albums are about Amanda, and those that aren't sound like songs trying not to be about her. It's extraordinary how much she possessed him, and how public he was willing to make his need for her known. Song after song aches for and invites her return, and many of them – 'The Dark Side Of Town', 'Stones For You' and 'Things Will Change' – are beautiful. 'Riddle In The Rain', sequenced last on *Fireboy*, was his line in the sand. He is still trapped forever – 'But I'm still a long way/ I'm not even close/ Tell me who do I pay to get rid of your ghost?', as each chorus laments – the tone in the verses swinging between resignation and sarcasm, an attitude he carried in life that surprised people expecting the sincere romantic. With nothing to lose he turns on his subject and the past. 'You rock and roll schoolgirl/ You said the mechanism was fixed/ You let your lips curl/ It's funny how some things stick.' The swoon of the tune has him reckless. Was this the last twenty-four hours in their home? 'A genuine proposal/ A shifting of skin/ Then a quick proposal into the cut-off bin.' There's even a fascinating passing take on The Go-Betweens before Amanda joined – on Lindy, Robert, myself and Grant in order: 'A reluctant bitter feminist/ A boy with thin wrists/ A tall man with a gift/ And I'd never been kissed.' The song, played with a guitar strum and vocal I knew so well, sounds like it was recorded live and late at night. Grant dying to get this six-minute-plus epic that he knows is brilliant – an exorcism, a cry of freedom – out of himself and into the world. It's one of his greatest songs, and with a minimal arrangement: Dobbyn lets him go, only trailing an organ to the songwriter's guitar; Grant bursts into focus.

*

While I'd been in Melbourne toiling on my covers record, Grant was in Athens, Georgia, recording his third album, *Horsebreaker Star*. The album's opening line, 'Simone rings and tells me all about her problems', tolls the changes – he's back telling stories, and he's billed as Grant McLennan. There are songs of heart-break and betrayal but they don't come so consistently, nor do they have the almost ghoulish revelatory sizzle of the Sydney albums. The bigger story of the record is its length; it's twenty-four songs long, as if Grant wanted to record every piece of material he had in the drawer, running back to 1989, and finally get his unrecorded song count down to zero. A house-clearing that might also have been inspired by the abilities of the roots-rock musicians assembled by the album's producer, John Keane. The double album is one of rock's great romantic quests, so irresistible to Grant, who'd been hinting that The Go-Betweens should make one since the mid-eighties. 'Freakchild' the one time it might have worked.

The best song on the record he again sequenced last. The album's title track is confessional, and made even more powerful by being brief in lyric and majestic in sound, the band making a great explosive entry after the second verse. The mood, though, is subdued from the start – a voice with all bravado shaved from it singing, 'Got a mouth full of feathers/ Bit off more than I could chew.' And a verse later, 'Thought that I'd been broken/ Finally been brought down to my knees.' There it was laid bare. A similar devastation was evident in another song, this one directed at me. The narrative of 'Coming Up For Air' begins with Grant receiving a copy of *Calling from a Country Phone*; it gets him reminiscing. 'Sometimes I think about that night/ Two actors full of wine and a burning car/ You said we'd take this land/ I said that I agreed, but I'm the one with the scars.' Grant had declared himself 'the lonely one' as long ago as 'The Wrong Road', and the key line in 'Streets Of Your Town' can be missed: 'But I still don't know what I'm here for.' But there was now seeping into his work a fatalism, a deeper distress that made listening to his material, especially for those of us who knew him, very difficult, and which made his appeal on 'Coming Up For Air' all the more affecting for me. 'Will you pull me up, drop a rope down the hole/ Coming up for air, playing that jazz called rock and roll.'

By now there could be no mistaking the change in him. The person I'd known had unravelled, and was in trouble. Easy evidence was his appearance. Every photo of him until at least the mid-eighties has him looking stylish, in smart shirts and pants, coats, the odd tie. The T-shirts and jeans worn low on his arse began in the early nineties. Did grunge inspire this, or did his mental state just happen to coincide with a cultural moment?

Perhaps years of having to compete with the finery of Lindy, Amanda, Robert, and the great preening ponce that I was meant the only place left for him to go was down to jeans and sweatshirts, which over time got less and less of a wash. From the outside he could have been seen as someone ageing into another style, but the greater shift, the moving of earth, was within. Grant, prim, held, correct, like a favoured bachelor English teacher at a high school, was the one I'd turned to on matters of conduct and propriety. And if his songs had melancholy to them, and the idea of an ongoing relationship with another person was a work-in-progress, he still projected serenity and a crisp, businesslike attitude to things, including the running of the band.

In the months leading up to the split with Amanda he was fraying a little, and his reaction to their separation and his subsequent behaviour surprised me; I thought he would move on quicker. But in a way, he never fully recovered from that. It took me a while to pick this up, the clues filtering through phone calls, faxes and letters, second-hand stories from Bob and friends, and of course seeing his songs take the turn they did. That was where he couldn't, or didn't want to, hide it – music was his confession box.

He became less predictable. Rock'n'roll had got him too, and he was in a rock'n'roll town. His mood swung. At times he had a pumped-up ecstasy, usually connected to his work. 'I am Fireboy,' he once proclaimed to me over the phone, 'When Word Gets Around' off *Watershed* his 'Born In The USA', and for Grant, the latest record he'd made was, endearingly, always the best thing he'd ever done. Other times he was despondent; it was a deep place he'd gotten himself into, lonely, afraid, which I could on most occasions pull him out of with a call. It meant I walked to the phone in dread. What would I find? Karin would leave the room. I'd emerge an hour later with a smile: 'It was a good call.' Or I'd come out truly shaken: 'Grant, oh my god.'

In late '94 he and I were standing at the front of the Paddington house waiting for his cab. He'd been in town a few days, a gig perhaps, and he turned to me and said, a little self-consciously, 'I met a woman last night that I am in love with. She's called Julieanne Lawson.'

He savoured her name and the flourish of the pronouncement; I was most likely the first person he had told. My reply probably not hitting the level of confidence he was looking for. I often did that with him. 'That's great,' I said. And I *was* pleased, I just didn't want to fool him or myself with false exultation. It was the first woman's name I'd heard since Amanda's, and we both knew the significance of that. Also, there was the lurking belief, clichéd as it was, that a new girlfriend could save him.

He went back to Sydney, packed his bags and books and moved to Brisbane.

The Dendy

The film, or what I can remember of it, went something like this: a set of jewel thieves in Sydney, wanting to transport the proceeds of a recent robbery to Brisbane, decide to build an underwater tunnel linking the two cities. It sounds improbable, but then this is Golding Street talk and, as we would hear Edwyn sing from an Edinburgh stage a year or two later, 'Worldliness must keep apart from me.' Grant and I were batting around ideas and plot constructions as we sat in the green fifties lounge chairs, the Fellini *Amarcord* poster across from us, before moving to notepaper and then typed pages in Grant's bedroom. The film, to star a favoured sixties actor of ours whom we thought in need of rediscovery, James Garner, was the most prominent of a number of projects – a fanzine, an advertising agency – that Grant and I planned to spring upon a startled world (Hello! We're geniuses) once the band became famous, which we thought would be sometime in the middle of 1981. Film was running on a parallel track to music, and it was the aesthetic of filmmaker Billy Wilder – cynical yet warm-hearted, wisecracking and real, manifested in *Sunset Boulevard*, *The Apartment*, *Some Like it Hot* and *Double Indemnity* – as much as any musical influence, that we hoped to draw into our band.

Music won. Grant's subscription to *Film Comment* lapsed, and the cinema books couldn't be taken city to city, or to another country. He would still talk with authority on whatever he had seen, and I remember walking out of an ornate Manchester cinema astonished by *Blue Velvet* – relieved, too, to know that someone could penetrate the mediocrity of eighties Hollywood and get something this forceful and weird onto the screen.

In 1990 a film idea popped into my head with a dream-like intensity. Its echo of recent events in my life, and of the locations and movements of that earlier script, not immediately apparent to me. The idea was this: the hero, forced to leave Sydney quickly, dashes to the airport on a stormy late afternoon. His relief at being on the plane is shattered when two gangsters in his pursuit board the aircraft as the cabin doors close. Rushing off the plane in Brisbane, he sees a young woman holding a sign with a name on it. He says he is this person and she escorts him to a two-seater plane which she pilots into the night. The two in pursuit, having lost their chase, meet the person who was to be picked up, in a shared taxi to the city. The hero wakes next morning on a pineapple farm three hours north of Brisbane. And so it went on.

When did I tell Grant? It might have been on the Lloyd Cole tour, or during a phone call. If it was on tour, the scene would doubtless have been a dressing room, with hours to kill. 'Hey, have I told you about this film idea I had?' We'd have each poured a shot of bourbon, lit cigarettes, and off I'd have gone. I didn't proffer the film to impress Grant or rope him into the project; it was something to talk about to pass the time. But as soon as I started the story, the crackle between us was there: him listening, nodding, pursing his lips to indicate a false turn or doubt, making a remark here and there. And at the end a loaded silence. Then, as with the songs we wrote for The Go-Betweens, even at the moment of the break-up of the band, the potential to take things further immediately sprang up. Grant being a frustrated director, he was putting thoughts to the film outside the script. He was talking about how the movie should look. Colours. Shooting style. Camera motion.

Over the next couple of years, mainly through faxes, improvements to and development of my draft script bounced between us. To complete a final version we knew we needed a few months together, and that didn't look like happening soon. When I moved back to Brisbane we got closer. When Grant moved up, well, there we were. Now we needed a place to write. Not at either of our homes – too predictable. It had to be a bare room with a desk, a location where we could summon up the ghosts of Billy and his co-scriptwriters laughing on coffee and cigarettes in a fifties Hollywood backlot. We found it through Peter Fischmann, an Estonian-born photographer Glenn had recommended for the cover of *Calling from a Country Phone*.

Peter and his girlfriend Christina were now managing the old George Cinema in the city, which had been renamed The Dendy. They offered Grant and me a room. It was almost too good to be true – we'd be writing a film *in* a cinema.

For three months, starting in August '95, as morning patrons entered the foyer to buy their tickets and chocolate, Grant and I peeled off through a side door and descended the stairs to a disused storeroom. We worked there five days a week, from eleven till four, writing our script.

We got off to a bumpy start. The master copy of the draft, the one with all the alternatives and re-plotting, particularly important to a film about mistaken identity and chases, had been in Grant's possession. Somehow, in the move from Sydney to Brisbane, it got lost. (This would not have happened in the eighties.) 'We can write it out again,' he said. We did, but it was never as good as the first version. It also meant we spent the early weeks redoing that instead of jumping straight into dialogue. After this hiccup we got down to writing scenes and here we hit another hurdle. Grant was meticulous in his attention to detail, and tenacious in defending his meticulousness, each line, each word a labour. It gave our characters consistency, but a certain flow that went with the feel of the film was being lost. Having never written songs together from scratch, our different approaches to the creative process hadn't been exposed before. The film script, which we titled 'Sydney Creeps', did progress, and a side benefit of our enterprise became apparent – it was great to be working together again, and on something other than music.

We finished a new draft and over the next year tinkered on it. We had a number of copies printed and sent them to the few contacts we had in or near the film business. The reactions we got were the same – the script was good, and we'd successfully avoided many of the pitfalls associated with first-time screen-writers; no one wanted to take the film further. I could see why. The dialogue didn't sparkle enough and we were working on a story that was five years old. The white-hot feelings of 1990 were gone. And meanwhile Tarantino had come along and blown the gangster genre apart – his dialogue sang. Grant and I would have to write more scripts until we got good.

*

Another development, more predictable, came with us living in the same town. While Brisbane was changing, it wasn't happening fast enough for two young women, Joc and Cee, who wanted to open a music venue. The collusion between the government and the strong arm of the hotel- and liquor-licensing associations kept the serving of alcohol and the city's drinking culture stuck in the 1950s. The main turf was The Valley – a downtown 'entertainment precinct', in truth one of the scariest places on earth. Amidst the grotty pubs, fire-hazard discos, and 'we can't pay you tonight' rock clubs, The Zoo, the venue Joc and Cee opened in 1992, was a blast of fresh air. Grant and I had both done solo shows at the club, and an offer stood that if we ever wanted to do anything together we could. Perhaps a Christmas show?

The pieces had fallen into place without pressure being applied. I had a rhythm section Grant knew and liked. He and

I had done one or two acoustic shows since Lloyd, and were wanting to try something different. And with the intention of only giving one performance, we decided to do a show billed as The Go-Betweens. A name Grant and I, while acknowledging all who had played in the band before, felt entitled to. We opened with 'To Reach Me' off *Liberty Belle*, and this set the tone of the show: a wild wander through our back catalogue with solo songs included. It was a classic Brisbane summer night, hot and humid, and the large windows along the side of the second-storey venue afforded a view of our music floating out over the city. It meant a lot to me to be playing these songs electrically again with Grant, and with Adele and Glenn at our sides, Karin in the audience – whenever she'd seen the band we'd always played strong shows. Here we were doing it hometown-style, to a sweaty, boisterous crowd full of familiar faces.

Two months later I was in a London recording studio waiting for a phone call from Paris. A 'here's a thing' project was in motion. Christian Fevret, editor of *Les Inrockuptibles*, had a proposal he wanted to run by me. I knew him from interviews; he was a serious and intelligent guy, and, like most Europeans involved in rock'n'roll, a keeper of promises. His dry manner was further tuned by having to communicate in a second language. The call came through and he outlined his pitch.

He wanted to put The Go-Betweens on the front cover of a forthcoming edition of the magazine and commission a number of his journalists to produce a multi-page spread on the group. It would be the most comprehensive story on the band yet in print. There'd also be a cover-mounted CD of our music, and, as

the cherry on top, he offered to fly the band to Paris to do a concert promoted by the magazine. I listened knowing the French
dream was being placed before me. I also realised that this
would be a small but important first step in a broader acknow-
ledgement of the group, and that this process, which could fan
out to other countries, often began in France. I thanked him
while explaining that Grant and I weren't in a position to play
with any eighties line-up of the band. What we could offer was
the group that had recently performed in Brisbane – a show he
wasn't aware of – a formation with its own sound and chemistry that Grant and I were happy to call The Go-Betweens. 'It is
this or nothing,' I said to him. He told me he'd think about it,
and phoned the next day to accept. Late May '96 was set as the
publication date for the front-cover issue, with the show to follow soon after.

It was the Hollywood twist to our tale. In Paris I kept turning my head expecting to see a twinkle-eyed godmother, Angela
Lansbury or Julie Andrews, orchestrating the whole thing. On
arrival we were presented with copies of the magazine, the front
cover a *16 Lovers Lane*-era photo, the headline 'Is this the most
underrated group in the history of rock?' A fair question. You
know my answer. The image and the query stared out at us from
every corner kiosk we passed. There was also a television show
to do. On the Canal Plus channel. Playing 'Spring Rain' to six
million people on a Saturday-night talkshow – live. The other
guest was tennis player Henri Leconte, 'the Frenchman', as the
BBC's Wimbledon commentator Dan Maskell used to call him.
Leconte was a hyper-emotional, extravagant player who always

lost in the quarter- or semi-final. A Go-Betweens tennis player, you could say, to go with golfer Ballesteros. Were the spirits most compatible with us in the eighties to be found in sport?

The concert was in a beautiful old theatre with a staircase descending from the dressing rooms to the stage. There were a thousand people waiting for us, and they exploded as we strode down to perform. After a few songs we realised that this was like no audience we'd played to before. Not only did they cheer in verses and sing through choruses, at the end of each song they wouldn't stop clapping. Where had these people come from? We had to pound our heels, Dylan electric at Albert Hall '66 style, to hear ourselves counting songs in, inspiring the feeling we could do no wrong. A forceful 'Bye Bye Pride' took the roof off. Then encores. More trips up and down the stairs. One final diva wave and then off. Decompression backstage. Disbelief, relief and exultation in a mix. Bob there. Karin. English and German friends. The *Les Inrockuptibles* crowd. Christian smiling at me: 'You did it!' Drinks. Laughter. Praise. More drinks. I was drunk before we even started out on the town.

The Weight

After three albums with Beggars I was on my last roll of the dice. Fortunately, the ambitions I had for the coming record coincided with a feeling from the company, and Bob, that something had to be done. London was to be the recording location and Edwyn Collins the producer. Since the break-up of Orange Juice, he had released two quality solo albums while immersing himself in the techniques and tools of recording. The result, 'A Girl Like You', was a worldwide hit recorded in his bedroom. When I arrived in January '96 he was the season's unexpected pop star, and the gods were smiling as I walked down the lanes from my Hampstead hotel to his West Hampstead studio, built from the proceeds of his latest single and album.

I'd come alone, and leaving Adele and Glenn behind was the hardest decision I'd made in my solo years. The budget was stretched and the recordings would be staggered to allow Edwyn to answer the last calls of his record – flying off for an appearance on South Korean television; visiting Rod Stewart, who was covering 'A Girl' in concert.

'Oh hey Robert, you're here,' he said. I immediately clocked the cosmic significance of the scene in front of me. Edwyn crouching on the floor before a set of speakers, not listening to John Fogerty this time, as he had been those sixteen years before, but with a soldering iron in hand, wiring the boxes. I must have looked surprised. The gurgled Collins laugh prefaced his lovely next line. 'As you can see, we've almost finished building the studio for you.'

The studio was vintage, before vintage was in vogue. There was a silver-coated, science-fiction feel to it that, with Edwyn's enthusiasm and expertise and the pulse of the band – Dave Ruffy from Aztec Camera on drums and Claire Kenny on bass – leant itself to the dry-boned sound I was after. 'We're chugglin',' said Dave after a take. We were recording my Highgate Hill songs and 'Cryin' Love'. Edwyn's approach to producing was not dissimilar to Mick Harvey's; he favoured band takes and overdubs, he played and sang too, and the choice of studio and a faithful engineer dictated the sound. With Edwyn that was a gritty, rhythmic tone with effect-laden guitar and keyboard on top. The LP was titled *Warm Nights*, and was perhaps not as commercial-sounding as expected. 'Cryin' Love' was the single, a monster track that I had been closing shows with. In hindsight, 'I Can Do', with some great bottleneck guitar from Edwyn, would have made a better choice. Still, the reviews were good, Beggars and Bob energised, and a world tour was booked.

*

Karin and I gave up the Highgate Hill house soon after my return from recording, and with her having completed two years of work, a prerequisite for gaining full registration as a psychologist in Australia, we took to the road. The first stop was the Go-Betweens Paris show in May, then a German-family holiday in Italy, before reassembling Glenn and Adele for the three-month tour, with Jeff on sound and Karin on merchandise. We were a happy party, and the band refined its sound and approach to a point where the shows could start at any moment, moon phase, song or strum.

Ironically, the worst show we played of the tour provided the best off-stage memory. Woodstock was dangled before me. I'd never been there, and a small cafe show was offered. It was horrible. But from among the ten people in the audience and the grumpy old bastard who ran the gig there stepped up a saviour – the hip local radio person.

'You're a fan of Dylan and The Band, right?' he said to me as I dejectedly packed my guitar into its case. 'I work in the basement at Big Pink. Do you want to visit?'

He drew me two maps. One was for Byrdcliffe, Dylan's home from 1965 to '68, and the other was for Big Pink – the pink-coloured house where some members of The Band had lived between '67 and '70.

The next morning was pale blue and cloudless. Byrdcliffe

was ten minutes from our hotel and easy to find. We parked at the end of a forested, deserted road and looked up in the direction of the house. Karin and I felt the significance of this: we'd traced Dylan to the source. There was a thrill to the proximity, and a desire to go no further – to leave the magic at the top of the hill and not trespass. We headed to Big Pink, and moving off from the end of Byrdcliffe's street made me think that Dylan must have done this drive himself many times in '67. Maybe on one of them he had the conversation he recounts in his memoir *Chronicles*, where Robbie Robertson asks him, 'Where do you think you're gonna take it?' For Dylan to reply, 'Take what?' For Robertson to say, to Dylan's annoyance, 'The whole music scene.' Years later, when I read that passage, I thought of the roads we were on that day.

Big Pink was outside Woodstock, in West Saugerties, and much harder to find. You really did need a map. We pulled up and there was the house looking very much like it did when the world first saw it, on the back cover of The Band's first album, *Music from Big Pink*. The radio guy came out to greet us. The basement was now the storeroom and distribution centre for a company selling mail-order records. He invited us inside.

Here in essence was the Bob Dylan and The Band practice room of 1967. The place where keyboard player Garth Hudson had set up a reel-to-reel two-track recording unit to capture some of the music. For months Dylan would come over with new songs to informally record with The Band. The tapes soon bootlegged, and became known as *The Basement Tapes*. And it had happened in this room almost thirty years ago. Were the drums set up over in that corner? Did Garth have the two-track on a table by that wall? And where was Bob standing? Where I am now, with his back to the door? There were long lines of shelving and office tables, but it was all very easy to imagine – the dimensions of the room were unchanged, the major revelation how low the ceiling was for recordings that sound so ethereal and big. The air was dank-o above the concrete floor; it really was a basement.

Another, closer brush with a hero came in LA, where we supported Jonathan Richman and his band. The guy who'd soundchecked Jonathan earlier in the afternoon was incredulous. 'He wants the volume so low people can talk over it,' he said to me. 'He wanted his mother to feel comfortable here.' Jonathan was still a genius, and I thought that with the pulled-back *Warm Nights* sound we made a compatible bill. That night I watched him charm the crowd with his uber-sincere folksy way and songs, and later Adele and Glenn went backstage. I couldn't; there was the awkward imbalance of all backstage meetings, and the greater fear that the golden picture I had of Jonathan, whose songs had shaped me, would in some way be tarnished. The brilliant first line of 'Hospital', from the Modern Lovers debut album, 'When you get out of the hospital/ Let me back into your life', had opened worlds to me. Why she was in hospital was never made clear, and to start a song from deep inside a story was to honour your audience and take them to a place most songwriters feared to go. It was a piece of craft I never forgot.

By November Karin and I were back at The Gap, preparing

to leave for Germany in January. The two-country pull built into our relationship, which Karin, in frustration, dubbed 'the curse', had us continually examining each location and its suitability for a lifelong stay, knowing that whatever decision we finally made was bound to disappoint one set of parents and friends and consign one of us to bouts of homesickness. But for now, unburdened and young – I was thirty-nine, Karin about to reach thirty-one – we were ready to bounce again. In the new year, as last tasks were being ticked off, Karin suggested I take a blood test. A week later the doctor gave me the results.

Hepatitis C.

A breathless moment. A definite gut-to-bowel pull.

She went on talking and I tried to concentrate as my brain split between receiving information and running wild with its implications. I had a chronic disease, she told me, and by law she must pass my details on to the Queensland Health Department, where my name would be put on a register. She started taking literature from a drawer while outlining some bottom-line facts. The disease had only been identified in the late eighties. Millions of people around the world had it and didn't know. Symptoms of lethargy and depression could come when the condition was more advanced. A year-long treatment was available, akin to chemotherapy, with a success rate of ten percent. The virus was seemingly indiscriminate in its effect; some people shook it off, others ended up with liver cancer – that group stood at over thirty percent. It was a blood-borne disease; 'Like AIDS,' she said.

The doctor was nursing me through the results while not sparing me the seriousness of my predicament. She asked how I thought I'd got it. I told her it was probably through drug use and needles. When had I started? In Melbourne in the early eighties, and then sporadically through the decade. I was a dabbler, never owning a needle and always having someone else shoot me up, which wasn't helping me now. Heroin and amphetamine use was an occasional social thing with friends; a lot of people did it, and no one would have known, had not an undetected blood virus been dancing between us all. Karin, aware of my drug history, had pushed me to take the test. Thank god she did. My last emotion as I sat in the doctor's rooms was to curse myself for having been weak-willed enough to take drugs. They'd come and got me, like a hand coming through a curtain in a horror movie.

I walked out thinking I had five years to live. Now to go back to The Gap as if nothing had happened. Mum in the kitchen, Dad reading the paper. That night, as the TV droned in the front room, Karin and I sat in bed in each other's arms in tears. A shadow was over me and our future. Two things were clear in the gloom: Germany would provide sanctuary, and our wish to have children took on a new urgency.

Grant was on the phone, disappointed. We were to have made one final sweep by him and Julieanne to say goodbye and I was cancelling. I couldn't tell him why, not from my parents' house, and not with my diagnosis a day old and still hurting. He took it as a snub, adding it, no doubt, to other feelings he had about me leaving town. That didn't matter *so* much – our paths would always cross – it was the mystifying cancellation that rubbed on old notions he had of kept promises, which, when not honoured, got him frosty. I could hear it in his voice and it pained me. An odd, unsatisfying farewell.

Illusion Reigns

When Karin and I lived in Alteglofsheim, Regensburg was our playground, and we'd decided then that if we ever moved back to this part of the world, Castra Regina, as the city had been known under Roman occupation, would be our home. Through a lucky real estate break, and after surviving a grilling on our professions – I didn't mention music, calling myself a journalist; Karin won the day – we got a two-bedroom attic flat in a nineteenth-century villa at the edge of the old city. Opposite us was Herzog Park, a green gorge, and at the end of our street coursed the Danube on its way to Vienna and Budapest. Raw nerves would be soothed, and for songs I had atmosphere.

I had two in my back pocket. One was 'German Farmhouse', whose lyric had been spurred when an interviewer asked what

I'd done after The Go-Betweens broke up: 'I lived in seclusion for a couple of years/ In a German farmhouse just drinking beer/ And every morning I'd wake up, with a smile from ear to ear.' The other was 'When She Sang About Angels'. In mid-'96 Karin and I had blagged our way into Patti Smith's first performance in Europe since coming out of a sixteen-year retirement. It was a media-only event held at the Serpentine Gallery in London, a few weeks after our Paris show. Smith had Lenny Kaye and Oliver Ray on acoustic guitars, and from the stage she gestured, talked, charmed, dropped names ('Dylan's well'), and sang songs from her forthcoming album *Gone Again*. One was 'About A Boy', and seemed to concern Kurt Cobain. Inspired as I always was by Patti, I jotted down a poem-like impression of her performance. Months later it became a song: 'When she sang "About A Boy"/ Kurt Cobain/ I thought what a shame it wasn't about Tom Verlaine.'

So, two good songs, and in style and content they were the next step after *Warm Nights*. But they were all I had, as Beggars had dropped me, and with that the second phase of my career was over. I'd given it everything I could, but a required level of popularity hadn't been reached and it was time to let it all go. As I strode the medieval alleyways in the cold, pull-the-collar-up weather, a new persona was born. Self-preserving, forgotten, withered, proud, discarded – glorious emotions, for how you *imagine* yourself to be is as important as talent when writing songs. I'd try and write great ones, and I didn't care how long it took me. Someone, I hoped, would be there to finance their recording.

Karin had a part-time job helping children with learning difficulties. I got six-monthly publishing cheques and some performance royalties from Australia, and we played the odd acoustic show together around Germany, with Karin on violin and vocals. The gigs stopping at a late stage of her pregnancy. Our lives were simple – on foot, on bikes to the city to shop. Another saving was alcohol. Upon receiving my diagnosis I'd stopped drinking, and having quit smoking a few years back, I was clean. The first sensation – feeling nineteen again. It took months of waking up without a hangover to finally realise I'd never have to go through that pain again. One more thing abandoned. And the second part of my waking ritual was swinging my feet from the bed to the floor and thinking, I've been given another day.

My blood test results had been forwarded to a hep C unit at the Regensburg University Clinic, where an American doctor was urging me to begin treatment, his chilling pitch, 'You could be in trouble by the time you reach fifty.' I had a biopsy the following year, the result indicating that my liver was not yet cirrhotic. Some comfort to mingle with the doctor's warning, leaving Karin and me uneasy and guessing.

*

The Go-Betweens' appearance and reception in Paris had not gone unnoticed, and an offer had come through to play Roskilde in Denmark, one of Europe's biggest summer festivals. Grant and I decided to add other dates to the itinerary, and concerts were booked in London, Dublin and Glasgow. Glenn couldn't make this round of gigs, having joined Custard; his replacement on drums was Ross McLennan, a friend of Grant's. In hindsight, we needed more time in the practice room and with each other to confidently play a run of shows as big as these. Not that it mattered at Roskilde. We'd been bumped up from a tent venue to the main stage, and found ourselves on a rainy day playing to a thousand scattered people holding plastic sheets over their heads in a field that usually held seventy thousand. It was like looking out over the Somme. Then the power cut out during 'Karen'.

The other gigs were drier, but not much better. I stood onstage at the Town and Country Club in London silently exhorting the band to get lift-off. But this wasn't Paris or Brisbane. For the first time I thought we weren't doing the band's name justice, and Adele knew it too. With Grant it was harder to tell. I had visited him and Julieanne in their room at the Columbia Hotel late one night, to find that he was travelling with four bottles of spirits. A few friends were there and Grant, always a warm host, was dispensing drinks. Being around people who drank didn't tempt or annoy me; the feeling in the room, though, was the mood of the tour. A bit woozy and boozy. Grant, as ever, was professional onstage, good in interviews and fun to be around. (I'd told him of my hep C; a sad, unreadable nod was his response.)

This was the first tour we'd done where one of us was sober, and I don't think my clearer eye was the sole basis for my dissatisfaction. I just thought we'd taken the band a step too far, and the woolliness that came from the alcohol was part of a bigger problem of us not thinking these shows through as well as we should have. The Go-Betweens was a rare thing, a Fabergé egg, and had to be treated as such.

*

Our son Louis was born on 18 April 1998. A healthy, blond-haired boy looking up at us intently from blankets and cushions. Karin had had a difficult pregnancy, premature contractions leading to white-knuckled weeks as we listened to doctors charting, when pointing at her scans, what needed to develop for the child to survive in health. No wonder we had the dew-eyed adoration of parents in their early twenties when he was born. In a step we were a family, a three-piece, and I was ready for fatherhood. Rock musicians often speak of the arrival of their first child as a massive correction to their lifestyle. Whereas my ego had already been checked, my career was parked, or perhaps sinking in a lagoon, and my party days were over. Louis hadn't landed as a bomb, but as someone to be embraced and placed into an ordered, loving world.

The next person of significance to enter Regensburg was Andreas Schaffer a year later. He was a large man in height and girth, and as he sat opposite me at our meeting in the elegant atmosphere of the Orphée Cafe, enjoying his morning coffee and apple strudel, I could see he was a person of his pleasures. Having finished the strudel he lit up what has to be the world's strangest cigarette – a Marlboro menthol. Andreas was from a Frankfurt record label called Clearspot. He was keen on my work. Was I signed to anyone? Did I have any new material?

The meeting was not without its timing. I'd recently demoed songs with Karin at Schinderwies, a hippie farmhouse in the hills above Regensburg. Archie Müller, who lived there, was an engaging, Beck-like character who could play twenty instruments and knew how to work a four-track. Karin and I had visited his bedroom studio in early '99, and in one live session we'd cut everything of worth I'd written over the past three years ('German Farmhouse', 'When She Sang About Angels', 'Caroline And I', 'Spirit', 'He Lives My Life', 'Surfing Magazines', 'Daybreak Woman', 'In Her Diary', 'Don't Touch Anything', 'Woman Across The Way', 'Sleeping Giant' and 'The Freedom').

Andreas and I moved on to lunch. I told him I thought I had enough songs for a record.

'Does it have a title?' he asked, looking up from his plate.

'Herzog Park.'

*

Back in Brisbane, Grant had recorded a batch of new songs with Glenn and Adele in a day at Sunshine Studios. The tape he sent me sounded so fresh and loose, in a stroke unlike him and yet *exactly* him, that I suggested he release it as it was, as his next album. This was the Grant I knew from practice rooms and guitar sessions – pushing his voice, lost in the music; a side of his musicianship he tended to tone down for a perfectionism he thought the studio demanded. The songs became *In Your Bright Ray*, his fourth solo album, recorded in Sydney with local musicians and Wayne Connolly as engineer and producer.

It's as contented a group of songs as Grant ever wrote, yet at thirteen numbers, to my taste, ten minutes or three songs too long. I now realise that when working with Grant I edited him, a conscious procedure in our day-to-day song reviewing sessions before recording whereby I'd keep returning to the songs of his I thought strongest. He knew what I was doing as his song count was whittled down to five, and would give an occasional smirk or annoyed tightening of the lips in recognition of my manoeu-vrings, and naturally there were times I couldn't budge him, but it did mean Go-Betweens albums had focus.

Pop ballads were his metier, where he always sounded com-fortable and sure, and there are at least three of top standard on the album, including the title track, 'Lamp By Lamp', and 'One Plus One'. In the latter, Grant and Julieanne are at home in Brisbane (the lyric laid out below as in the CD booklet):

In the house
smell of tulips
and peppermint
cotton sheets
candle smoke
and a mosquito net
making love
making waves
and not making sense
everyone's gone
what everyone said
sure seems like

we went and

lost our heads

one

plus

one.

In late '89, when Grant and I were in a Sydney bar breaking up the group, he said to me, 'I've never been in a band with anyone but you.' Two years later, he teamed up with Steve Kilbey to form the rock duo Jack Frost. Kilbey, blessed with an ego, a love of poetry and pop, and a view of the rock star as exalted seer exempt from the responsibilities of reality, was a match for Grant, whose willingness to support someone who threw grand gestures (while retaining a strong sense of his own talent) had also benefited me. Jack Frost did two albums, their eponymous debut the better, containing some of Grant's best solo songs.

A project of a different kind was the Far Out Corporation, a jammy rock collective that Grant started in 1998 with Adele, Ross, and guitarist Ian Haug, whose band Powderfinger was beginning a decade-long reign as the biggest rock group in the country. FOC, as they were known, recorded a good self-titled album and single, 'Don't Blame The Beam', and importantly provided Grant with the camaraderie of an around-town gang, something he missed when solo. In total, between 1991 and '98 he was involved in the making of seven albums, one of them a double – when not touring, he loved the locked-away world of the recording studio.

A song that stood out amidst the riffy rock on *FOC* was Grant's 'Suicide At Home'. A pretty melody setting off a storm. 'No one's there when you need them/ Friends and family they cave in', to end, 'Illusion reigns, channels change/ I just tried suicide at home.' Whether this was written as an exercise in despair or after Julieanne left him, I don't know. Nor was I aware of the circumstances of their split, only that Grant was alone again. And as with Amanda, it sent him on a downward spiral. On his forty-first birthday, not long after the break-up, I phoned him, and following the call I wrote in my diary. There is precious little reflection on my own state of mind through its pages, nothing on Grant's, but here is that entry in full, blunt and fresh: 'February 12th 1999. Just spoken to Grant for his birthday. The most disturbing conversation I've ever had with him in my life. He sounds at the end of it. Repeating himself, small voice, "Smashed," he said. "Grant is fucked" and "I'm tired of being a fake." He sounded really bad. The only thing he's looking forward to is the tour. David McComb's death has thrown him too. I suggested he go to Cairns. But he doesn't want to go anywhere. Why? "Because of people here." But where are the people on his birthday? He is alone.'

The passing of David McComb, lead singer and songwriter of The Triffids, at thirty-six shocked me, and for Grant, adrift and unhappy, it hit even harder. The tour he was looking forward to, a three-month, around-the-world set of dates to promote *Bellavista Terrace*, a best-of album proposed by Beggars to fill a hole in The Go-Betweens catalogue, was my response to Bob's query, 'Beggars want to know what you want to do to promote the record.' I'd suggested we do interviews on the road by day and an acoustic show in the same town at night. 'Making a fuss', as Bob liked to call it. I also wanted us to be billed under our own names. And with our friendship now honed to one-word sentences and gestures, there was the opportunity, this time with a note of urgency, to check on Grant. To get him out of town, on the road, where he could lose himself in music once again.

Room 508

The first show of the Australian tour was a disaster. Instead of snaking down the coast from Brisbane to Sydney playing small halls, learning our act again, and the vital rhythm two people need onstage when armed with just acoustic guitars and voices, we walked straight into the biggest venue of the tour, and we weren't convincing. No command. Nervous. A lukewarm review in the *Sydney Morning Herald* got it right and told the world.

We improved, starting the next night at the same venue. In Canberra a day later, we leapt another twenty percent. In Perth for two shows, we jumped in confidence and quality again. Ninety percent, I'd rate us, and by the time we reached Melbourne for a three-night stand at the Continental Cafe, we were on fire. The Conti was managed by an enthusiastic young man named Bernard Galbally; his club was a joy to play, with waiter service backstage and a door at the end of the dressing room leading to a curtained stage, which when parted revealed a room of two hundred people at ringside tables, with a further tier of listeners standing on a raised level at the bar. I loved playing there, and it made me realise just how good Grant and I were. Our Go-Betweens songs were amazing, and a pick of them, plus an unrecorded song each, and the fun of synthesising our solo material – I'd sing a verse of 'Haven't I Been A Fool' off *Watershed*; he put Johnny Cash riffs to '121' – allowed us to build an impressive set.

On the cab ride to our hotel after the first Melbourne soundcheck, Grant asked if he could come to my room for a chat. Sure. I thought it concerned his mother, who'd been sick. Maybe he'd have to fly to Cairns soon. We were staying at the Novotel, on the waterfront at St Kilda. I was in room 508 with a view deep out over the bay, where I could see waiting ships. Grant came in and the first thing he said was, 'I think we should restart The Go-Betweens.'

I wasn't totally surprised, and yet the gasp in my heart showed I wasn't prepared for the request – it wasn't a question. The tour had just begun. We were settling in to what we could do. But Grant was streets ahead. Historically I saw the fit, the turn of the wheel. I'd had to ask him twice to start the band, and he'd saved me back in '77 and I'd never forgotten it. Eternal gratitude and brotherhood for that. I'd been in a jam, with two classic songs in a town where no one understood me but him, and now in return he wanted what he'd given me. I was aware, too, that we wouldn't be starting from scratch. (Not 'Lee

Remick' this time; instead, the album after *16 Lovers Lane*.) There was a legacy attached to the group's name, and it was building; if we recorded, which was obviously part of Grant's plan, then not only would what we did now be measured against what we'd done before, but we'd be seen to be tampering with the legacy. In effect, juggling fire. This didn't seem to bother Grant. For him, one set of songs led to another, fished as they were from a great pond of poetic intent, and in conjunction with this was his spirit, blithe, blind, full of self-possession, qualities that drove many mad but which, when hitched to an artistic adventure, were pure gold. He didn't even consider the possibility that we could fail. I'd have to worry about that, and in doing so, guide the direction of our group as best I could.

Grant gave me room to think as I paced the floor. For once my lack of emotional spontaneity wasn't counting against me. I mumbled 'yeah's and 'okay's as he tried to elaborate on a proposition that really needed no more elaboration. I was leaning to a yes, and he was happy to leave without a firm answer. I phoned Karin that night, and there was as much shock in her voice as when I'd phoned in late '89 announcing that Grant and I were breaking up the group. We discussed the changes Grant's proposal would bring to our lives and growing family, both of which were in need of financial security.

The next dates were in Europe and by then the decision was made – Bob was happy. The tour now had another purpose, and as we travelled from city to city Grant and I looked for a location to record a new Go-Betweens album. Not that we visited studios or had discussions with producers backstage – that's what a normal group would do – we were looking for signs in the sky, a carving in a tree, a David Lynch moment, some person or clue to reveal itself to us. And if that didn't work, there was the phone book.

Nothing came to us during our 24-date European tour, and we were down to the last three shows of the three-week US leg when the puff-of-smoke event we'd been hoping for happened.

*

Musicians hate doing interviews at soundcheck on tour. It's free time; the day's travel is done, and theoretically no one from the record company or management or the public can reach you. You've got a show that night, and the nuts and bolts of checking sounds and playing a few songs is the best preparation you can do for it. I was strumming a guitar at our Seattle venue, the Crocodile Cafe, coffee and apple-and-cinnamon muffin at my side, when an employee said, 'There's someone here wanting to do an interview with you.'

Waiting in a booth at the back was a curly-haired chubby guy with a tape recorder and a stack of magazines. I slumped down. Three questions in, I knew this was unlike any interview I'd done before. Larry Crane had no interest in the meaning of lyrics, or biographical data, or even how the tour was going. Instead he wanted to talk about the sounds of the records I'd been involved with. What was the difference between Mark Wallis's and Richard Preston's working methods? What was Hansa like? What had been my thinking when returning to Brisbane to record at Sunshine? We talked about reverb, guitar sounds, studio size and the producer's role. All the stuff that interests musicians but no one ever asks. Larry wrote for and edited *Tape Op*, a magazine which, like his questioning and cheery, unpretentious manner, cut away from the glossy journals on hi-tech studios and sound. *Tape Op* covered the four-track and eight-track waterfront, plus the groovy bigger studios, and the articles, free of brochure-speak, concentrated on hands-on tips and advice, a fraction of which came from interviews with recording artists.

Talking done, Larry gave me a few back issues, and in parting told me he was a recording engineer with a studio in Portland. To gauge its scope I asked him who had recorded there, and out of a few groups I knew, one was Sleater-Kinney. My interest in Larry had been tweaked; now it positively twinged.

To rewind: I'd first heard of Sleater-Kinney in London in mid-'97 when on the Roskilde dates. Bernard MacMahon, our tour publicist, and Ben Watt, via Geoff Travis, had both name-checked the band when I asked who they were listening to. I bought a copy of the group's new album, *Dig Me Out*. It Knocked Me Out. The nineties were a good decade for music, to my mind better than the eighties. Good bands dotted the scene: Tindersticks, Pulp, The Auteurs, P.J. Harvey, Dirty Three, Grandaddy, Portishead, The Jayhawks, and Mercury Rev. There was a whole army of groups; *Dig Me Out* was the rifle shot. Its songs and sound were brittle and fierce, with smart, emotive lyrics, not word games, fitted to hooky melodies. This was not flannel-shirted fuzz or sixties garage-rock revivalism. The fact that the band was made up of three women, Corin Tucker and Carrie Brownstein on guitars and vocals, and Janet Weiss on drums, seemed to help in wiping the rock history slate clean. Yet I had the feeling that the sensibilities firing the group were somehow near my own. They'd obviously listened to Television, and they just might know, although I couldn't guess how, *Before Hollywood*.

The Seattle show done, Grant and I were at the airport next morning waiting to board a plane for San Francisco, when a mischievous-looking, dark-haired girl with a drink in her hand walked up to me.

'I saw the show last night and I thought you were great.'

'Thank you.'

'I'm Jessica and I work for a record label called Kill Rock Stars.'

'Oh uh . . . and what are you drinking?'

'Scotch and soda. I read somewhere that it's Richard Hell's favourite drink.'

I thought, This is the first person I've met from an American record company on my wavelength.

'You're flying to San Francisco?' I asked, nodding at the departure gate.

'Yeah. I have to pick up Sleater-Kinney from the airport.' She looked to see if the name registered. I played it cool. 'They're coming in from Japan today. They're fans of yours, and we're coming down to the show tonight.'

After Larry, this was Cosmic Signal number two.

In the press and on the internet, rumours were circulating that Grant and I were going to relaunch the band. To meet the whispers head on, and with Grant's agreement, I made our secret public from the American Music Hall stage that night, adding that we were planning to record an album. The response was cheers. We weren't too long offstage when we saw someone standing at our dressing-room door. It was Janet Weiss. 'If you haven't got a drummer I'll record with you.' Things were now falling into place with drop-from-heaven ease. We met all of Sleater-Kinney that evening, who enlightened us further on Larry and Portland. When I mentioned Television to Carrie Brownstein she brushed past *Marquee Moon* and raved about 'Days' from *Adventure*, one of just two songs, the other being 'Venus De Milo', that Grant and I would play air guitar to while standing on the arms of the lounge chairs at Golding Street. And of course we took up Janet's kind offer.

The seventh Go-Betweens album, born out of a greatest-hits tour, took twenty-four hours to assemble and came from a part of the world that had played little role in the band's history. Things could have gone differently. We could have demoed our new songs, shaving them to an enticing four-song set for Bob to shop around for a big deal, then do the producer hunt, apply gloss with session musicians, and come out hot and heavy, panting for a hit. That didn't feel right. That was not our way. With the addition of Adele on bass, the one component we had in place before meeting Larry, we would emerge from a studio built in the back of a storefront in Portland, in the first days of a new millennium.

The Second of Three Acts

The Orphée Cafe had recently opened a boutique hotel. The vibe: Paris 1910. Grant was right at home, his narrow, single-bed room with a wooden desk by the window reminding him perhaps of boarding school, or St John's College days. On my first visit to him after he checked in, familiar tokens were in place – the leather-bound notebook on the desk, the guitar with capo attached nestled in its open case, a bottle of red wine and a stained glass on the windowsill; cigarettes, an ashtray and books by the bed. All he ever wanted.

Outside, snow sat on the market square. The oldest bridge across the Danube was a street away. Church bells rang on the quarter-hour as we worked on the songs to take to Portland in early February. Two of them we knew – my 'He Lives My Life' and his 'Magic In Here' were in our touring set – and as routine as our preparation was, there was a subtle difference in the dynamic between us. While I had plenty of songs (this had been one of my reasons for committing to re-forming the group; as in '77, I was loaded, this time with unrecorded 'Herzog Park' songs), Grant, having recently recorded *Bright Ray* and *FOC*, was scraping to get his five. I'd cherry-picked 'When She Sang About Angels' and 'Spirit' as ballads, 'German Farmhouse' for punch and backstory, and the pop of 'Surfing Magazines' (Louis's favourite), a fond look back at another time: 'We used to wet our fingers on surfing magazines/ Going to throw school and follow those scenes/ Going to get a Kombi and go from beach to beach/ Be the kind of people the authorities can't reach.' Grant's guitar sounding great under all of them. He had 'Heart And Home' and 'Orpheus Beach', which were similar in feel to 'Magic In Here', drifty pop with no great personal revelation. 'The Clock' was the best rock song he'd ever written, and 'Going Blind' an unconvincing pop song that I was trying to manoeuvre out, for another spiky rock number to slide in.

Grant and I flew to Portland to meet up with Adele. She was crucial to the relaunch of the group: a Manchester-born, working-class girl who'd migrated with her family to Brisbane in the early eighties, she had performed with her father, a professional piano player, and his bands in leagues clubs as a teenager. She could play, and was a great harmony singer. Adele was also warm-hearted and true, virtues that Grant, in his up-and-down days after the break-up with Julieanne, recognised and leant on. Like Grant's sister Sal, Adele was up for a bevvy and a laugh, and could say things to him that no one else could, home truths, close-to-the-bone jokes, and words of concern. And he listened too, knowing they came from a genuine and loving place.

The one hitch in Portland came early and was easily fixed. The low-rent hotel we'd been booked into was near strip clubs and screams in the night – rock'n'roll atmosphere for some – which we quit for quieter rooms in the city. Near our new hotel was the three-storey haunted house of Powell's bookstore, with cafe attached, and it was there we'd breakfast before heading off to Jackpot Studios. Larry, having repair work to do, had set up a makeshift practice space in the recording room with drums, amplifiers and a vocal PA, and as he pottered around with a ladder or soldering iron, he familiarised himself with the songs we were knocking into shape. One morning, his jobs done, he looked up from the console and said, 'I'm pressing record.' The transition from rehearsal to recording seamless.

We did nine takes in the first day. Four of them in five hours. Such was the swing of the session. We were aided by the extraordinary support we got from the studio and local musicians, including Sam Coomes, from Janet's second group Quasi, on keyboards; and Corin and Carrie sang and played on 'Going Blind', making the song infinitely better. The irrepressible Larry, who'd gone from interviewing to recording The Go-Betweens in months, captured us with his crunchy homemade sound. After three weeks *The Friends of Rachel Worth* (a mysterious phrase lifted from a story in my diary, and a break from the double 'l's featured in our previous album titles) was finished; one final day was dedicated to making rough mixes, and had we been more far-sighted or bolder, we'd have kept them all and not done any further mixing.

Although it was our seventh album, Grant and I regarded it as the first in the second part of our career. We were in Act II with, we assumed, another four or five albums to come. To return, we joked, for one last record when we were seventy, which would be our masterpiece. We saw an arc of albums before us, its narrative partly built on experience gained from the first six. *Rachel Worth* was the re-emergence, the face from behind the curtain, and as raw and real in its way as *Send Me a Lullaby*. In keeping with lessons learnt from record companies past, and wanting to proceed gently, we entrusted the release to those close at hand – Andreas Schaffer in Europe; Robert Vickers in the US, where he was label publicist at Jet Set; Roger Grierson, now running Festival Records in Australia; and in the UK we had Bernard MacMahon, who with his partner Allison McGourty had begun Lo-Max, recently successful with the Magnetic Fields' *69 Love Songs*. Bernard, an Englishman, in appearance and manner resembling a tall Hugh Grant or a slim Oscar Wilde, had a prominent position over the following years, remaining as our genius London publicist.

We were ahead of a wave of bands re-forming to undertake long tours, or one-off shows performing their best known album, whereas *Rachel Worth* was a fresh start. It was well reviewed, and Grant and I did many interviews with journalists eager to hear about our decade-long break. Some wanted to know the mechanism that had brought our bitter warring selves back together, having presumed that an angry split between the two songwriters was the reason for the break-up. I'd been asked in a phone interview in Alteglofsheim whether it was true that Grant and I no longer spoke to each other: at the time he was upstairs writing 'Riddle In The Rain'. We were also aware of another distortion, this one pertaining to our public roles: I was still the flamboyant wild man, spending my nights in bars, landing in trouble, bewitched by women and dawn visions, while Grant was in bed by ten with herbal tea and books. *If only they knew.* We tried to say this wasn't so, but perceptions are hard to shift and both of us came to enjoy the peculiar twist to our personas.

With the album released, we toured the UK and the US, and finished in Australia at Big Day Out. Glenn was with us again on drums, Custard over, and we were on the road with Coldplay, P.J. Harvey, Rammstein, and a plane load of other acts flying from town to town. I knew I was back in the game when, opening my newspaper after take-off from the Gold Coast, I saw that the lolling, sleeping head that had just fallen onto my shoulder belonged to Happy Mondays' lead singer Shaun Ryder.

*

It may not be the first day, it might be days or weeks later, but at some point after a tour, fidgety musicians ponder, What's next? For Karin and me, it was the arrival of our daughter Loretta, on 3 July 2001. She too landed in a loving, ordered world, one where her father was back in a rock group. The growing family was shadowing the demands of the band, and a nagging feeling came that if Grant and I were to continue on full steam, we'd have to be in the same city. We weren't musicians with home-studios, sending demos to each other, to complete or polish and return for more adjusting; our working method was no different to John and Paul's, knee to knee with guitars in a Liverpool front room circa 1960. It was the late-morning drive over to Grant's place, his mystifyingly frosty greeting at the door, then the 'Watcha reading? Watcha hearing?', state-of-the-Australian-cricket-team chat, until the guitars came out – 'This one's in G' – at which point the mood suddenly wheeled back to the warm camaraderie of the afternoon before and we'd sail off into the mystic with our first song. You couldn't do that from Regensburg, and Grant was embedded in Brisbane and his ways. A man in his early forties unperturbed by, even proud of, his distance from the business of the world, possessing neither computer, watch, wallet nor driver's licence. It meant that Bob and our new Australian manager, Bernard Galbally, often turned to me for answers and instruction, simply because I was the one awake and available at eleven in the morning or eight at night.

Karin and I huddled on our decision. We had pulled up at another crossroads, a child in our arms and another just above our knees. Australia seemed *very* far away, but we decided to go, in a mad, sad jump, the only way it could be done. The deal being Karin would give her time to the children, I'd give full gas to the band and Grant, in the hope that a more secure, or even prosperous, financial future would also come with the move.

So we were back at The Gap. Louis running around the yard with his cousin Tate, Loretta crawling down the hallway, Mum busy in the kitchen, Dad reading the paper on the verandah. We were passing through, having taken the biggest mortgage we could get to buy the cheapest house in – The Gap. One advantage was my familiarity with the area, important with young children in tow; the disadvantage, if it could be called that, was that I had to reconcile myself, the grand adventurer, the rock star poet, to the fact that after twenty-three years I'd managed to relocate myself to a house a kilometre and a half from where I'd grown up. We assured ourselves we wouldn't be there long.

If our relocation pleased Grant it was hard to know – another in the sea of things that went unsaid. He was in groovier, inner-city New Farm, at the end of a cul-de-sac that led to the banks of the Brisbane River, the house he shared with friends unseen from the street and only accessible via a garage door at the back of a block of flats. It was a hideaway, and one blessed with spectacular river views. Grant had a book-lined flat under the house, with its own entrance.

Visiting him regularly after a five-year break allowed me to measure his changes, and he wasn't in good shape. He had no steady girlfriend, and from what I could gather his romantic and sexual life consisted of scrappy relationships with women he met in and around Valley bars. His watering hole of choice was Ric's, and friends wishing to see him knew they'd find him there. His favourite drink was a Long Island Iced Tea, an eighteen-dollar concoction whose lengthy list of ingredients Grant proceeded to detail as I sat beside him at the bar one evening after practice. I was reminded that he was never a sloppy drunk; he maintained an etiquette of dignified imbibing, and tut-tutted any loud or wasted behaviour from those drinking with or near him as bad form. He was a great person to drink with, and some of our best conversations had been had while moving through the slow, delicious stages of drunkenness. Alcohol was not a demon for him, but one of life's necessities, and often treated as such – he sipped his iced tea like a schoolboy with a milkshake. But drinking was also eating him out, destroying him, and he knew it, and sometimes at the end of our afternoon songwriting sessions there was a restlessness about him, and I could tell he wanted to start the numbing.

And what did he make of me? Was there frustration? Envy? Occasionally I caught him looking at me bemused, in search of the man I'd been in the eighties. As if the sober family guy beside him were a con. As if I might spring from my straitjacket to guzzle drinks, pontificate floridly, and accompany him to more dangerous pleasures out there in the night. It was not to be, and it pained me to imagine him thinking this. The man he was looking for was gone. I was closer now to the person he'd first met in the seventies than the one I was for much of the grand detour that was the eighties. In part it came down to the myths of the artist. I could be straight and create, while Grant associated music with a chemical tweaking of the mood, and with night rituals. I was happy with my life, and blessed with a generous, wise, loving wife and two children I desperately wanted to see grow into adulthood. Grant was in a dark place. Songwriting sessions, especially in the first twelve months I was back, sometimes became talking sessions – the guitars didn't come out. He'd be in a ragged state when I arrived, and in tears not long after. He spoke of depression, the first time he'd put a word to what had been festering in him for years.

I talked to Karin about these visits. Her objectivity, her compassion for Grant, and her psychology background were a guide; she suggested, as had a medical friend of Grant's, that he seek professional help. We found a psychologist. I gave him the number and urged him to phone. He never did.

*

For the first half of 2002 we were working on songs for an album to be recorded in the second half of the year. I had judged 'Caroline And I', 'In Her Diary' and 'Something For Myself' from Regensburg as suitable foundation numbers, but I'd arrived in town expecting new songs, to again be disappointed. Grant had a trove of material, and a fantastic, fresh-off-the-press chord sequence that I grabbed. He was generous, and happy for me to provide lyrics and set up our first co-write for a Go-Betweens album. 'Too Much Of One Thing' leant itself to storytelling. My aim, perhaps in return for acquiring the tune, was to write a portrait of him. I started in fine fettle:

Nothing in my life is numbered
In my life nothing is planned
You might think you see purpose
When what you're seeing is a band

A thin line like from a spider
Upon which I dance
Nothing in these days is constant
Come home to chance

The lines popped out and I was sailing close to the wind.
I think I was trying to send subliminal messages to him. Things
I wanted to say but couldn't, and which came out in song as
borderline cruel. I backed away. The first line of the next verse,
'In the distance is a bridge, and on the bridge a rail', literally has
distance built into it. (The bridge was the Story Bridge, in view
from Grant's loungeroom.) I further confused things by throwing the song over to the first person in the next two lines: 'I have
known a hundred women, and part of me loves to fail'. Was that
him or me? It was him, I guess. By now I didn't know who the
song was about, which is what makes it work. Later, on tour,
I'd occasionally introduce the song to baffled audiences as 'The
Ballad Of The Go-Betweens'.

The sonic approach to *Bright Yellow Bright Orange* (the
two colours in an L-shaped painting John Nixon had done
for Louis) was similar to *Rachel Worth*; we eschewed a producer and worked with an engineer, Tim Whitten from Sydney,
achieving a natural, warm sound. Nothing more complicated
than that. There was still a sense of us finding our feet, and we
weren't ready to shift to producers or a greater experimentation
just yet. We had demoed twelve songs and intended to record
them all, breaking a run of ten-song albums that went back to
Before Hollywood.

Few groups go into a studio knowing they're going to make a great record. The staggered processes of writing, rehearsing and recording obscure the larger view. The perspective from the recording studio, a month of ten-hour days in a black box, akin to the one you'd get from a submarine parked on a seabed. I can't remember feeling much different going in for *Spring Hill Fair* than I did for *16 Lovers Lane*. The unveiling comes after. We approached *Bright Yellow Bright Orange* with confidence, and yet the album, like *Tallulah*, didn't quite emerge with the frame or size we thought it had before recording began. Two songs, 'Ashes On The Lawn (another co-write, with Grant and I singing the verses as a duo) and a storytelling folk tune of mine, 'A Girl Lying On A Beach', were unable to be recorded to our satisfaction, bringing a more ambitious album back to earth.

As You Like It

I had registered with a specialist at Royal Brisbane Hospital, my birthplace, and was having six-monthly blood tests and liver scans to track the progress of my hepatitis C. Due to newer, more effective medication, the success rate from treatment had risen to forty percent, and I was being urged to consider it. But it would be tough, with the side effects including hair and weight loss, energy completely sapped, and depression, and they'd have to be endured for a year. Karin and I were contemplating this option, while appraising the touring and recording commitments of the band. Life had become a set of equations. Some things, thankfully, still ran free.

I'd heard about a lecturer at Queensland University named Peter Holbrook who was teaching interesting ideas in the English department. He knew of me through the band, and a signal came via mutual friends that I was welcome to enrol in one of his classes if I wished. His specialty was nineteenth-century poetry; this coincided with Grant and I having recently been on a Richard Holmes binge, reading his excellent biographies of Coleridge and Shelley while on the road. Unfortunately, Holbrook's course for the first semester of 2004, my four-month window of time, was on Shakespeare. I took it, to hear what he had to say and to shake the pattern of my days. So I was back at uni at the age of forty-six, as – and the term was a shock when I first heard it – a mature-aged student.

Although the university had changed drastically – the revolution was definitely over, and my relationship to the texts and the analysis afforded them had altered (Marxism and feminism now gone, postcolonialism the new squeeze of the lemon) – miraculously the plays remained the same. As much as I admired them, and found Shakespeare's 'sugared' sonnets a revelation, the most fascinating aspect of the course was the life of the writer. There were only postage-stamp-sized pieces of information on him, and every one had been turned over and over through a thousand biographies. In essence, the bard had left in his wake, apart from an avalanche of work, a missing decade and many other missing years, no letters or diaries, no record of his schooling, a few signatures, some disputed portraits – did he have a beard, did he wear an earring? – and an older wife abandoned in the country with two kids. He was possibly a gay blade in town, an actor and businessman too. Virtually nothing was known about the man himself – Shakespeare, I had to conclude, was more interesting than any of his plays.

Grant looked on in wry amusement, an attitude he often had with me, and perhaps one I prompted him into assuming: I must admit I took delight in surprising and entertaining him. He had his degree; I was trying to finish mine. Half-heartedly, at times when boredom and dissatisfaction had settled on him, I suggested he go back to university too. 'Why don't you do a PhD?' He'd purse his lips and hang his head to the side. He thought I was taking the piss. 'It's nice out there,' I'd say. 'A lovely secluded world. Why don't you think of academia?' 'No,' he said.

As had been the case in the late seventies, the inspiration I got from study and the time I had to respond to it bounced into my songwriting, and I wrote a clutch of good songs. One of them was 'Here Comes A City'. It was the kind of songwriting moment you dream of, that the years are put in for, a spine-tingling half-hour when I jumped from a chord-driven guitar riff to having the rough structure of a super-charged song in place. The lyric needed to move as fast, so I turned to the train trip from Regensburg to Frankfurt airport that Karin and I and the children had taken on our way to Australia in late 2001. It had been a traumatising event leaving Germany, the causes of which were too complicated to get into a song, but the course of the journey I could cover. Our life in suitcases, our faces turned to the switching scenery out the window – stretches of black countryside then the freeze of white lights and distant skyscrapers as we passed through every oncoming city.

*

'Here's a thing.' Bob on the line. 'We've been offered a show at the Barbican in London. You know the Barbican? Big theatre. It's in late June and it's good money.'

'What do they want?'

'It's your show. Do whatever.'

'But, but . . . University won't be over. I've got an assignment to get in and an exam to do.' How rock'n'roll was this conversation?

'That *was* the plan.' (Pause) 'It's a big gig, and the money would allow us to bring over Glenn and Adele. You could record a single with Wallis, and see what he'd be like as producer for your next album.'

And so I made my second ignoble exit from university, and once again it was The Go-Betweens that spirited me away.

We structured the Barbican show as a retrospective played over two sets. The first as a three-piece with Grant on bass and Glenn on drums, the raw-boned sound sitting up in the grave to embrace 'The Sound Of Rain', 'Your Turn, My Turn', 'Karen', and other early songs. It was great to look over and see Grant on bass again, and how I loved the trio – the elements of a band playing for their lives with no rhythmic cover from a fourth person. For a part of the second set, Audrey Riley joined the group with her string quartet for some *Liberty Belle/Tallulah*-era songs. We also flashed the future, playing 'Here Comes A City', which we'd given ourselves three days to record and mix with Wallis in his new South London studio.

Short visits to London were Groundhog Day, governed by always staying at the Columbia Hotel. I proceeded late the next morning to a small Chinese restaurant I frequented at the top of Queensway. After lunch I walked back to the hotel along Hyde Park, noting the familiar summer sights – squirrels hopping up trees, lewd sex-worker cards spilling out of telephone booths. I considered going to the Peter Pan statue in the park and touching the bronze-plated hem for luck, as I often did, and decided against it. But I should have gone, as a storm was brewing in my stomach, to unleash itself that night in multiple trips to the toilet and a violent, cold shaking of my body. The hotel summoned a doctor, who gave me a handful of tablets in exchange for a hundred pounds in cash. Nice work if you can get it. I had food poisoning, one day shy of my forty-seventh birthday and our recording session.

The next two days passed in bed in agony. Grant popped his head around the door to check on my progress as I cancelled yet another day in the studio. The second night, a Sunday, the bug cleared. We had a day to cut a record. A van picked us up early and we tore through the tight London streets. Wallis had the drums and amps miked, and everything was switched on and ready for our arrival. He looked the same – very Black Sabbath. We whipped through the song. Our deadline was five in the afternoon, when Grant, Glenn and Adele had to leave for the airport to fly home. Being the sensible one now, I had allowed a fourth day for contingencies. Overdubs were done in relay. Grant not only recorded a fantastic lead line, but also came up with a two-note push that did wonders for the verses. He really was a genius on the guitar, and gave so much to my songs. With the track almost done, the three of them jumped into a cab, Glenn calling out that the track needed a theremin line. Mark mixed that night, ready for Bob and me to hear the finished version as we drove to the airport the next morning. It sounded incredible – our best single since 'Streets'. Wallis had worked his magic, and in the process updated our sound yet again.

*

I mustn't have seen Grant for at least a couple of weeks, because he had six songs to show me. We were sitting in the large upstairs loungeroom above his flat; before us, through a wall of glass, a millionaire's view of the river and the city.

Still nervous after all these years when playing new numbers to each another, we would occasionally preface them with quick, coughed-up introductions. This day Grant was referencing groups.

'This is a kind of Roxy Music number.'

And it was.

'This is kind of a Rolling Stones-type thing, I guess.'

A kind of . . . 'Jumpin' Jack Flash'.

He played me two more songs with group taglines, and each was well structured with a chorus lyric and improvised mumbled words in the verses. Before the fifth number he said, 'Oh, and I've got this.' It was 'Finding You'. At least that's what I thought it was called after hearing the first chorus. 'Don't know where I'm going/ Don't know where it's flowing/ But I know it's finding you.' I was aware of the song's potential from the first strum, a steady, percussive stroke with a touch of country, a touch of pop, which with its balance of major and minor chords amounted to his signature feel. So convinced was I of the song's worth that I was thinking as he reached the second chorus, Please let there be a great middle part to this. And there was. It began: 'But then the lightning finds us/ Burns away our kindness/ We can't find a place to hide.' No third verse, just a doubling of the chorus, and it was over.

I didn't leap up, wave my arms and scream, 'You've written a classic,' although he'd just played me one of the ten best songs he'd ever written. A considered 'Wow, that's good' may have been what I said. (To put this in context, after proudly playing him my latest song, the epic 'Darlinghurst Nights', some weeks before, he had rubbed his chin on its conclusion, letting agonising seconds hang in the air before finally admitting, 'I think we could work on that.') I later wondered if he'd set me up with 'Finding You'. Playing the inferior songs first and then slipping it in to mess with my head. But I knew he hadn't. To Grant, all songs were of worth, and he put exactly the same amount of effort into each, and played them to me in the order that seemed natural to him. The 'Oh, and I've got this' was as genuine as he was. There was no caprice.

Years later I would wonder what the sixth song was that day – the one we didn't get to work on.

As I drove home the melody of 'Finding You' was as incessant in my head as incoming ideas for lyrics. Even at this stage of our songwriting partnership, I still had the urge to add lyrics to some of his melodies. It was our long-time predicament – he had too many melodies, I had too many words. I'd asked before leaving if he had verses in place for what was a chorus with a fairly open meaning; he said he hadn't. In the car a scene came to me. Imagine you're living alone in a distant city, far from friends, family or lover, and suddenly you look up and see someone you know pass by. They don't greet you, or even see you, and stranger still, they move as if on daily business in the city. How might that feel? A seed for the thought may have come from knowing that Grant was in a long-distance relationship with a woman who'd been living in the house and then moved to Tasmania to study. He'd recently visited her. 'What would you do/ If you saw me driving by in a car/ The quickest you've ever seen me spin?/ Would you smile and wave/ Or would you bow and get in?/ Don't know where I'm going/ Don't know where it's flowing/ But I know it's finding you.'

That was the second verse, with chorus, and having also written the opening verse that night, I phoned Grant to ask if I could bring the words over the next day.

He laid my lyric sheet beside him, scanning the words as he tuned his guitar. I was getting personal on him again, but he said nothing while he ran the metre of the words through his mind. He then played the song, patching his words to mine. It was an amazing thing to hear, which didn't necessarily mean he'd go for it. 'They're good,' he said with a smile. 'Okay.' There aren't many Forster/McLennan songs like this – real old-fashioned co-writes. And I have come to appreciate that we wrote one as good and as meaningful as 'Finding You'.

*

Satisfied with 'Here Comes A City', we were recording our ninth album with Mark and his co-producer Dave Ruffy in a studio as far from the comforts of *16 Lovers Lane* as it was possible to contemplate – in Duckton, a rough, on-edge part of South London. Up on the hill at Crystal Palace was our hotel, a large, Victorian, wedding-cake building with views out over the surrounding suburbs. It was a slice of England – dusty, a disco in the cellar, breakfasts of warm orange juice, toast and strong tea, bare carpets, groaning water pipes, and a whisper that Russian prostitutes were working in a far wing. On my bedside table was Susanna Clarke's *Jonathan Strange & Mr Norrell*, just out with fantastic reviews, my reading soundtrack for the album. The late-autumn streets, the hotel, and Clarke's tale of magicians, altered states and creepy, cloaked, early-nineteenth-century phantasmagoria swirling together to colour and place the recording experience in memory.

There was a bar on the ground floor where we gathered with friends after a day in the studio. Over beers sat Australian photographer and long-term London resident Bleddyn Butcher. He and his wife Jude, in their East London council house, had been generous hosts to a generation of bands – The Birthday Party, The Moodists, The Triffids, and ourselves. Also at the bar was the urbane Jonathan Turner, creator of The Go-Betweens' website, and Bernard and Allison. Bernard, the quintessential publicist, never venturing out without at least three journalists in tow, was a boosting presence. Realising that the best way to manoeuvre and please Grant and me was to play to our vanity, he would place whatever we did on the top shelf of Go-Betweens lore, flicking off any slip of confidence we might have.

After two albums of *audio-vérité*-style recordings we were ready for the pulse of London and some production, a pop shimmer that recording in the city always seemed to bring. *Oceans Apart*, named after a nearby bar that Grant frequented, took two months to record and mix, which seemed to be the time Wallis needed to make an album, even though the single was done in two days. We weren't complaining, and it was in the middle of the recording time range; some bands take years, others days.

For the first week Grant was not well. He'd done the flight to London many times, with drinking on the plane usually bubbling over in the excitement of arrival and meeting old friends, extending the binge for a day or so. But he was still drinking to excess after a week, and it was affecting his mood and performance in the studio. He phoned me late one night in my room, questioning Wallis's behaviour and commitment to the album. It made no sense. He'd phoned Bob too, who'd phoned me worried about Grant's mental state. Finally he could drink no more, he got an early night, a very long sleep – he'd landed, and was better from then on. He had reasons to be clear-eyed, having brought his best run of Act II material, 'Boundary Rider', a strummy, country cousin to 'Finding You', with an absolutely key line: 'To know yourself is to be yourself.' A deceptively obvious piece of philosophy that I thought signalled an understanding of his predicament. Besides this and the chorus of 'Finding You', which was also heart-warming for those of us used to songs of resignation from him, there was 'No Reason

To Cry' (almost covered by Glen Campbell on one of his last albums) and the maze-like psychedelia of 'The Statue'. 'No Reason' resurrected old subject matter – Amanda ('Fifteen years since we last spoke'), rolling through the tumult of the '89 tour ('For days we fought across the globe/ You bit my tongue on a Lisbon Road') and its messy aftermath ('December sun didn't make us sing/ Wounds too deep to keep anything'), before finding reconciliation ('The wounds have healed on my throat').

I was craning my neck too, but further back and to happier times. 'Darlinghurst Nights' was a snapshot of Sydney 1985, the cafes with Space Invaders machines and industrial-strength cappuccinos. A restaurant named No Name up a flight of stairs, where, after a day of cigarettes and a chocolate bar, the fuel to soldier on was a bowl of pasta with a brick-sized loaf of white bread on the side, washed down with beer in tallies. 'Gut rot cappuccino, gut rot spaghetti/ Gut rot rock and roll through the eyes of Frank Brunetti.' Frank being the first keyboard player of Died Pretty, who always played in wraparound sunglasses. Nineteen eighty-four was a sunglasses-after-dark kinda scene – friends lounging in the front rooms of Crown Street houses listening to records with the door open to the street. A time when you didn't consider one consequence of your deeds, a time so unusual Dylan was making bad albums. A time so new there were still years of promise to be fitted and filled with all the splendid things we'd do after the rock'n'roll party had spun to its end. 'I'm going to change my appearance every day/ I'm going to write a movie and then I'm going to star in a play.' I told Mark I wanted brass at the end of the song, some Laughing Clowns swing.

Mojo magazine a few years later, in a top-ten list of our albums, had *Oceans Apart* at number one. The record earned us our first ARIA award, for Best Adult Contemporary Album of 2005. We stepped off to tour. How big were we now? It was a solid following: some theatres, full clubs, the odd festival. The strange thing was, and here it is again, that after all these years there was still a sense of potential about us. We were hungry too, not sloth superstars defending a patch, but two singer-songwriters with a great rhythm section pushing ourselves towards rewards and regard we believed we deserved. A staggering amount of people still didn't know who we were. On our first round in the eighties *Liberty Belle*, our fourth album, was a peak we hit and sustained for the next two records. Grant and I thought we were in the same place again, and the songs he wrote over the next year told me that he was ready to take the whole thing up another level.

*

At the end of 2004 he moved to Highgate Hill. The address put him in a more suburban context, although it was still inner-city and his habits didn't alter. He had a two-storey flat at the back of a large-verandahed Queenslander; in the house lived two women he'd met through the New Farm residence. The change a reminder that Grant was still in share houses, essentially living the same life as when I'd first met him. Alternative arrangements were hard to imagine; he didn't want to be by himself, and if he was ever going to buy a place it would have to be done in true rock star style – walking into a real estate office and plonking the cash down on the table. How he would have loved that.

Our touring had finished in Spain in November 2005: four dates with the Teenage Fan Club, who may or may not remember the shows for a drink Grant invented – a tall glass half filled with vodka, topped with Coke and a slice of orange, that he christened the Go-Between. Try one. In the early new year he was phoning me, asking if I could come over and hear some new songs. He was persistent and so one January night, without a guitar, I drove to his house, climbed the stairs to his room and sat at the end of his bed. He played me five numbers and they were the best group of songs I'd heard from him since *16 Lovers Lane*. And he knew it. A grinning, almost bewildered sense of his own accomplishment. It was less a songwriting session than a private performance, my attention focused by habit on his moving fingers as he softly sang his songs. Each number seemed to tip to a highlight – the high melodic exuberance of 'Let Your Light In, Babe' and 'It Ain't Easy', the country-rock power of 'Into The Rising Sun', a very tender ballad whose title I didn't catch, and the gem-like 'Demon Days'. The latter was the third song he played, so I was already under the spell when the strum hit in heavy three-four time, capo high up the guitar, a death-defying certainty to Grant's intent. The familiar tricks of his composing fell into place – fingers descending in melodic steps on chord shapes, the swoon given to a minor chord when it breaks majors, the invented two-note chords that he'd suddenly place to build or relax tension, all there at the service of a grand, grand melody.

At the end he looked at me a little dumbfounded – where had these songs come from? My thought was they were a return to the core strengths of 'Finding You' and 'Boundary Rider', no 'this song sounds like that' this time. Amidst a bubble of praise I told him his half of the album was already written, and added – and I'm so glad I did, in light of how cool we'd been with each other's work, and what was to come – 'I've got a lot of catching up if I'm even going to get close to you.' I said that straight to him and it went in. We were standing on his front porch, Brisbane asleep as I was leaving. What I didn't say, what he knew anyway, was that the next album was going to be his.

There were two shows to play in the new year. The first was an offer from the Sydney Festival, who were after 'something special'. I came up with 'The Story of The Go-Betweens', a big title for a concert that consisted of Grant and me on acoustic guitars roaming through our back catalogue, stories and patter aplenty, tying our history to our songs. As it happened, this was Grant's and my last public appearance together. The Sydney Theatre was sold out and the show, nerve-racking as it was, a triumph. Grant, who could be stiff onstage, more comfortable *in* songs than out of them, was chatty and warm, pitching gallantly to support the tales-bursting-out-of songs concept. The mood tumbled backstage, where a meaningful collection of friends were gathered: Bernard Galbally, Glenn and Jane, Emma Pursey – Grant's new girlfriend – and Tony and Sal, brother and sister of reckless older brothers in a famous partnership, who, on the rare occasions they met, got on well.

Our last show was a private performance, also in Sydney and

also unique. Andrew Upton, theatre director, playwright and scriptwriter, wished to have The Go-Betweens play at his fortieth birthday party in February. His house was in a thin North Sydney lane, with views from the back lawn to far-off hills; a tentacle of the harbour passed by at the bottom of the garden. The stage was on the stone stairs at the rear of the house, with a full sound system and operators. We were soundchecking in the early afternoon, having met Andrew, when his wife, the actress Cate Blanchett, came to join her husband. They stood arm in arm watching the group play – a moment for us, and an opportunity for them to dig the band in peace before guests arrived.

We played two sets to a large garden-party gathering in the late afternoon. Our brief was not to fill a dancefloor with thumping rock noise, but to complement the occasion with a lean to the gentler side of our music. Given this approach, and the unusual venue, the show couldn't help but remind Grant and me of some of our first performances. A few guests smiled in recognition and delight at our appearance – we hadn't been announced – Hugo Weaving flopping down on the grass before us with his children. Others, including Clive James, preferred to stay on their side of the lawn chatting in chairs with food and drinks. The surprise of the party was its informality, the cast of friends and family outnumbering famous or near famous faces. No photographers hustling people into groups for snaps either. Yet Hollywood, its spirit, was there, if only through Cate, and I thought how for Grant, who was enjoying himself enormously, smoking and yakking with Andrew between sets, music had finally, in the most roundabout of ways, brought his two worlds together.

The Missing Statue

It is curious that our last three trips, spaced a month apart, were all to Sydney. In early March 2006 Grant, Adele and I flew down to join Glenn as finalists in the inaugural Australian Music Prize, based on the UK's Mercury Prize. *Oceans Apart* was one of six albums up for the award, to be presented at the Museum of Contemporary Art by Circular Quay. It was a big rock'n'roll and media event, the kind I dislike, happy as I was to sprint down any red carpet or use a side door. Still, an interesting evening was promised. Bernard was coming up from Melbourne, and Lindy and Amanda were to be there too. My contact with them both had been brief through the years. I'd played a few songs with Amanda in 1996, when she was in a support band on a bill with me, and she'd graciously invited Karin and me to her home the next day.

The floor cleared when Amanda and Grant inevitably met; the

torn romance tied to *16 Lovers Lane* and the dramatic crack-up of the group had long been the stuff of Sydney rock folklore. 'They're *talking*,' people whispered in thundering voices around me, and yes indeed, there they were, and it was good, and Grant came away happy, not hurt – no reason to cry. I wasn't so lucky, as Lindy had chosen the moment of the announcement of the award, as the nominees were about to be read out, to sidle up to me and tip a cup of poison into my ear. 'Whatever happened to that lovely young man who had so many dreams when he began his band and then lost his way . . .?' I tuned out, while berating myself for letting my guard down in her presence. The second the winner was announced, The Drones for *Shells*, I walked away clapping.

Our party gathered outside. Grant, having negotiated the night's emotional dips, was already very tipsy. A meal in a restaurant with our new Australian record label, EMI, followed and then the scraggling group moved on, to settle around a table in a pub opposite our hotel. We'd been presented earlier with a tiny wooden statue as a consolation prize, and between the ceremony and the pub either Grant or Adele had lost it, and now they were having a squabble. 'You had it last.' 'No, no, I'm sure I gave it back to you.' 'No *you* . . .' Grant was spilling drinks on his jeans, to stagger up and flick off the remains, as drunk as I'd ever seen him in public. Ever. The breaking of his code. An image that flashed to mind when the time came to look back.

*

In late March I began hep C treatment. The plan was to stop live appearances for a year; the next date on our calendar was for October the following year, when, with months of recovery behind me, we'd return to London and record our next album with Wallis. (The treatment didn't succeed, and I would undergo it again some years later, with a new drug added in the mix, to be declared clear in 2012.) Until then I had songs to write and music journalism to compose, having been enlisted the previous year by Christian Ryan, an adventurous editor for a new national publication named *The Monthly*, to be the magazine's music critic.

I had tried to write in the nineties, my diary subsequently clotted with false starts to stories. Damian, Grant and me in a car. Myself as observant second character to the wiles and wit of a Bill Arning or Pierre figure. A long prose poem of Lindy and me in Spring Hill, living on my mother's boiled fruit cake. I'd be excited for a few days and then abandon them all in disgust. Never thinking I could write criticism, the gong not ringing, even though most of my reading was in nonfiction, biography in particular. I'd accepted Christian's offer on the proviso that, by submitting my first piece early, another writer would be engaged if I failed. But I didn't fail, and had been submitting 1500-word articles, some of them written when touring – a Franz Ferdinand piece done on the fly in Spain, a review of Smog's *A River Ain't Too Much to Love* composed on motel coffee in Canberra in a day. Now I would have time to craft and improve my writing.

With the appearance of the reviews, there was in the time of my retreat a widening of my public profile. I was asked to contribute to a rock'n'roll issue of the literary magazine *Meanjin*, and forwarded a story written from an invented first-person perspective that placed me as a friend to a real Australian pop star recording in mod London in the mid-sixties – it was called 'The Coronation of Normie Rowe'. I showed it to Grant and received an appraisal that amounted to a compliment for one image amidst three thousand words. This didn't upset me, as I knew my writing stepped on a perception he had of himself as 'the author'. I trod lightly, but I valued his reaction, as I did with my songs, no matter how hard a pill it was to swallow. Perhaps my writing would push him, with a year off, to do something outside music too.

So, taking six tablets of Ribavirin a day, and injecting myself in the stomach once a week with five hundred milligrams of Interferon – that irony not lost on me – I shivered and shook through the first weeks of treatment, unable to visit Grant for a month. I was to see him one more time.

I'd packed a keyboard with my guitar, and we set up in the sun-filled loungeroom of the main house. There were a lot of songs to go through: Grant's five stunning January-night numbers, '6 Days In A Town Called Hell', and a shuffling soul number that he'd written since, the floodgates open. I had 'Did She Overtake You', which had been road-tested in Europe, 'Pandanus' and 'A Place To Hide Away'. For an album eighteen months away we were holding a strong hand. We worked on most of the songs over the next hours. Grant was sipping rosé with ice cubes, always the connoisseur. We broke for coffee and in the kitchen I flicked through the pile of new records beside the CD player. 'What's the new Vashti Bunyan like? You've got The Shins?' He covered the current scene better than I, and though his responses were often not much more than a distracted 'Yeah, it's good,' the fact that he had a particular album was enough for me to investigate.

In the late afternoon I packed up to go, to beat the peak-hour rush and be home for dinner. Before I left, Grant mentioned a housewarming party to welcome Emma, who had just moved in. He wasn't sure of the exact date – he'd phone. Emma was a tall, thin, redheaded actress, almost twenty years younger than Grant. The age difference and their contrasting appearances made them a striking pair. (It was seeing them at a party, where Grant was sitting in a chair, cigarette in hand, Emma gliding across to deliver him his drink, when a cog clicked for me: *Bogart and Bacall.*) Grant, who'd been looking a little older of late, a tearing at the body that only enhanced the seen-it-all, done-it-all demeanour of a man who had achieved great things, was enlivened by his glamorous new partner, and seemed to believe that life and his career had more in store. He was satisfied, the best I'd seen him in years. Not only was he in a new relationship, and The Go-Betweens on song, but after years of hard times there was some money. He'd proudly shown me suits bought from a local tailor. To go with the new threads, he'd also acquired a guitar, and what a guitar it was – a brand-new black Les Paul. The first electric guitar he'd purchased since the eighties. Was that where the new album was going?

He was outwardly, as opposed to what must have been happening inside his body, well. There'd been pains in his arms and fingers – the artery trouble that would move to his heart – his inability at times to properly grip the guitar prompting him to take the rare step of seeing a doctor. The diagnosis was sketchy, clouded by Grant's obtrusiveness and my reluctance to probe. Magnesium tablets were prescribed, his diet adjusted, and on a visit in March, Emma had made us a salad for lunch. Was she aware of the doctor's advice or did she just live healthier than he did? That wouldn't be hard, as he never ate regularly or well. At New Farm his first food of the day was often after we'd finished playing – a pie from a shop at four o'clock in the afternoon. Eating was like other signs of domesticity, something he liked to do when no one was around.

I carried my instruments to the car. He was standing on the verandah. I noticed a bulging packet in the letterbox; it was an airmailed copy of the *New York Review of Books*. I called out that I hadn't known he was getting the magazine delivered again. He called back that Sal had given him a subscription for his birthday. He then said one more thing: 'I'll lend you some.'

'Thanks,' I said and got into my car.

I'll lend you some. Our friendship was grounded in that. And more often than not, the outstretched hand was his. The first thing I gave him, I think, was the sight of a person he knew doing something artistically valid: playing 'Karen' in a Battle of the Bands competition, at a very particular point in his life. He then did what I did – wrote and sang songs – and we created the most romantic thing two heterosexual men can, a pop group. Between us it was always an exchange, and his last words to me in person honoured that.

I drove off thinking about little more than negotiating the curve at the end of his narrow street, hoping that nothing was coming quickly at me from the opposite direction.

6 May 2006

A few days later Grant called to give me the details of the party. 'Come at four-thirty,' he said. 'There'll be other people with kids here then too.' The conversation was short – we'd see each other on Saturday. Bye. *Click*.

On the Friday Louis fell sick, and the next day Karin and I decided he wasn't well enough to attend. So I went by myself, still at the agreed time, to be with other friends and their children. I arrived to find no one there. No party, no kids running around. I walked down the front hall of the main house quietly calling Grant's name. The loungeroom furniture had been rearranged and glasses were stacked in rows on a table. I was moving slowly, expecting the party to burst to life around any corner. A child to come rushing out and freeze in fright when seeing me. I went into the kitchen, and it too had been set up for guests but there was no one there either.

Then a man I didn't know came through the back door from the direction of Grant's flat.

'I'm looking for Grant,' I said. 'Where's the party?'

'It's starting later. They've been preparing all afternoon. Grant's lying down, he could be sleeping.'

I was a little annoyed, and glad I hadn't brought my family. But now I didn't know what to do.

'Why don't you come back at six? That's when people are arriving,' the man said.

With an hour to spend I went to West End and browsed through Avid Reader – time goes quickly in a good bookstore – and it was a full hour later that I drove back. I decided not to park on the hill near the front of the house, where it would be tight with cars, instead settling for a place I could drive away from easily and early. I found a spot and walked up the hill. It was early evening and getting dark; the stars were gaining their twinkle.

The first vehicle I saw in front of Grant's house was a big white ambulance with orange lights flashing. Something was wrong. I felt the chilled, gut-to-bowel pull I had when hearing of my hep C diagnosis.

I stood at the front gate and saw an ambulance officer walking quickly up the stairs to the house. People were huddled together on the verandah. Then Emma came running down the path and into my arms. She looked up at me with tears streaming down her face and cried out, 'My baby's gone.'

Jesus Christ.

I held her close. I didn't know what to say. The shock had

sent me into shutdown. We went into the house, where she was comforted by other friends.

I was back in the same rooms I'd been in an hour before. People were weeping in groups, holding onto each other. Some were on their phones, trying to stop more people coming to the party. Others were calling friends far away.

It seemed that Grant had suffered a massive heart attack. His mother and stepfather had been reached, and the rest of his family. I moved around telling various people that I loved them; it was something we were doing. There was a need for it. Everything was fragile, even though things were being handled well. There were perhaps thirty people there – the first to arrive were many of Grant's closest friends in Brisbane. They were looking after him still.

Someone asked me if I wanted to see his body. I said no. There were a thousand images I had of Grant, and I didn't want that to be the last. Ten days ago, I'd been here playing songs with him and he'd waved me goodbye with a smile from the verandah. That would do.

I stayed for an hour or so, and then I wanted to get home. I said a few deep goodbyes and left. The ambulance was still there. His body would be taken out soon.

I walked back over the hill to my car and got behind the wheel. I was so traumatised I perhaps shouldn't have driven, but I wanted to get away, be alone. I drove off with my eyes focused miles into the distance. Traffic moved around me as if in a dream. I drove back over the river, through the Normanby intersection, along Musgrave and Waterworks roads, out to The Gap.

A drive I'd done a thousand times.

I went up our driveway and stopped. I'd made it. Karin opened the front door. She had an inquisitive look on her face. Why was I back so soon? I got out of the car. She was standing before me.

'Grant's gone,' I said.

This didn't register. I had to bring myself to say it.

'He's dead.'

*

It was incomprehensible. The children stood in the loungeroom, cognisant of a drastic turn of events but unaware of the implications. They hadn't seen us like this before. Karin, in tears, tried to absorb the news. I was white as stone. I phoned Bob: the news had jumped so fast, he already knew.

Lying in bed that night, our faces to the ceiling, Karin and I circled his life and death. Searching for clues to the heart attack, while acknowledging the shadow that ruled it all: the sour condition of Grant's soul.

'He walked to it,' I kept saying. There had been times when he could have turned back, could have stopped the punishment he inflicted on his body, the neglect, but he kept on going. The week he'd planned in Melbourne with Emma after the party would have been another feast of restaurants and drinking. There was the comfort that he hadn't died at a cafe table or in a hotel, but at home, in bed, with those he held dearest nearby. Later, friends, independently of each other, told of chance meetings or phone calls with Grant over the last weeks, and each time he was drinking. There seemed to have been an acceleration of his already heavy intake in these final weeks of his life.

As Karin and I murmured our convulsions of confession, this notion came – Grant had had no anchor. No life-grounding weight at the end of the long chain we all drag. For some it's family, it's love, it's self-acceptance and self-preservation. Grant floated in calm waters, through the good years and the dangerous, the bad. He had a weak point that made it difficult for him to say, 'No, I won't do that,' and he seemed to conspire to allow conditions for that attitude to prevail: shared households, few responsibilities, a remote sense of time – the rock life. Yet through it all he was a gentleman, and most people knew him as such – polite, caring, and highly intelligent. The most gifted person I will ever know. But he drifted on his back, his face blissful to the sky, free to the currents.

Looking for reasons can sound like pat psychology, but we said them anyway. Losing his father at six. Boarding school at eleven. An eldest child with no older sibling as protector. He was a country boy who could only live in the city, he was a city boy who knew that part of his true self belonged in the country. He was the precocious, approval-seeking schoolboy jeered for having a David Bowie poster on his wall, who knew he was different not only to his fellow students, but to most of his family. And maybe he lacked a little love. He took refuge in academic achievement, which flowered into grander passions. And he needed a skin to protect that boy fired with enthusiasms, one that took the form of an arrogance, never checked, which attracted and repelled those he encountered. He had no father to guide his behaviour, and a mother who never saw him perform, whose letters, filled with the plain-spoken minutiae of rural life, he read to me with amusement and pride under a Visconti film poster in his bedroom at Golding Street.

Through the burst of teenage years and the first decade of the band, little of this mattered. It was the stuff of his songs, but he managed his life. A life lived full and fast, on tour, in foreign countries. These were the years when I looked ragged beside him, when I turned to him to ask the readings of the compass cupped in his hand. And then, on the ping of midnight, the clock striking the last days of the eighties, there was a change in us both. A reversion to our truer selves, it could be said. For me, it was a quieter home life with a woman I loved. For Grant, it was being alone and in need of a place to run to, but he stayed for punishment in Sydney, much of it inflicted by himself. A naive boy, he thought the world was fair.

And circling all of this, on an orbit further out still, I saw another aspect of my own role. I was one of a number of men that Grant orientated himself to, who could all be shorthanded as 'bad' boys. Grant knew good boys too, but he didn't often gravitate towards them. And the orientation to the wilder types started before he was in a rock'n'roll band. It's how I got in.

Going

I found out that when someone dies the conversation with them doesn't necessarily end there. How can you listen and talk to a close friend, exchange songs with them, for almost three decades, for their voice to vanish in a moment? There's an echo. For four days I had Grant in my head. It was as if an earpiece were plugged in, with him intermittently on the line.

I woke the morning after his death with him telling me two things. The first was that I must put to paper everything that had happened to us, write our adventures down, which was the moment this book was born. The second was more abstract: Go to the biggest place of worship you know and think of me. The impracticality of this, the morning after his passing and with a fresh infusion of hep C medication raging through my body, certainly lent credence to the notion that these words weren't coming from me.

I got out of bed. Shock and utter sadness upon us in the house. Guilty about leaving a grieving Karin, I had to follow Grant to the end. I told her of my need to get to a church. She suggested asking Tony to drive me.

We were travelling towards the city when the directive seemed to pop out of my mouth. 'St John's Cathedral,' I said. He dropped me off at the stairs.

A service was ending; worshippers were rising slowly and dispersing from the pews. I moved down an outside aisle to the altar and lit a candle, arching my neck to view the vaulted ceilings and breathe the air that hangs around old sandstone churches, inspiring serenity and peace. I wasn't undergoing a religious experience, it was simply the awareness of Grant's presence, and the presence was happy. *Here I am,* he said.

Monday was when reality set in, beginning with the funeral arrangements. Bernard Galbally, who was magnificent throughout the following week, organising Grant's funeral with as much care and commitment as he'd given his career, was already in contact with Grant's family, who'd chosen a site for the service near the Gold Coast. This didn't feel right to Bernard and me, and we thought that although the family realised the importance of Brisbane in Grant's life – the funeral could have been held in Cairns – the venue suggested they may have underestimated the number of people he had touched with his music and person.

'Leave it to me,' said Bernard.

He called a few hours later. 'There's been a change of venue.'

'Good, where to?'

'Do you know St John's Cathedral?'

*

Due to a lack of available accommodation, Grant's family were staying in a low-set motor inn off a busy road in Woolloongabba, near the Story Bridge. When I visited them on Wednesday, any concerns I had about the standard of the rooms and the location were brushed off with a smile. 'There's a good steakhouse around the corner.'

They were like that, practical, adaptable people, and standing among them I could imagine Grant in their company, and I couldn't – there was a side of him that would have been on display at the Oak Park Races and Christmas in Cairns that I never saw. His mother Wendy was in a wheelchair now, diminished by ill health, time, and the death of a son. I'd met her only once before, in the late seventies, when she'd come down to visit Grant and her brother, who was a minister at the Toowong Anglican Church. She'd risen to greet me from the settee in the rectory, and I remember the surprise of being welcomed by this stocky, strong woman, a cigarette in hand (Grant didn't smoke then) and a raspy voice. Her cinema-loving son was almost dainty beside her.

I knelt down and passed on my condolences. She grasped my hand. I was a trusted if not familiar face, Grant's working partner and lifelong friend in a town of strangers.

There was a group of us drinking and chatting on a terrace outside the motor inn rooms. Grant's brother Lauchie and cousin Bram were there, beers in hand; they were still joking and warm, but this was tinged now with brittleness. Between them was Sal, who was closest in temperament and personality to Grant. She lived in Sydney, and had made an album of her own songs with Grant playing and producing. She had the swagger of her mother, handy in dealing with unruly country men, but dosed with a vulnerability and a streak of melancholia in common with her elder brother.

A new face amidst them, broad of shoulder and with long black corkscrewed hair, was Nathan Wallace, Grant's son. In the all-consuming rush of The Go-Betweens' eighties career, a whisper had it that Grant had fathered a child with a woman in Brisbane during Dahrl Court days. Nathan entered Grant's life gradually, in the mid- to late nineties. The first time I saw him was backstage at a festival in Brisbane where Grant was performing. I shot a photo of them grinning arm in arm to take back to Karin. Over time Nathan had been drawn into the family, culminating in an Oak Park Races stay; he was a quiet and observant young man, still familiarising himself with his new relatives when the passing of his dad threw him further into their embrace.

Emma was there too, pale and ethereal, struggling, along with her grief, with a kind of culture shock, trying to match the city musician she loved to his country family. (Years before, Amanda had experienced a similar disconnect on a Christmas visit to Cairns.) I was talking to Emma when we were called into a reception room at the motel. Wendy sat at the head of the table, with family and friends fanning off in an order that reflected their relationship to the matriarch – I was about halfway down the table. With her notes before her she went through the details of the service, allotting duties. I was to be one of a number of people giving a eulogy, and, in conjunction with Nathan, program the music for the service.

It was held on Friday. Robert Vickers, Bob, Bernard MacMahon, Andreas Schaffer and Jonathan Turner had flown in from overseas; songwriter peers Peter Walsh, Paul Kelly and Steve Kilbey were there too. Lindy and Amanda, whom I passed with a nod when arriving with my family and parents, were seated together. A thousand people in attendance, and if I didn't know all of them by name it felt like I did. The minister conducting the service was a friend of Grant's family. He had phoned me during the week to outline the eulogy he would be presenting. To prepare it he'd been listening to The Go-Betweens, and a lyric had jumped out that he wished to elaborate upon. It was from a song of mine on *Oceans Apart*, called 'Born To A Family'.

> Born to a family, a family of workers
> Born to a family of honest workers.
> Then I came along, golden boy who belonged
> And changed the system of honest workers.
> I was square into the hole, there was something in my soul
> What could I do? But follow the calling.

It was my story and Grant's too: wayward eldest sons who 'belonged', yet had to go their own way.

'I booked this gig thirty years ago,' was Guy Clark's laconic opening line at Townes Van Zandt's memorial service in 1997. Townes had gone at fifty-two, another prolific singer-songwriter who'd chased his demons down through melody and rhyme. As I rose to speak, there was nothing as hard-bitten on my mind – I'd never thought it would end like this. Perhaps that was wishful thinking. I'd seen Grant so many times, after a night lived to the edge, appear the next morning waxy and pale in sunglasses, walking across a hotel lobby in Munich or Melbourne or Boston, guitar and suitcase in hand ready to head for the next show; or sleepy and distant at eleven a.m. for song sessions. On many occasions dark rock bands would encounter The Go-Betweens expecting namby-pamby, book-besotted, cocoa-drinking wimps, to find themselves par-tied under the table. We were a rock'n'roll band. Grant had a strong physique, the broad shoulders of a champion swimmer, and he seemed capable, deceptive as that was, of more years. There was, too, the long-held hope that a girlfriend would help him get there. Emma had the will, the love for him (and he for her), and youth. There was the belief he would make sixty.

At the pulpit, I held my composure. I told the story of wak-ing with Grant's voice in my head, his instructions to go to church, and Bernard's call the next day. Again, I felt Grant's presence, looking down on us all. Like a floating figure in a painting by Chagall, whose palette of red and crimson, Prussian-blue and snow-white were *so* Grant. I saw him up high amidst the eaves, in a ridiculous pose I admit, reclining on a cloud with a smug, pursed-lip smile, eyes alight, saying silly things to himself like, Oh yes, he's turned up. And, Umm . . . she's here, that's good. And, Oh my god, what's he doing there? The final performance, dare I say it.

He was heavy. The afternoon sun hit our eyes as we carried the coffin out. Lauchie, Bram, Andrew Wilson, Ian Haug, Nathan and me. The cathedral steps were bare; a white limousine was parked below, waiting. Just as we were out of the door, The Monkees' 'I'm A Believer' started to play through the church. Golden pop sung in the creamy purr of one of Grant's favourite singers, the indomitable Micky Dolenz, the song written by Neil Diamond, and with Neil there's always a burr in the lion's paw. The opening lines are 'I thought love was only true in fairytales/ Meant for someone else but not for me.' Sure, that was Grant, but the chorus breaks with 'And then I saw her face/ Now I'm a believer.' And Grant *was* a believer. A believer in all the good, fine, uplifting, wonderful things of life. Lines of poetry, the shadows of a film, the majesty of a great song. He was high-romantic. Singular. A complete one-off.

People were coming out as we placed him in the limousine. I hung back. I touched the coffin, knowing Grant was listening inside. The Go-Betweens were being buried too; we both knew that. Never, though, the spirit of collaboration of the two young men who started the band.

'Goodbye, mate,' I said. 'I'll carry it on.'

Then he was gone.

ACKNOWLEDGEMENTS

'8 Pictures', Words & Music by Robert Forster & Grant McLennan © Copyright 1982 Domino Songs Limited. All Rights Reserved. International Copyright Secured.

'After The Fireworks', Words & Music by Robert Forster & Grant McLennan © Copyright 2002 Union Square Music Songs Limited, a BMG Company. All Rights Reserved. International Copyright Secured.

'All About Strength', Words & Music by Robert Forster & Grant McLennan © Copyright 1982 Domino Songs Limited. All Rights Reserved. International Copyright Secured.

'Apology Accepted', Words & Music by Robert Forster & Grant McLennan © Copyright 1986 Union Square Music Songs Limited, a BMG Company. All Rights Reserved. International Copyright Secured.

'Apples In Bed', Words & Music by Robert Forster & Grant McLennan © Copyright 2004 Complete Music Ltd. All Rights Reserved. International Copyright Secured.

'Arrow In A Bow', Words & Music by Robert Forster & Grant McLennan © Copyright 1982 Domino Songs Limited. All Rights Reserved. International Copyright Secured.

'As Long As That', Words & Music by Robert Forster & Grant McLennan © Copyright 1983 Domino Songs Limited. All Rights Reserved. International Copyright Secured.

'Ask', Words & Music by Robert Forster & Grant McLennan © Copyright 1983 Domino Songs Limited. All Rights Reserved. International Copyright Secured.

'Attraction', Words & Music by Robert Forster & Grant McLennan © Copyright 1984 Domino Songs Limited. All Rights Reserved. International Copyright Secured.

'Bachelor Kisses', Words & Music by Robert Forster & Grant McLennan © Copyright 1984 Domino Songs Limited. All Rights Reserved. International Copyright Secured.

'A Bad Debt Follows You', Words & Music by Robert Forster & Grant McLennan © Copyright 1983 Domino Songs Limited. All Rights Reserved. International Copyright Secured.

'Before Hollywood', Words & Music by Robert Forster & Grant McLennan © Copyright 1983 Domino Songs Limited. All Rights Reserved. International Copyright Secured.

'Born To A Family', Words & Music by Robert Forster & Grant McLennan © Copyright 2005 Union Square Music Songs Limited, a BMG Company. All Rights Reserved. International Copyright Secured.

'Boundary Rider', Words & Music by Robert Forster & Grant McLennan © Copyright 2005 Union Square Music Songs Limited, a BMG Company. All Rights Reserved. International Copyright Secured.

'Bow Down', Words & Music by Robert Forster & Grant McLennan © Copyright 1986 Union Square Music Songs Limited, a BMG Company. All Rights Reserved. International Copyright Secured.

'By Chance', Words & Music by Robert Forster & Grant McLennan © Copyright 1983 Domino Songs Limited. All Rights Reserved. International Copyright Secured.

'Bye Bye Pride', Words & Music by Robert Forster & Grant McLennan © Copyright 1987 Union Square Music Songs Limited, a BMG Company. All Rights Reserved. International Copyright Secured.

'Caroline And I', Words & Music by Robert Forster & Grant McLennan © Copyright 2003 Union Square Music Songs Limited, a BMG Company. All Rights Reserved. International Copyright Secured.

'Casanova's Last Words', Words & Music by Robert Forster & Grant McLennan © Copyright 1988 Union Square Music Songs Limited, a BMG Company. All Rights Reserved. International Copyright Secured.

'Cattle And Cane', Words & Music by Robert Forster & Grant McLennan. © Copyright 1983 Domino Songs Limited. All Rights Reserved. International Copyright Secured.

'The City Lights', Words & Music by Sushil Kumar Dade © Copyright 2005 Universal Music Publishing BL Limited. All Rights Reserved. International Copyright Secured.

'The Clarke Sisters', Words & Music by Robert Forster & Grant McLennan © Copyright 1987 Domino Songs Limited. All Rights Reserved. International Copyright Secured.

'Classic', Words & Music by Adrian Gurvitz © Copyright 1982 RAK Publishing Limited. All Rights Reserved. International Copyright Secured.

'The Clock', Words & Music by Robert Forster & Grant McLennan © Copyright 2000 Union Square Music Songs Limited, a BMG Company. All Rights Reserved. International Copyright Secured.

'Clouds', Words & Music by Robert Forster & Grant McLennan © Copyright 1988 Union Square Music Songs Limited, a BMG Company. All Rights Reserved. International Copyright Secured.

'The Clowns Are In Town', Words & Music by Robert Forster & Grant McLennan © Copyright 2002 Domino Songs Limited. All Rights Reserved. International Copyright Secured.

'Cracked Wheat', Words & Music by Robert Forster & Grant McLennan © Copyright 2002 Union Square Music Songs Limited, a BMG Company. All Rights Reserved. International Copyright Secured.

'Crooked Lines', Words & Music by Robert Forster & Grant McLennan © Copyright 2003 Union Square Music Songs Limited, a BMG Company. All Rights Reserved. International Copyright Secured.

'Cut It Out', Words & Music by Robert Forster & Grant McLennan © Copyright 1987 Union Square Music Songs Limited, a BMG Company. All Rights Reserved. International Copyright Secured.

'Darlinghurst Nights', Words & Music by Robert Forster & Grant McLennan © Copyright 2005 Union Square Music Songs Limited, a BMG Company. All Rights Reserved. International Copyright Secured.

'The Devil's Eye', Words & Music by Robert Forster & Grant McLennan © Copyright 1988 Union Square Music Songs Limited, a BMG Company All Rights Reserved. International Copyright Secured.

'I'm A Believer', Words & Music by Neil Diamond © Copyright 1966 Tallyrand Music Incorporated, USA/EMI Foray Music. Universal/MCA Music Limited/EMI Music Publishing Limited. All Rights Reserved. International Copyright Secured.

'I'm Alright', Words & Music by Robert Forster & Grant McLennan © Copyright 1988 Union Square Music Songs Limited, a BMG Company. All Rights Reserved. International Copyright Secured.

'I'm Gonna Knock On Your Door', Words & Music by Aaron Schroeder & Sid Wayne © Copyright 1972 Rachel's Own Music, USA/Holly Hill Music Publishing Company New Songs Administration Limited/Memory Lane Music Limited, a BMG Company. All Rights Reserved. International Copyright Secured.

'I'm Stranded', Words & Music by Edmund Kuepper & Christopher Bailey © Copyright 1977 Mushroom Music PTY Limited. BMG Rights Management (US) LLC/Christopher Bailey. All Rights Reserved. International Copyright Secured.

'In Her Diary', Words & Music by Robert Forster & Grant McLennan © Copyright 2003 Union Square Music Songs Limited, a BMG Company. All Rights Reserved. International Copyright Secured.

'In The Core Of A Flame', Words & Music by Robert Forster & Grant McLennan © Copyright 1986 Union Square Music Songs Limited, a BMG Company. All Rights Reserved. International Copyright Secured.

'It Could Be Anyone', Words & Music by Robert Forster & Grant McLennan © Copyright 1982 Domino Songs Limited. All Rights Reserved. International Copyright Secured.

'Just A King In Mirrors', Words & Music by Robert Forster & Grant McLennan © Copyright 1983 Domino Songs Limited. All Rights Reserved. International Copyright Secured.

'Just Right For Him', Words & Music by Robert Forster & Grant McLennan © Copyright 2002 Domino Songs Limited. All Rights Reserved. International Copyright Secured.

'Karen', Words & Music by Robert Forster & Grant McLennan © Copyright 1978 Domino Songs Limited. All Rights Reserved. International Copyright Secured.

'Lavender', Words & Music by Robert Forster & Grant McLennan © Copyright 2005 Union Square Music Songs Limited, a BMG Company. All Rights Reserved. International Copyright Secured.

'Lee Remick', Words & Music by Robert Forster & Grant McLennan © Copyright 1978 Domino Songs Limited. All Rights Reserved. International Copyright Secured.

'The Life At Hand', Words & Music by Robert Forster & Grant McLennan © Copyright 1986 Complete Music Ltd/Union Square Music Songs Limited, a BMG Company. Union Square Music Songs Limited, a BMG Company. All Rights Reserved. International Copyright Secured.

'Little Joe', Words & Music by Robert Forster & Grant McLennan © Copyright 1986 Complete Music Ltd/Union Square Music Songs Limited, a BMG Company. Union Square Music Songs Limited, a BMG Company. All Rights Reserved. International Copyright Secured.

'A Little Romance', Words & Music by Robert Forster & Grant McLennan © Copyright 1987 Union Square Music Songs Limited, a BMG Company. All Rights Reserved. International Copyright Secured.

'Locust Girls', Words & Music by Robert Forster & Grant McLennan © Copyright 2000 Union Square Music Songs Limited, a BMG Company. All Rights Reserved. International Copyright Secured.

'Love Goes On', Words & Music by Robert Forster & Grant McLennan © Copyright 1988 Domino Songs Limited. All Rights Reserved. International Copyright Secured.

'Love Is A Sign', Words & Music by Robert Forster & Grant McLennan © Copyright 1988 Union Square Music Songs Limited, a BMG Company. All Rights Reserved. International Copyright Secured.

'Magic In Here', Words & Music by Robert Forster & Grant McLennan © Copyright 2000 Complete Music Ltd/Union Square Music Songs Limited, a BMG Company. All Rights Reserved. International Copyright Secured.

'Make Her Day', Words & Music by Robert Forster & Grant McLennan © Copyright 2003 Union Square Music Songs Limited, a BMG Company. All Rights Reserved. International Copyright Secured.

'Man O'sand To Girl', Words & Music by Robert Forster & Grant McLennan © Copyright 1984 Domino Songs Limited. All Rights Reserved. International Copyright Secured.

'Marco Polo Jnr', Words & Music by Robert Forster & Grant McLennan © Copyright 2002 Domino Songs Limited. All Rights Reserved. International Copyright Secured.

'Mexican Postcard', Words & Music by Robert Forster & Grant McLennan © Copyright 1988 Complete Music Ltd/Union Square Music Songs Limited, a BMG Company. Union Square Music Songs Limited, a BMG Company. All Rights Reserved. International Copyright Secured.

'Midnight To Neon', Words & Music by Robert Forster & Grant McLennan © Copyright 1982 Domino Songs Limited. All Rights Reserved. International Copyright Secured.

'Mountain Near Delray', Words & Music by Robert Forster & Grant McLennan © Copyright 2005 Union Square Music Songs Limited, a BMG Company. All Rights Reserved. International Copyright Secured.

'Mrs Morgan', Words & Music by Robert Forster & Grant McLennan © Copyright 2003 Union Square Music Songs Limited, a BMG Company. All Rights Reserved. International Copyright Secured.

'Near The Chimney', Words & Music by Robert Forster & Grant McLennan © Copyright 1983 Domino Songs Limited. All Rights Reserved. International Copyright Secured.

'Newton Told Me', Words & Music by Robert Forster & Grant McLennan © Copyright 1984 Domino Songs Limited. All Rights Reserved. International Copyright Secured.

'No Reason To Cry', Words & Music by Robert Forster & Grant McLennan © Copyright 2005 Union Square Music Songs Limited, a BMG Company. All Rights Reserved. International Copyright Secured.

'Old Mexico', Words & Music by Robert Forster & Grant McLennan © Copyright 2003 Union Square Music Songs Limited, a BMG Company. All Rights Reserved. International Copyright Secured.

'The Old Way Out Is Now The New', Words & Music by Robert Forster & Grant McLennan © Copyright 1984